Natasha Farrant has a first-class degree in Modern Languages from Oxford University and an MSc in Social Anthropology from the LSE. She worked for various publishing companies and now runs her own children's literary scouting agency. Natasha lives in West London with her husband and two children. She is a native French speaker and a qualified translator, and spends several weeks a year in France with her family.

DIVING INTO LIGHT

Every summer throughout her childhood, Florence would return to her family home on the west coast of France. There, joined by her exotic, glamorous cousins, life as she knew it would begin under the benevolent eye of her grandmother Mimi. It was a heady existence of illicit drinking, stolen kisses and the bittersweet pains of first love. But now Florence is living completely alone with her new baby. Haunted by nightmares, she cannot open the letters from her grandmother accumulating on her mantelpiece. What devastating truth do these letters hold? Why has Florence turned her back on her past? And will she and Mimi ever be able to escape the guilt that is tearing them apart and has shaken their family to its very core?

NATASHA FARRANT

DIVING INTO LIGHT

Complete and Unabridged

CHARNWOOD
Leicester

First published in Great Britain in 2008 by
Black Swan
Transworld Publishers, London

First Charnwood Edition
published 2009
by arrangement with
Transworld Publishers
A Random House Group Company, London

British Library CIP Data

Farrant, Natasha
Diving into light.—Large print ed.—
Charnwood library series
1. Single mothers—Fiction 2. Intergenerational relations—Fiction 3. Family recreation—France—Fiction 4. Domestic fiction 5. Large type books
I. Title
823.9'2 [F]

ISBN 978–1–84782–495–0

Published by
F. A. Thorpe (Publishing)
Anstey, Leicestershire
Set by Words & Graphics Ltd.
Anstey, Leicestershire
Printed and bound in Great Britain by
T. J. International Ltd., Padstow, Cornwall

This book is printed on acid-free paper

For Ameé, in loving memory
And for Steve

Acknowledgements

Writing is by definition a solitary exercise, but I owe a particular debt of thanks to the following for helping to make this book possible: Jean-Luc Labour, who committed an act of selfless charity when he bought the German underground bunker beneath the Hôtel des Etrangers in La Rochelle, and turned it into the Musée de la Dernière Guerre. A born storyteller, he was incredibly generous with his time when I was researching the Occupation in La Rochelle, and the insight and information he gave me were invaluable. My grandmother Jeanne Moorsom, and family friends Edith Rheims and Didier Béraud for sharing stories about La Rochelle before and during the war. My agent Laura Longrigg, for her consistently wise advice and unflinching enthusiasm. And most of all my family, for their continuing patience and support.

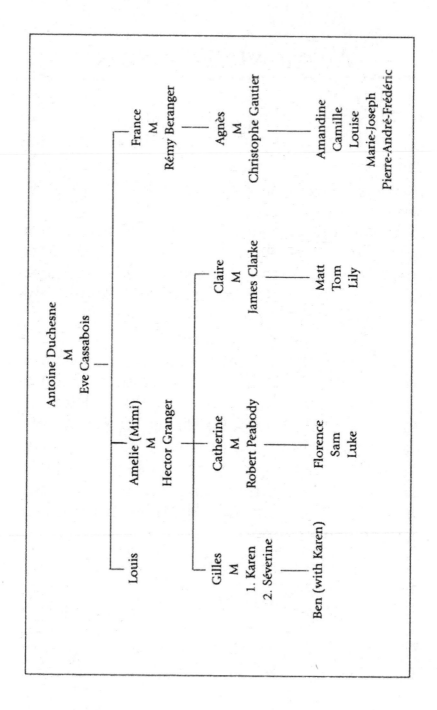

Antoine Duchesne
M
Eve Cassabois

Louis

Amelie (Mimi)
M
Hector Granger

France
M
Rémy Beranger

Gilles
M
1. Karen
2. Séverine

Catherine
M
Robert Peabody

Claire
M
James Clarke

Agnès
M
Christophe Gautier

Ben (with Karen)

Florence
Sam
Luke

Matt
Tom
Lily

Amandine
Camille
Louise
Marie-Joseph
Pierre-André-Frédéric

PART I

London, 2005

Florence is dreaming.

In her dream, she rests her head against the window of the train, hoping for a better view. 'Not long now,' she thinks happily, and at that moment, as if to prove her right, the coast suddenly appears. Eyes half shut against the light, concentrating hard, she can just make out *their* beach on the far western tip of Ré, the lighthouse dominating the curving sweep of pale sand, waves rushing in from the Atlantic pounding the shore. The train accelerates around a bend and they are treated to a full, glorious view of the old harbour, its ancient towers standing proudly to attention, yachts and pleasure-boats sailing gaily in and out, people waving madly as they race past. The train screeches through the station, picking up speed, and Florence's mood swings from excitement to fear. In a dim recess of her mind she realizes that even the view is all wrong, that the sea and the harbour should be no more than a glimpse, the island invisible. And now they are racing towards the fortifications of the old town. There is no sound, except for a baby crying. No feeling, except for overwhelming sadness. A sense of loss, and a baby crying. A baby crying . . .

'Darling, you're going to have to feed her, you know. I can't do it for you.'

Florence wakes weeping, drenched in sweat.

3

The large West Indian agency midwife, the one called Cassandra, is looking down at her kindly.

'I was dreaming . . . '

'Dream all you want, darling, but your baby's hungry.' Cassandra smiles, a broad flash of sunlight in the plain hospital room. 'I'll bring you tea. Then you and me can talk about your dream.'

★ ★ ★

Since the baby's birth, Florence's normally creamy complexion has acquired the grey pallor of anaemia, and dark purple shadows underline her green eyes. Though she is still slim, there is no denying the post-partal sag of her formerly washboard stomach, nor the gravitational pull on her breasts, always heavy and now swollen with milk, barely supported by her soft maternity bra. But her thick mane of tawny hair is held back by a scrap of vivid scarlet silk, her dressing-gown is made of thick old-rose linen, her slippers are soft embroidered leather. She looks incongruously elegant, and her glamour is compounded by her solitude. None of the staff on this private ward can remember a new mother being so completely alone. Not one friend has visited, not a single relative, let alone a husband or boyfriend, and yet she does not seem to mind, even to notice. She fits no stereotype. Even her voice, soft and educated, defies classification with its occasional inflections, sometimes American, sometimes foreign. The hospital staff, whom she fascinates, have cast her as a widow and an orphan.

4

Florence gossip is rife on the midwives' station, though she herself is utterly unaware of this.

The baby, Zélie, does not feed for long. Florence rubs her back gently. Zélie lets out a gentle burp, yawns delicately, and falls asleep again with the ease of a kitten. Florence waits a moment, then rises with difficulty and places her back in her transparent hospital cot, her fishtank. She gazes at her, her expression wistful.

'I wish you could talk,' she says. She kisses the fingertips of her own right hand, and carefully brushes the kiss on to the cheek of the sleeping child. Her baby is so new, hunched together like a bud still waiting to uncurl, tight fists, screwed-shut eyes, knees folded to her chest. They measured her in bits to check her length, all twenty-three centimetres of her. Florence still does not think that it is possible to be so small and live, yet the baby, even fast asleep, radiates life. The room seems to pulse with energy emanating from her, this minuscule child who does not move, who appears not even to breathe. Florence, despite her discomfort and her exhaustion, is beginning to understand what it could mean to be religious.

She is still sitting, watching her baby, when Cassandra returns to her room with two cups of tea. 'So quiet out there,' she beams. 'So different from the public wards. A nice break.' She settles comfortably in the armchair next to Florence's bed. 'I said to myself, I'll take my tea with that sweet girl. Then maybe she'll tell me why she cries so much when she dreams.' She drinks her tea, closes her eyes and sighs. 'That's better.

5

Now darling. I'm listening.'

Florence is baffled by Cassandra. She would like to tell her to mind her own business and leave, but somehow that is impossible. Cassandra is too large, too determined. Too sure, really, that Florence will comply. And also . . . Florence wants to talk. She has managed to hold herself together so well, for so long, but over the last few weeks of her pregnancy she has felt herself coming apart, almost literally unravelling, seam by seam. Her nightmares have returned, different each night but all linked by this terrible, choking sense of loss and the memories she once hoped she had escaped. She takes a sip of tea, and begins.

La Rochelle, 1995

She was not always alone.

When Florence was twelve years old, her mother gave birth to twin boys. Their conception had been an accident, but her parents rose to their new challenge with gusto. Not so, however, Florence who, try as she might — and she did try, a little — could not muster any enthusiasm for the new brothers who had robbed her of her single child status. Her role had been assigned to her prior to the birth: she was to be a Great Help, a Little Mother, a Big Sister — everything, it seemed, but herself. And as life with its challenges — superfluous siblings, puberty, secondary school — gradually ate away at her grasp on what exactly that self was, she grew grumpy and recalcitrant. A *problem*, sighed her mother, Catherine, viewing the end of term with trepidation. She had been looking forward to a restful summer at home in London, but soon realized that this would not be possible with a bored and angry Florence in the house. 'Send her to me,' declared Mimi, her own mother, from her airy home in La Rochelle, that medieval jewel of a town on the south-west coast of France. 'I'll look after her.'

And so it was that Florence — gangly legged, bushy haired and not yet remotely glamorous — arrived for lunch at the old family property of

La Pommeraie one sunny August day, accompanied by her grandmother but missing the
protection of her parents, to find her Great-
Uncle Rémy, grey haired and bewhiskered,
standing on the porch in a pink terry-cloth
dressing-gown, brandishing a hunting rifle and
shouting orders at his grandson across his
extensive front lawn.

Three of his granddaughters, all blond and
blue-eyed, were on the porch with him, the
smallest on the floor with her arms tightly
wrapped around a squirming cocker spaniel.

'Let me guess,' sighed Mimi. 'The coypu
again.'

'Between the Canadian maple and the
sycamore!' yelled Rémy. 'What's wrong with the
boy? The maple and the sycamore, I say!'

'Tell him the sweet tree and the old swing,'
suggested Marie-Jo, the youngest granddaughter,
from the floor. 'Yuk, Oscar, stop licking me.'

'THE SWEET TREE AND THE OLD
SWING!' bellowed Rémy. 'Ridiculous!' he
added. He turned to Mimi, and his face lit up.
'You're here! Look, everybody, Mimi's here.
With little Florence!'

Five pairs of eyes — three girls, one old man,
one small dog — turned towards them.

'What's happening?' Tante France, Rémy's
wife and Mimi's younger sister, walked towards
them from the vegetable garden, a wooden
gardening basket over her arm, her usual serene
smile playing over her fine-boned face. 'I heard a
gunshot. Mimi, *chérie*, you've arrived. And little
Flo! Come and give me a kiss.' Florence

8

embraced her obediently. 'Even prettier than your mother,' whispered Tante France, and winked.

'Never mind all that,' interrupted Mimi, who was as tall and thin as her sister, but rather more imperious. 'Why the hell is Rémy shooting coypu in the middle of the day?'

'What's a coypu?' asked Florence, only just off the plane from England and feeling rather lost.

'Paf saw one!' Everybody knew Rémy's six-year-old grandson by the acronym of his full name, Pierre-André-Frédéric, an impossible mouthful bestowed on him by over-enthusiastic parents delighted to finally produce a boy after an uninterrupted run of girls. 'I've been waiting up for it every night for a week, and blow me if it doesn't turn up bold as brass in the middle of the day while the boy's playing down by the river!' Rémy turned to Florence. 'A *coypu* is a semi-aquatic rodent, not dissimilar to a large rat, *allegedly* herbivorous, and *allegedly* crepuscular. Except for the ones in Pommeraie, which eat my chickens, and come out to sunbathe when they ought to be asleep. *Alors?*' he hollered at Paf, who was rooting around in the woodland bordering the river, aided by an enthusiastic chocolate Labrador. 'Have you found it yet?'

'Nothing!' called Paf in a small, reedy voice. 'Can I come back now?'

'*Chéri*, I don't understand why you're wearing my dressing-gown.'

'I was in the bath,' answered Rémy simply.

'Oh for God's sake!' said Mimi.

9

'You do look awfully odd,' smiled Tante France fondly.

'I think he looks gorgeous.' Another blonde granddaughter, older than the others, slipped on to the terrace, wearing a very short tennis dress, trainers and a conker brown tan. 'You should wear it always, Papi,' she drawled.

'It was perfectly safe,' insisted Rémy, turning to Mimi. 'I knew where everyone was. I made sure of it, before I took my shot. There was nobody in the garden. Except you, my dear,' he added to his wife, 'but I knew that you were out of range.'

'Oh look,' said Mimi sarcastically. She pointed down the path past the vegetable garden, where a small slim woman was hurrying towards them. 'Here comes Agnès.'

Rémy turned pale. '*Merde!*' he muttered. 'I'd forgotten about Agnès.'

Agnès, France and Rémy's daughter, was quite unharmed. She appeared not to have noticed the gunshot, and nobody chose to mention it to her. She was prone to twitter, and it was an unwritten law among her family to keep as much from her as possible.

'Little Flo!' she exclaimed. Florence gritted her teeth, and tried to look older. 'Has everybody said hello? Lunch is ready. Amandine, do get changed, you can't possibly have lunch in a tennis dress.'

'I don't see why not,' said Amandine.

Agnès ignored her. 'We're having lunch at mine,' she said graciously. 'Are we waiting for Claire?'

Claire was Florence's aunt, Mimi's other daughter, due to arrive with her family that afternoon.

'They won't get here till later,' answered Mimi. 'They called from Tours to say they were stuck in traffic.'

'What about Gilles?' Gilles was Mimi and Hector's son.

'He's on the afternoon train, he said he'd come here from the station.'

'Then it's all ready. Papa, why on earth are you wearing *maman*'s dressing-gown?'

Camille and Louise, her two middle daughters, seized her by the arm and marched her firmly away. The others followed in dribs and drabs, Florence keeping close to Mimi.

'I think you'll find,' whispered her grandmother, 'that it helps to think of them as individuals, rather than as a pack. Less *overwhelming*, somehow.'

'I'm not over . . . ' But Mimi had already turned towards France, and engaged her in a detailed conversation about gardening which was to go on for most of lunch.

★ ★ ★

La Pommeraie was Mimi's childhood home. Here she had been born. Here she had grown up with her sister France and her brother Louis. And here she had lived until the end of the war, when she had left La Rochelle for Paris and met an Englishman called Hector who swept her off her feet, married her and took her off to live in

11

Hove before returning ten years later to build the light modern house on the avenue Carnot where they still lived now. La Pommeraie in contrast was ancient and a little gloomy, built in 1826, all pale grey *pierre de taille* and slanting blue slate roofs, casement windows and tall white shutters, wide stone steps leading up to a vine-clad terrace and the glass panels of the front door. Its kitchen dated back almost to the last war, and the smell of nearly two centuries of wood fires burned in the marble fireplaces lingered throughout the entire house. Inside, a creaking wooden staircase led upstairs to a maze of interconnecting rooms and antediluvian bathrooms. Outside, in the acres of parkland, dark oak woods once dotted with manicured clearings were now thickly carpeted with ivy. The grounds boasted a fish-pond full of frogs, two disused gardener's cottages, a stagnant river, a bursting vegetable garden, two dogs, three cats, and innumerable geese, ducks and hens.

Ten years previously, when Agnès and her husband Christophe's reproductive zeal showed no sign of abating, Tante France had realized that even her large and rambling house could not accommodate her tribe of grandchildren comfortably every summer. She had offered them the old stable block instead, which they had converted into a pretty, low-lying summer house, with their bedroom in the old grain store under the eaves, and the children in two long dormitory-style rooms below. Agnès referred to it as her Petit Trianon, but the rest of the family knew it as the Warren.

'Because,' explained Matt, Auntie Claire's eldest son, who had first coined the name, 'they breed like rabbits.'

Lunch was served in the grassy courtyard in front of the house, in the overlapping shade of a walnut and a fig tree. Even out of the sun, the air temperature was in the low thirties. People, animals and plants wilted. With an unspoken but complete conversational ban on the great coypu hunt, the children retreated into silence, solidly working their way through their potato omelette with glazed expressions, with the exception of Amandine, who ate nothing but left the table periodically, returning a few minutes later trailing a scent of cigarette smoke and perfume. Of all the sisters, only she was at all intimidating when considered outside her pack. Still in her tennis dress but now barefoot, with her lithe figure and sheet of white-blonde hair, she exuded eighteen-year-old cool and sexiness and confidence. The others were dressed like miniature versions of their parents, Paf in Bermuda shorts and polo shirt, the girls in traditional summer dresses. Nine-year-old Marie-Jo looked sweet enough in her cap-sleeved flowery print, but it was a strange choice for Louise and Camille, aged thirteen and fourteen respectively, both sporting budding curves and long legs and eyeing Florence's denim cut-offs with envy. Mimi's advice worked, thought Florence as she started to relax. Taken one by one, the cousins weren't scary at all.

'Dear, how are the twins?' Agnès brought her back to earth. Florence, lost in thought, choked guiltily on a piece of potato, and coughed loudly.

'OK,' she hiccuped eventually. 'Sort of . . . twinnish, really.' Camille and Louise giggled.

'Do you hate them?' asked Marie-Jo. 'I *really* hated Paf when he was born.'

The cousins perked up.

'You were *awful* to him,' said Camille.

'A terror,' agreed Louise.

'She tried to drown me,' confided Paf.

'In the bathtub,' confirmed Marie-Jo.

'We felt so sorry for you, when we heard they were born,' added Camille.

'We thought how *tragic* it was, after being an only child for so long,' sighed Louise. 'We all *long* to be an only child.'

'They're not *that* bad,' said Florence, surprised at her own new-found loyalty. She turned to Agnès, who sat with one elbow on the table, her hand gently massaging her temple. 'I mean, when they're asleep and everything.'

Agnès smiled faintly. 'I bought some apple tarts for dessert,' she said. 'Why don't you all go and eat them in the garden?'

They took their cakes into the woods, and ate them sitting on the low branches of an old holm oak.

'You *are* so lucky not to have to wear stupid dresses,' said Camille.

'*Maman* still buys all our clothes, except for Amandine who's got a job and can buy her own,' grumbled Louise. 'I swear she just goes into a shop and buys the same thing in all our sizes. That's if we're lucky and don't wear hand-me-downs. It's hell being in a big family. I mean *look* at us.'

'I think your dresses are pretty,' lied Florence. Marie-Jo snorted. 'They're *babyish*.'

'I can't wait for Matt to get here,' said Camille dreamily. 'You are *so* lucky that he's your first cousin, and you get to share a house with him and everything. He's *so* gorgeous.'

'Not *that* lucky,' said Louise. 'You can't snog your first cousin. Ooh, talk of the devil . . . '

Through the trees, they made out a battered Mercedes estate driving up to the house. It stopped, the back door opened, and a small girl shot out, followed at a more leisurely pace by two teenage boys.

'They're here!' yelled the cousins. They slid out of the tree in one lithe, coordinated movement, and ran towards the car.

★ ★ ★

Florence had dreaded and longed for this moment.

When Catherine had first raised the question of going to La Rochelle for the summer, Florence had resisted. She had protested that she did not want to go, that they could not make her go. In short, that she *would* not go. She loved La Rochelle, the house and her grandparents, but she was not a chattel, she announced to her startled mother, to be used and disposed of. She had feelings. She had rights. She intended to exercise those rights, and stay. She had protested all the more because she knew that Catherine

15

would hold firm, and that chattel or no chattel, there was a very compelling reason for her to go to La Rochelle, that reason being her gorgeous, apparently unsnoggable, totally delectable first cousin Matt, at this very moment spilling out of the back of his parents' ancient car along with the rest of his family, who were collectively referred to with great affection as 'Claire's lot.'

Like her mother and her sister, Auntie Claire had married an Englishman. She now lived in Cambridge, but remained very attached to her childhood home. She and her husband were both teachers, and they took advantage of their long summer vacations to descend on La Rochelle *en masse* for a good month every summer, filling every nook and cranny of Mimi and Hector's pristine house. And here they stood now, Claire's lot, on the lawn which earlier today had seen such excitement, watching the children approach. Auntie Claire herself, all long brown hair and soft smiles and vaguely hippie clothes. Uncle James, looking fat and jolly, with thirteen-year-old Tom, pale and bookish, his glasses slipping down his nose. Lily, six years old, golden ringlets and a face like an angel. And Matt.

The Pommeraie cousins crowded round, jostling for prime position, while Florence held back diffidently. Lily flung her arms adoringly around her waist.

'I'm sharing a room with you!' she announced.

'Only if Flo doesn't mind,' warned her mother.

'She doesn't mind,' said Lily firmly. 'Do you,

16

Flo?' She dropped her voice. 'If you say you mind, I'll cry.'

'I don't mind,' said Florence quickly. Lily beamed.

'Ahoy there!' They all turned to see a taxi making its way slowly round the gravel drive, a large bearded man in a garish shirt hanging perilously out of the open window.

'Perfect timing as usual,' murmured Auntie Claire as she greeted her brother Gilles. 'We've just arrived as well.'

'Darling Claire,' answered Oncle Gilles, kissing her fondly on both cheeks. 'Lend us the money for the cab fare, will you?'

Claire complied, grumbling. Gilles stretched, grinned, and prepared to engage with his family. 'How's my favourite niece?' he boomed, seizing Florence by the waist.

Florence laughed. It was impossible to be timid around Gilles. Would-be artist, enthusiastic supporter of doomed business projects, leader of adventures and expeditions, he was a big, over-sensitive bear of a man, adored by everyone except his two ex-wives and his only son, Ben.

'Oncle Gilles,' reminded Lily darkly, '*I'm* your favourite niece.'

'You, young lady, are my favourite *little* niece. Flo is my favourite big niece.'

'What about us?' demanded Marie-Jo.

'Strictly speaking, you lot aren't nieces at all. Where's your mother? Where's *my* mother? Take me to them.'

They moved off together towards the Warren. Florence followed in their wake, and was surprised when Matt fell into step with her.

'So,' he asked easily. 'When did you get here?'

He was even more god-like than she remembered. He was fifteen now, and had grown again since Christmas. He had that look of teenage boys, of a body not quite in chime with its sudden growth spurts, a tangle of long limbs, a face neither adult nor childish. There was nothing gawky about him though, and unlike his brother he carried his adolescence with grace. Matt was an athlete, a swimmer, a sailor. His hair was already turning fair from the summer sun, and his blue eyes were bright in his suntanned face. She tried to speak, but discovered that her tongue had twisted itself into a knot.

'This morning,' she stammered finally.

'I'm glad you're here,' he said, and her stomach flipped.

'Really?'

'We'll have fun. Loads of things we can do.'

Like what? she wanted to ask, her imagination running wild, away from the cosy, chaotic family group to a place inhabited only by Matt and herself.

'Shall we go and find the others?' He was smiling, a Matt smile, patient and sympathetic and dazzling all at once.

'Yeah . . . oh, er . . . sure.'

She would have liked to walk on with him, into the cool dark woods where they could continue as they were, deliciously alone. Surely she must be able to find something to say, something to slow him down. *What, what, what,* she thought desperately. *What can I say?*

The Warren came into view. Lily pounced on them the moment they appeared, dragging an anxious-looking Paf. A duck had nested on the roof of the porch of the big house. Paf had seen it. The ducklings had hatched, they were safe for now, but what would happen when they were ready to leave the nest? Would they not break their necks, falling so far to the ground?

'They'll fly, won't they?' said Matt.

'No, but their tiny tiny wings . . . ' Lily held her hands out in front of her to indicate just how small the ducklings' wings were. 'We have to build a slide.'

'For the ducks?' asked Florence.

' . . . *lings.* For the duck*lings.*'

'But what if the coypu climb up the slide?'

'They won't,' said Paf. He had not spoken until now, but this was not unusual. With four older sisters, he found that there was little point speaking unless he had something really worthwhile to say. 'Coypu can't climb.'

'You're sure of this?' asked Matt.

'Absolutely,' said Paf with more assurance than he felt. 'Quick,' he added, looking over his shoulder. 'Before the others.'

'Before the others *what?*' Marie-Jo bounced up. '*What* before the others?'

'We're going to build a slide. For the ducklings.' Paf drew himself up as tall as he could. '*We're* going to. With Matt. Right, Matt?'

'Right,' said Matt.

'And Florence,' added Lily.

'What are you talking about? What are you

19

going to build?' Agnès waved them over, smiling.

'Oh no,' muttered Paf. 'Now we'll never get it done.'

And indeed the likelihood of the ducklings' ramp ever being built seemed to grow increasingly remote, as suddenly everybody wanted to express an opinion on the matter. Oncle Rémy pronounced the idea ridiculous, Tante France thought it delightful, Gilles — who had been drinking *pineau* while the others had coffee — actually cried with laughter, Agnès mentioned that the building was listed, and had anyone thought of that, Amandine told her not to be absurd. Marie-Jo, who was rather enterprising, found her father's address book and telephoned his cousin Régis, who was a vet and quite used to this sort of call and confirmed that a ramp *could do no harm*. 'Régis says . . . ' reported Marie-Jo, but it took a while to make herself heard. By the time they had all agreed that a temporary ramp was in fact a good idea, and that it would not contravene any city planning laws, Matt, Florence, Lily and Paf were already hard at work on the porch of the old house, with several planks of wood, some gardening twine and an old paddling pool, 'to put at the bottom,' explained Lily, 'so they can have a nice splash.'

★   ★   ★

No, Florence was not alone, in the summer of 1995, when she was twelve years old. The ducklings' ramp built, the afternoon passed, as

20

so many had before and so many would again, in a lazy haze of games on the lawn and in the woods, of groups lying on the grass to talk and plan. Among the cousins there was little catching up on the months passed since their last meeting. Their common ground was here and now, this garden, this town, the surrounding islands and beaches. The sun began to dip lower in the high August sky, and shadows grew longer. Hector, Florence's grandfather, arrived on his bicycle, every inch the English gentleman in his linen shirt and straw boater, and was universally fêted. Tante France brought out iced tea and packets of biscuits, and later a bottle of *pineau*, with a bowl of cocktail crackers. Plans were made for tomorrow's expedition to the nearby island of Ré, shopping lists made, picnic menus drawn up. Florence watched and listened, enjoying herself but too shy still to contribute much to the conversation. With her parents far away, she was dimly aware of a new chapter opening, in which a new self emerged, as yet indistinct and out of focus but clearly separate from them, no longer their little girl nor yet her own young woman but something in between, yet to be discovered.

Matt moved from one group to another. He never stayed long with anyone, she noticed, and yet he seemed to please them all. She knew, at any given moment, where he was, and who he was talking to. Out of the corner of her eye, she watched him organize races for Paf, Lily and Marie-Jo; with a pang of jealousy, she saw him lean against Amandine's sun-longer and talk with her in low voices. She knew when he moved over to the grown-up circle, heard him laughing with Gilles, answering Christophe's questions about school and exams, teasing his grand-mother and France. As late afternoon melted into evening, the low-lying light turned the garden and all within it a deep glowing gold, but in Florence's eyes nobody on that first rich evening of the holidays shone more brightly than her cousin Matt.

London, 2005

A pinch-faced midwife sticks her head around the door of Florence's room.

'There you are,' she says disapprovingly to Cassandra, who sits comfortably installed, cradling her mug of tea. 'I've been looking for you. You're needed.'

Cassandra peels herself out of her armchair. 'I'll be back later, darling,' she smiles at Florence, who smiles dreamily back.

A new mother has been wheeled down from the delivery suite. Two nurses push her bed along the wide corridor to her room as she sits proudly clutching her baby. Her husband walks beside her, weeping openly, clutching a spectacular bouquet of roses. Behind him comes a little girl, solemn face shining, holding her beaming grandmother by the hand. *A normal family*, thinks Cassandra with a pang of pity for Florence.

The pinch-faced midwife keeps her busy for the rest of the afternoon, but is eventually called away. As soon as she has gone, Cassandra tiptoes back to Florence's room. On the way, she stops by the other new mother. Her family have gone home and she lies asleep, pale blonde hair splayed out on the pillow, still smiling. Every available surface is crowded with the flowers which have been arriving in a steady stream throughout the afternoon. Cassandra feels no qualms at plucking two dark red roses from their vase.

'One for you,' she tells Florence. 'And one for the baby.'

Florence is sitting up in bed, holding Zélie to her breast. 'You're a very unusual midwife,' she remarks.

'Well that's good,' says Cassandra. 'You're a very unusual patient.'

She finishes putting the flowers in water, then fusses around Florence, checking her pulse and her temperature.

'They sound nice,' she says. 'Your family.'

'Yes,' says Florence flatly. 'Yes, I suppose they do.'

'What happened to them?'

'Oh.' She looks vague. 'We lost touch.'

'Want to talk more?'

Not really, thinks Florence. She puts the baby down tenderly and closes her eyes, hoping Cassandra will take the hint and leave.

She opens her eyes again. Cassandra is still here, ensconced back in her armchair, waiting expectantly.

Oh why not, thinks Florence. After all, what harm can it do?

La Rochelle, 2005

'Have an eclair.'

'What, now?'

'Why not?' Mimi, rather overdressed for market in a flowing orange pyjama suit, peered at Florence over the top of enormous sunglasses which gave her the look of an elegant beetle.

'It's like . . . breakfast time.'

'Best time for cakes.'

It was the morning after everyone's arrival. Florence had woken early and lain for a long time in her bunk above a gently snoring Lily, listening to the eerie silence of the sleeping house, until a painful wave of homesickness compelled her to climb quietly out of bed and creep downstairs, armed with a vague plan of calling her mother. Mimi, also rising early to go shopping for the picnic, had found her curled miserably on the stool by the telephone, unable to remember the dialling code for the UK and struggling to overcome her pitiful certainty that even if she did remember it, Catherine would not appreciate a tearful early morning call from the daughter she had so conveniently disposed of. Mimi had taken one look at her, understood the situation perfectly, bid her get dressed, handed her a banana and a large piece of baguette smothered with apricot jam, and swept her off to market. By nine o'clock, they had bought *tartes au gruyère* and cold *rôti de porc*, *clafoutis aux cerises* and mountains of fruit for the picnic, as well as two sea-bass, half a kilo of tiny *crevettes grises*, *moules* and two dozen oysters for dinner. Florence, unused to such a bustle of activity so early in the morning, was exhausted.

'With coffee,' said Mimi, eyeing the *pâtisserie* display lasciviously.

'I don't drink coffee,' said Florence.

'Best for dunking, though.'

Resistance, in the face of Mimi's determination, was always futile. Installed at a tiny table on the pavement, their heaving shopping basket at their feet, the pungent smells of the market rising to greet them and the summer throng beginning to press around them, Florence and Mimi sat beneath a green and white striped awning and delicately nibbled at chocolate éclairs dipped in steaming cups of black coffee.

'You see what I mean,' sighed Mimi, and Florence, the feather-light pastry melting on her tongue, the creamy chocolate filling sliding down her throat, the bitter heady scent of the coffee intoxicating her senses, nodded in blissful agreement.

'I always think,' continued Mimi, 'that the holidays are a time for excesses. For doing things you wouldn't normally do. A time of possibilities.' She took off her sunglasses and leaned forward, the expression in her clear hazel eyes uncharacteristically gentle. 'I want you to have a splendid summer here, Florence. Do you think you will?'

A recent memory flashed through Florence's

mind. Catherine at the airport, entrusting her to the air hostess, for once ignoring the twins howling in their double buggy, looking very hard as if she was trying not to cry herself. 'Be brave,' she had said as she kissed her goodbye, and for the brief moment when they held each other's eyes it felt to Florence like old times, before the twins and growing up made life complicated, when she and her mother were the best of friends. She felt her way cautiously around the memory, anticipating melancholy, surprised to find instead a sort of courageous resolve. *Be brave*.

An elderly woman walked past, trailing a ribbon of small grandchildren. Standing against a shady pillar of the covered market, two lovers embraced, thinking themselves invisible. A collarless dog loped by, tail held high, a scrap of meat in his drooling jaw. Overhead, the morning sun climbed higher into the blazing sky, while on the table in front of her the last fragment of éclair nestled against her half-full cup of bittersweet coffee, demanding to be eaten. Florence let out a small involuntary sigh of satisfaction.

'Yes,' she said, smiling gravely. 'Yes, I think I will.'

Back at the car, they found a parking ticket stuck to the windscreen. Mimi sighed. 'There's no respect any more,' she said sadly. 'Flo, *chérie*, will you? While I load the car?'

Florence had no need to ask what her grandmother wanted from her. She plucked the ticket from the windscreen and then, with a sense of great daring and adventure, crossed the road to throw it in the bin.

* * *

The smell of Ré rose to greet them before they even left the bridge which connected it to the mainland, warm pine mingled with the musty scent of the *immortelles*, the little yellow flowers which dotted the dunes. The first few kilometres of road were bordered with clusters of low whitewashed houses, pink-roofed and green-shuttered, hollyhocks standing proudly to attention in neat front gardens. These gave way gradually to pine groves, then to salt marshes. The sea, never far away, shone an inviting turquoise. They drove with the windows open. 'Feel the air! Feel it, feel it!' ordered Auntie Claire ecstatically, basking in an environment the memory of which kept her going through the long damp Fenland winters. It was impossible not to be infected with her high spirits, in this light and pretty place which breathed freedom and holidays and well-being. Even when they ran into slow traffic, and the sun beat down relentlessly on the hot metal of the car, and Tom grumbled that he didn't understand why they must always, *always*, drive right to the end of the island when there were plenty of perfectly good beaches closer to the bridge, even then Florence's spirits kept up. They finally turned off the main road, and took a winding track through the woods, leaving main car parks behind to stop in a tiny shady glade nestling between the tree line and the sand dunes. They spilt out of the car, stiff and sticky with sweat, and would have run for the water if Claire hadn't sharply called them to order, and loaded them up with the mountain of beach apparatus which in the cool of the house had seemed so desirable.

Florence walked alone, weighed down by a large beach bag. She was torn between the immediate, primitive desire to run to the water as fast as possible, and the more sophisticated wish to make her pleasure last. She chose the latter, and so walked slowly — trudged, almost — through the hot sand which burned her bare feet, and slipped away from under her as she began her ascent through the narrow thistle-ridden path leading up through the dunes. She kept her eyes on the ground, deliberately staving off the glorious moment when she would reach the top, and the warm still sweet air behind the barrier of sand would be replaced in one breath by the salt-buffeted breeze coming off the Atlantic. She looked up then, standing as tall as she could and for a short yet timeless moment she felt that she was flying. The wind lifted her, blowing back her hair, her clothes, wrapping itself lightly around her thoughts, her emotions, everything which made her *her*. She gazed down from her vantage point at the conch-shaped sweep of golden sand towards the lighthouse at Saint Clément des Baleines. From here the water no longer looked turquoise, but a more dramatic grey-blue, white horses galloping on the crest of breaking waves. The receding tide had exposed large expanses of dark rock pools. She knew that later Lily and Paf would prevail on her to explore these; that she would try, yet again, to ride the waves on one of the boards that Matt was lugging up behind her. But for now none of this seemed real. All that mattered was this feeling of elation she had at being totally disconnected from the world, and yet at the same time profoundly a part of it.

'Budge it, slowcoach!' Matt and his surfboards had caught up with her. 'You're blocking the way.'

'Flo star'd at the Atlantic with eagle eyes, And Matt and Tom looked at each other with a wild surmise, Silent upon a peak in Ré,' declaimed Tom, coming up behind him. Matt rolled his eyes.

'He's doing it again. It's from *Swallows and Amazons*. He always uses it.'

'It's an adaptation of Keats,' said Tom loftily. 'Actually.' He smiled, somewhat smugly, then without warning jumped from the top of the dune down to the beach and started to run. Matt whooped and went after him.

★　★　★

Florence had forgotten just how perfectly the Pommeraie cousins were made for the beach. They had already set up a noisy camp in the shade of the closest German *blockhaus*, the one which had tipped over so that it was almost perpendicular to the sloping ground. Gone were the demure old-fashioned dresses chosen by their mother: here they were in their element, Camille and Louise sporting scanty bikinis in acid colours, Marie-Jo in lime-green briefs, all showing off the deep dark tan which came so naturally to their olive skin and which contrasted so dramatically with their fair hair. Florence's mood — her happy state of grace — vanished as quickly as it had come. She thought of the plain navy Speedo she had brought for swimming, which showed off the pallor of her skin and clung unforgivingly to her nascent curves. Catherine had wanted to go shopping with her for beach clothes, had offered to book a babysitter for the twins in order to go out 'just the two of us,' but Florence had refused, moved by a combination of pride and modesty bordering on prudishness, far too ill at ease with her changing body to want to show it off.

Lily emerged from behind a windbreak, extravagantly attired in a pink flowery one-piece with a little ruffle on the left shoulder. 'D'you like my swimsuit?' she asked. 'It's new.' She pulled on a pair of lurid yellow armbands, then stepped into an inflatable duck-shaped rubber ring which she pulled up to her waist. 'Now I just need my mask,' she said.

Mimi gazed at her incredulously. 'When I was your age and I was learning to swim,' she said, 'my father tied a rope around my waist and threw me off the jetty at the beach at La Concurrence.'

Lily looked horrified. 'Didn't you drown?' she asked.

'No,' said Mimi. 'I swam.'

'If she'd drowned, you little goose, she wouldn't be here now, would she?' said Claire. 'Let's go for a swim. Is everybody coming?'

How easy to be Lily, thought Florence enviously. She took them all in, the little girl in her finery, Claire discreet but lovely in her old red one-piece, Agnès elegant in Dior, Mimi splendid in a black costume and white swimming cap. Matt, already running in the distance, his lithe fifteen-year-old body . . . It was ridiculous, she told herself sternly, to be so influenced by appearnaces. She would conquer her fears. She would don the dreadful Speedo, and wear it with pride.

Amandine had been lying on her front all the while, apparently asleep. She sat up now, and stretched out gracefully. She wore nothing but the briefest of orange bikini pants. Her waist-length blonde hair was twisted into a plait over one shoulder, half concealing one of her brown, bare breasts. 'I'll come,' she said. Gilles whistled. Claire frowned at him. Florence's courage deserted her completely.

She watched them wander off together, Gilles walking alone, Claire and Lily with Amandine, Mimi following with Tante France and Rémy. She heard Rémy say, 'Do you remember, old girls, when *we* were young, how we sometimes swam naked?' and Mimi and Tante France both telling him to stop being an old fool. She would never fit in here, she told herself dramatically. Feeling intensely sorry for herself, she curled up beneath a parasol and opened a book.

She was woken by a spray of cold water. Matt

32

was lying next to her, shaking his wet head. 'Good,' he said. 'You're awake.'

'You wet my book.'

'You weren't reading it. Anyway, it's one of Tom's. Listen. I have news. Amandine' — he paused for effect — 'Amandine has got a boyfriend.'

Florence was disappointed. Amandine *always* had a boyfriend. In fact the previous summer Amandine had had *two* boyfriends, at the same time, which everybody had found very confusing.

'So?' she asked.

'So,' said Matt, 'I know what you're thinking. But this one's different. *This* one has got a yacht.'

★ ★ ★

Together Matt and Amandine hatched a plan, and Amandine's boyfriend, a hapless twenty-year-old Parisian called Ludovic with butter-coloured hair and a puppy dog expression, was railroaded into accepting it. Mimi was harder to convince.

'Flo's too young,' she declared.

'I'll look after her . . . ' Matt smiled his most winning smile.

'You're hardly a responsible adult,' sniffed Mimi.

'Amandine will be there.'

'Oh, *that* makes me feel better.'

'And Ludo is *twenty*. Practically a *father* figure.'

'Matt really can be very serious, *maman*,' interjected Claire. 'He's promised to take good care of Flo, and I think we should respect that. Besides,' she added, lowering her voice, 'I think it would be *good* for her . . .'

'Er, *bonjour*,' said Florence crossly. 'I *am* here, you know. In case you hadn't noticed.'

Mimi ignored her and turned to her husband. 'Hector!' she demanded. 'What do you think we should do?'

Hector was older than Mimi, shy and prone to headaches. Much as he loved his family, he tended to keep out of their way, and it was a mystery to him now why they had chosen to have this conversation in his bedroom, when he was sitting at his desk and clearly trying to work. Naval history was his passion, and he was currently writing the memoir of a little-known but key participant of the battle of Trafalgar. A normally mild-mannered man, his answer for once was almost irritable.

'Well, *has* anybody asked Flo what she thinks? As she has just pointed out, she's right here.'

'Florence?' Three faces turned towards her, respectively hopeful, encouraging and disapproving. 'Well?' asked Mimi. 'You know I'll respect your decision,' she added unconvincingly.

Florence was in a quandary. On the one hand, she was excited at the thought of a proposed overnight sailing trip, mainly because it meant spending so much time with Matt. On the other . . . she suffered terribly from motion-sickness, and feared making a complete fool of herself by vomiting uncontrollably for twenty-four hours.

To add to this, she was terribly in awe of Amandine, and worried that this might render her completely tongue-tied, even if the seasickness didn't. And she had also convinced herself that Matt secretly fancied their older cousin, which rather negated her whole reason for wanting to go. On balance, then, there were more disadvantages than advantages to the plan.

'I . . . ' she started.

'Go on, Flo!' Matt smiled, that smile he had which told her that she was the most important person in the world. He couldn't possibly smile at her like that and harbour secret feelings for Amandine. And maybe on a *little* boat, she would be all right . . .

'I really want to go,' she said. 'I don't think I'm too young. I adore sailing. And Amandine and Ludo are really nice. I really do want to go.'

Mimi instantly tried to talk her out of it, but Florence remained adamant and did not change her mind.

★　★　★

Two days later, she sat huddled at the back of Ludo's father's tiny yacht, trying not to get in anybody's way and determinedly ignoring the steep incline of the hull as it cut across a two-metre swell. Amandine was steering, clad for once in both parts of her orange bikini, gleefully shouting out orders to the boys, and Florence tried to ignore her as well. The heat, even with the breeze and the spray, was intense, and her head ached. Her throat was parched, but she didn't dare go below for fear of being sick in the cabin. She closed her eyes, which dealt quite effectively with the problem of watching Amandine, but did nothing for her nausea. She opened them again and breathed deeply, trying not to think about her stomach.

'Go and sit up front if you feel sick,' said Matt. His obvious annoyance compounded her misery. She shook her head, too scared to move.

'*How* old did you say she was?' she heard Ludo ask Amandine.

'Twelve.'

'I thought you said fifteen.'

'*Matt* is fifteen. Don't fuss. She was miserable, poor *puce*. Her mother's just had these ghastly twins. This is an errand of mercy.'

'She's gone *green* . . . '

Florence closed her eyes again, this time not to bear witness to her own humiliation.

★　★　★

With a brisk wind behind them, they made the crossing to Ars-en-Ré in just over three hours, and reached their mooring in the early evening.

'Time for a drink!' announced Ludo. He disappeared below with Amandine to get changed. Almost immediately, light moans began to emanate from the cabin.

'Let's leave them to it,' said Matt, and Florence gratefully agreed.

He was in a sombre mood. Florence, worrying that she had let him down, dared not speak, and neither of them said a word until they reached the village, a good ten-minute walk from their mooring.

'Why didn't you say you got seasick?' asked Matt abruptly.

Hadn't that been obvious? She was thankful. 'I don't normally,' she lied.

'I wanted it to be nice for you,' he said peevishly. 'It was meant to be fun, something special for you.' She looked away so that he would not see her grin. 'I told Ludo you loved sailing. Now he must think I'm a total dweeb.'

'I'm sorry,' she said humbly. 'But I'm sure he doesn't think you're a dweeb. I'm sure nobody could think that, ever.'

His handsome features, which had been almost petulant, broke into a smile. That was the thing about Matt. He never could stay angry for long and then when he was happy again it was like the sun coming out.

'Flattery, flattery!' he mocked. 'So young, and yet so wily.' He held out his hand. 'Come on,' he said. 'I'll buy you an ice-cream, if you can stomach it.'

The terrace at the Café du Commerce was already heaving. Florence turned down the offer of an ice-cream, and they bought cans of Coke from the *épicerie* which they took to the edge of the tiny harbour to drink with their legs hanging over the water. The tide had gone right out, and boats and pontoons had sunk several feet beneath them. A pungent, brackish smell came up from the mud, but they didn't mind. The low, flat countryside glowed in the light of the setting sun, which bathed the little white houses of the village in new colours. Behind them the crowds grew thicker, and harassed waiters hurried to fulfil orders, but it was peaceful sitting there, leaning against an old anchor. Matt talked quietly about sailing. Florence closed her eyes and listened. Her head still ached and the heat of the day showed no sign of abating, but she was with him, and that was the most important thing. By the time they returned to the boat they were friends again, and she felt better.

They ate on board that night, a rice salad and cold meat, followed by yoghurts and fruit. Eaten out of context, it tasted exotic. After dinner, Matt and Ludo taught Florence to play backgammon and laughed as she grew more competitive with every game. Amandine draped herself across the prow of the boat and chain-smoked. Away from the open ocean, the night air was heavy and close. Florence wore nothing but a pair of white shorts and her new bikini (a present from Claire), too hot to care about her appearance. A lock of hair escaped from her scruffy half-ponytail, and stuck damply to her neck. She was tired, but the thought of going below was unbearable.

'This is awful,' declared Amandine. 'Ludo, we have to do something. We're all going to melt.'

'What do you want me to do? I can't very well make it rain,' answered Ludo helplessly.

'We could go for a swim.' She slid gracefully over towards him and wrapped her bare legs around his. Florence noticed with interest that his eyes seemed to darken, and that when he spoke his voice sounded hoarse.

'What, here?'

'No silly, not here. We could take the boat out, and swim off one of the beaches.'

'I . . . I'm not allowed to sail at night. I promised my father.'

Amandine smiled.

★ ★ ★

The sea, much to Florence's relief, was calmer than on their way over from the mainland, and she did not feel unwell again. They anchored just north of Sainte-Marie, on the more sheltered south-facing coast. The night sky was thick with stars and the moon, though not full, shone brightly. The still waters gleamed a soft ethereal silver around them, but the slightest disruption of their smooth surface revealed an inky blackness beneath.

'Well?' Ludovic lifted Amandine's heavy blonde plait to kiss the nape of her neck. 'What's the matter? Are you scared?'

She gave him a lazy, contemptuous smile. 'As if,' she said. She stepped deliberately away from him, and pulled her dress over her head. Underneath, she was completely, spectacularly naked. 'Your turn,' she said to Ludo. She glanced towards the others and winked.

Florence stole a look at Matt, who shrugged and raised his eyebrows as if to say *don't ask me*. Ludo tore off his shorts. Even though he stood with his back to her, Florence could see that he had an erection. She glanced away quickly.

They jumped in on the count of three.

Amandine screamed. Florence gave a little cry as they hit the water.

The sea, previously so still, so perfectly monochrome, exploded. Amandine and Ludovic, their bodies, their hair, the water around them all glowed an eerie green as phosphorescence bubbled around them. They hit the water with their palms, and it arced above them, glittering, jewel-like.

'They're beautiful,' murmured Florence. She turned to Matt. 'Don't you think?'

She had expected him to leap in after them, whooping and yelling as he dived into the light, but he continued to stand next to her, gazing at the swimmers, his face suddenly dark with an expression she had not seen before and which frightened her a little. 'Don't you think they're beautiful?' she asked again, not because she cared for his answer, but because she wanted him to talk, to reassure her that he was still *her* lovely happy Matt, and not this new cold and distant person gazing hungrily at Amandine.

His seriousness did not last long. When he turned back to her, his eyes were gleaming. 'Come on, then!'

'I'm not sure . . . ' She wanted to go with him, wanted to escape the oppressive heat and play in the luminous waters, but something held her back. It was too much, she thought. Too much beauty, too much perfection. Overwhelming, obliterating. She bit her lip. How could she explain it?

'I'm kind of scared,' she said.

'Of course you are,' he said calmly. 'It's bloody

scary. But that's not a reason not to do it. And anyway . . . ' — he took her chin in his hand, and wiggled it — 'I'm here to look after you. So if you drown, you can blame me.'

'Very reassuring,' she muttered. He had not understood her, and she was both relieved and disappointed by this. She peered over the edge of the boat. It *did* look an awfully long way down, but she had the feeling that if she didn't do this now, she would always regret it. *Besides*, she thought, *how would it look to him, to the others, if I cowered here alone?*

She stood up carefully and turned to face Matt again. 'I'll do it,' she announced, 'but I'm not going in naked.'

★ ★ ★

Later, Florence would look back on this night as one of the happiest of her life. When they finally pulled themselves shivering out of the water, they stayed on deck for a long time, wrapped in towels and blankets and drinking tea prepared by Amandine. The boat bobbed gently on the calm waters, and the night sky watched over them benevolently. They had used the engine to come out here but a breeze had picked up again and Ludo insisted on sailing back. The little yacht cut silently northwards through the sea growing milky with dawn. Florence lay curled on deck next to Matt and dozed. At some point, she was vaguely aware of him taking her hand. She did not dare move, did not even open her eyes. Joy coursed through her then, joy and something more. It started with her swelling heart and ran through her veins to the end of her tired, contented limbs. Here was the feeling she had had on the dune, 'silent upon a peak in Ré,' as Tom had put it. Life, she thought, pure and simple, and she smiled through her veil of sleep.

It was light when she woke, still on deck but under a sleeping bag, with a pillow beneath her head. They were back at their mooring, and Amandine and Ludo were climbing on board clutching baguettes and sweet-smelling paper bags.

'Breakfast,' smiled Amandine. 'Straight out of the oven, the *boulangerie* wasn't even open, we went in through the back.'

She tossed one of the bags over to Florence. Ravenously, with not a trace of latent seasickness, Florence pulled out a *pain au chocolat* and sank her teeth into it greedily.

London, 2005

It is growing dark outside. Florence has stopped talking. She is tired, and leans back against her pillows, lost in thought. The baby begins to fret, as though to fill the sudden silence. Cassandra picks her up, and walks over to the window. It is the beginning of the afternoon rush hour: a traffic jam is forming, lights are coming on. The stripped silhouettes of the trees are stark, their soft haze of new buds not visible from this distance in the twilight.

Florence's story does not make sense to the midwife. Her supervisors have reprimanded her in the past for prying too much into the lives of her patients, but it is not in Cassandra's habits to accept things she does not understand. 'You see, darling,' she says pensively, 'here's what's troubling me. This big family of yours . . . ' The baby burps, an indecently loud belch for such a small person. Florence laughs softly, but Cassandra is not to be deflected. 'All this family,' she continues, 'where are they? Why aren't they here with you?'

The young woman closes her eyes. *This is the problem with talking*, she thinks. *People inevitably ask questions*. She should have kept quiet, but it had felt so good, so liberating, to talk about them all again.

'I'll call them for you,' Cassandra is saying cajolingly. 'How about I call your mum for you right now? Or your grandma, or your auntie?'

Zélie begins to whimper again, and Florence holds out her arms. She leans her forehead gently against the baby's head, breathing in her sweet newborn smell. *Would it hurt to call them? Would they come if they were called? Mum would, I know, but would any of the others come now, after everything that has happened?*

Zélie is making pathetic little sucking noises, her face twisted towards her mother's breast, blindly searching. Florence feels an acute compassion for her daughter at this moment, a fierce desire to protect her. The future, which she has been approaching step by step, day by day, for the last nine months, seems suddenly impenetrable. Easier, on balance, to delve into the past, notwithstanding its many pitfalls. She puts the baby carefully to her breast, feels the now-familiar tug of pain, the cramping of her emptied womb. She waits for it to pass, then begins again.

'Once,' she says, 'when we were little — probably a couple of years before the summer I told you about — Matt made us all repaint Paf and Marie-Jo's bedroom in secret. They were the littlest, you know, and they went to bed before the others. There was a mosquito screen over the window — all the houses had them — but one night someone forgot to put it up, and went out leaving the window open. The room was full of mosquitoes when Paf and Marie-Jo went to bed. Tante Agnès burned one of those green insect-repellent coils, and told them that that would be enough, they wouldn't get bitten, but they didn't believe her, so when she went out they got out of bed and they killed all the mosquitoes, every single one. They squashed them with a book — I even know which book, it was *La Nouvelle Héloïse*, God knows what it was doing in a children's bedroom. By the time they'd finished, there were thirty-seven dead mozzies squashed against the walls. I know, because we counted them the following morning. The children were terrified. We were *all* terrified. Tante Agnès was really scary when she was angry — I think she had to be, with five kids — and we were convinced that this would make her furious. So Matt organized a secret painting party. He mobilized everybody: one party had to distract the grown-ups — only my Oncle Gilles was allowed in on the secret, we needed him to help buy the paint — and the rest of us painted frantically. We did quite well, considering. I never knew whether Tante Agnès guessed. That was the thing about Matt. He made things fun. He made you feel . . . he made you feel, when you were talking to him, that you were the very centre of his universe, that nobody mattered to him except you.'

'He sounds very charming,' says Cassandra. Her tone is not altogether complimentary. Cassandra mistrusts charm: her own ex-husband Albert was charming, and much good it has done her. Charm can conceal any number of lacking qualities, in Cassandra's opinion: kindness, generosity. Constancy.

Florence looks annoyed. 'Yes,' she says. 'But he was more than *charming*. He was thoughtful.

And he was right about the trip, you know. Everything changed, because of it. It was . . . it was a pivotal moment. It was like before I had been cowering in the wings, and after that I was happy to go on stage. I'd been so afraid of growing up, of things changing, and he showed me that really there was nothing to be afraid of.'

'You loved him,' says Cassandra sadly. In the articulation of this truth, she thinks that she has uncovered all the mystery of Florence's solitude. A love affair gone wrong, a scandalous pregnancy, a family rejection. It seems clear to Cassandra at this moment that the charming cousin must be the missing father. Why else, she thinks reasonably, would Florence be talking about him so?

At this stage of her small life, the baby never feeds long. She has fallen asleep at her mother's breast again, drunk on milk and warmth. Florence yawns. She has an overwhelming and immediate need to sleep. She curls herself carefully round the baby's tiny body and closes her eyes. There will be no more talking today.

Cassandra has been a midwife for over thirty years. Black babies, white babies, sick babies, healthy babies — she has caught and cared for so many, and yet this sight, of a mother sleeping peacefully with her child, never fails to move her. This is what she resents most about the charming Albert, that he left her before giving her a baby of her own, that she has been left caring for other women's offspring, in the first few days when they need her, before they grow confident and independent, before they understand that they know more than she ever will, than anyone ever will, about their own child.

The hospital bed is narrow. Cassandra lifts the sleeping baby from her mother's arms and places her safely back in her cot. She is about to tiptoe out of the room, when Florence speaks again.

'Thank you,' she mumbles sleepily.

The midwife would like to stroke the young woman's hair, to kiss her, as a mother would her daughter. But this too is forbidden by her supervisors.

'Maybe, if it's quiet again tomorrow, we can talk some more,' she offers.

'I'd like that,' says Florence.

'I'm going off shift soon, but if you need anything, just press on that button and the night midwife will come.'

Florence does not answer. Cassandra closes the door softly and leaves them together in the darkened room, mother and baby. She leaves them sleeping, and she hopes that tonight Florence will not dream.

La Rochelle, 1995

They saw dolphins on the way back. The sea was still calm. Florence leaned right out of the boat to touch them, while Matt hung on to her legs to stop her falling, and Amandine wiped away tears of laughter at the sight. Even Ludo, trying to maintain a semblance of discipline amongst his crew, chuckled. 'Phosphorescence *and* dolphins!' he repeated. 'Unbelievable!' On that sunny afternoon, out in the open sea, they felt that it was all there for them: the beating sun, the light breeze, the cool spray, the pod of silver dolphins racing alongside the boat.

Ludo dropped them home in the late afternoon. Anyone watching Florence as she crossed the courtyard towards the front door would have noticed the change in her, subtle but unmistakable. She seemed taller and less frail, as though in the past twenty-four hours she had grown somehow denser, as though her body and the space it filled had acquired a stronger physical presence. She walked with Matt, bone weary, her sunburnt face glowing, and she leaned in towards him, laughing. Mimi greeted them at the front door, and Florence fell into her arms. 'We saw dolphins!' she cried. 'It was too, too cool!' Words spilt out of her in a torrent, as she dragged her grandmother laughing and protesting across the room. At that moment, nothing seemed more important to Florence than to share her excitement about the trip, and she chattered for a full twenty minutes as Mimi plied them with tea and brioche left over from breakfast. It took her a while to realize that the atmosphere at home had changed. Tom waited for the adults to drift back to their assorted activities to tell them the news.

Gilles' son, Ben, was arriving the following day.

★ ★ ★

They crowded into the boys' room to hear the details. Karen, Gilles' first wife, had called three times that morning demanding to speak to her ex-husband. James took the first call, said Tom gleefully, and did not help matters by telling her — here Tom, who like his siblings was a cruel mimic, imitated his father's clumsy French — that *Gilles had gone to chat up the girls in the old harbour.*

'I don't believe you,' said Florence.

'I swear it's true. *Il est parti draguer sur le port.* I don't think he realized quite what he was saying, actually. Mum gave him a right bollocking afterwards.'

Gilles did not return until lunchtime, by which time Karen was hysterical. She was going to Italy, she said. She had been invited to stay with friends on Lake Garda, it was too good an opportunity, she'd been working so hard all year, he didn't understand what it was like bringing up a child alone, it was time he did his share, she was sending Ben to him for the rest of the

49

summer. 'Gilles said she's like that because she has red hair,' reported Tom. 'He said that should have been a clue not to marry her. He said she was beautiful, but mad. Mimi's furious, because apparently Ben was with her and heard everything.'

'She said Karen was a bitch,' confided Lily cosily.

'You shouldn't say words like bitch,' said Matt automatically.

'You do,' protested Lily.

'Actually, Mimi was really upset,' said Tom. 'Then Grampy told her to calm down, I think because of us, and she stormed up to her room, and he followed, and Mum and Dad were like, everything's fine, and Gilles' been on the phone or looking worried ever since, and drinking, and asking Mum if she thinks he's a really bad father.'

'Poor Ben,' said Florence, and the others assented glumly. That Ben deserved to be pitied went without saying. On the few occasions his mother had come to La Rochelle before the divorce, she had spent most of her time in her room, chain-smoking, only emerging to go to the beach on very hot days, when she sat under a parasol complaining that the water was too cold to swim and making it quite clear how much everybody, including her son, irritated her. And though they did all love Gilles they also knew, from having overheard their own parents talking, that since his second marriage, to a haughty Parisian called Séverine, he spent hardly any time with Ben at all.

'What did Mum say?' asked Matt.

'That of course he wasn't, but that he should think positively about this as an opportunity to spend some quality time with Ben, that everybody loved them, that we would all help. Typical Mum stuff. And Oncle Gilles — I think he was crying — was like he always wanted to do more for Ben only Séverine wouldn't let him because she was jealous, and he tried to see Ben more last winter since Séverine left but Karen won't let him, and Ben hates him blah blah, and then Mum noticed we were listening and made that face, you know, the *get lost or I'll kill you* face, so we left.'

'I wonder what he's like now,' said Florence thoughtfully. 'I haven't seen him for ages.'

'The way I remember him he was always a sulky little sod,' said Matt.

'Even so,' declared Florence firmly. 'We'll have to be extra-specially nice to him. Make him forget he's been dumped here.' She spoke with some feeling, remembering how she too had felt like she had been dumped only a few days before.

'Course we will,' said Matt cheerfully. Tom looked dubious. 'I think you've forgotten who you're talking about,' he said. 'I know *exactly* what he's like. He won't *let* you help him. That's the thing about Ben. He won't even let you be *nice* to him. He's horrible.'

'We'll charm him,' said Florence. Tom snorted, and she threw a pillow at him. 'You'll see, he won't be able to resist.'

★ ★ ★

Florence fell asleep at the dinner table that evening, and Mimi packed her off to bed. She tiptoed in later to check up on her, and found her reading.

'You should be sleeping,' she said.

'I couldn't. I'm tired, but I feel too . . . zingy.'

'Too much sea air, too much sun,' smiled Mimi. 'Your nose is burnt. Did you put any cream on it?'

'Auntie Claire gave me some.' Florence yawned. Mimi reached up and pushed back a strand of Florence's hair, tucking it behind her ear.

'I can't say I'm altogether delighted about this night swimming business. That cousin of yours has some wild ideas, I ought really to talk to Agnés about it.'

'You won't though, will you? You can't!' Florence sat up suddenly. 'I wouldn't have told you if I thought you'd tell! You'd have done the same if you'd been there. I mean, if you were young . . . ' She broke off, embarrassed. 'You must have done silly things sometimes,' she finished lamely.

A shadow, brief but vivid, flashed across Mimi's face. Memories played out on her handsome features like a dance. Florence, half remembering an overheard conversation, imagined a deserted beach, the feel of warm wind on bare skin, the shock of cold water. The possibility of more sensual pleasures flitted across her mind, startling, troubling. She dismissed it with an impatient little shake of her head, and looked hopefully up at her grandmother. Mimi reached over to kiss her.

'You'll be nice to Ben, won't you?' she asked.

'Of course,' said Florence quickly.

'It's not easy for him, you know, caught between his parents. And he doesn't know you all like you know each other.'

Florence was annoyed. 'We were *going* to be nice anyway, you know,' she said. 'Even without you asking.'

Mimi laughed. 'Sleep now,' she ordered.

Florence's mind was already on other things.

'Mimi?'

'What?'

'Do you think one day I'll be as beautiful as Amandine?'

'Oh, you'll be a beauty, *puce*,' chuckled Mimi. 'A regular beauty. But not unless you get some sleep.'

A beauty. Florence fell asleep savouring the words. *You'll be a beauty.* It seemed unlikely, but Mimi had sounded quite convinced, and Florence considered her an authority on the matter. She wondered what her grandmother *had* been thinking about, when she asked her about what silly things she had done. Once more that impression of sensuality, confused and confusing — her own, or the impression of someone else's? Ben arriving tomorrow, so different from the other cousins. A cat miaowing outside, a branch against her window . . . Her jumbled thoughts kept her awake a few moments longer, before her tired body banished them, and she slept.

★   ★   ★

'I want to play Monopoly!'

'No fucking way.'

'Tom, be nice to your sister!'

'She cheats! And she can't read properly! And it goes on for *hours*.'

'Well find something else to do then.'

'Will it *ever* stop raining?'

'One morning of rain. One morning! Surely you can find *something* to do?'

'I do NOT cheat! And I *can* read!'

The weather had broken the night after the sailing trip. On the morning of Ben's arrival, they woke to find that a low front had rolled in silently from the sea, enveloping the world in a thick, damp mist, and their moods had nose-dived accordingly. Florence, with nothing better to do, called home then curled up in a corner of the living room to watch the rain, brooding darkly on her conversation cut short by one of the twins throwing up over the phone, while Tom and Lily bickered, Claire tried to make peace, and Matt took his father's bicycle apart on the terrace, protected from the rain by the balcony above.

'You said it wasn't going properly!' he cried when James protested.

'Fuc — I mean, Jesus! It wasn't *that* bad, for Chrissake!'

'You really shouldn't blaspheme,' tutted Tom reprovingly.

James turned scarlet, Claire swept out of the room, Florence sighed. Lily, grim-faced and determined, rooted through the games cupboard. And into this atmosphere of family discontent walked Ben and Gilles, back from the station.

⋆　　⋆　　⋆

'You've arrived!' Mimi swept in anxiously after them from the kitchen, trailing scents of Guerlain and *tarte aux prunes*, the effect of her beautifully tailored cream trousers and cashmere sweater rendered more homely and a touch eccentric by the generous dusting of flour in her jet-black chignon. 'Ben *chéri*, do let me look at you! How you've grown since last summer!' She was not the sort to chatter, but the tension in the atmosphere was clearly making her nervous. 'I am *so* happy to see you. You're sharing a room with the boys.' Tom and Matt pulled faces at each other behind the others' backs. Florence, who had drifted over from the sofa when Gilles and Ben came in, glared at them. 'Will you like that?'

'Whatever,' muttered Ben.

'Well say hello to your cousin, children.'

Everything about Ben was awkward, from his badly cut black hair to his ill-fitting holiday clothes. He was smaller than Florence despite being a year older, and the overwhelming impression he gave was one of contained, contemptuous intensity. He did not move towards his cousins as they shuffled forward to greet him, but watched them approach with something like a sneer, his dark eyes flicking from one to the other, missing nothing.

'Do *you* want to play Monopoly?' asked Lily hopefully.

'I hate Monopoly,' said Ben.

Lily, finally defeated, burst into tears. Florence told herself firmly that Ben was being obnoxious because he felt intimidated, and moved forward to kiss him. He stepped back deliberately. She stumbled. He smirked.

Gilles' face grew dark with anger. Florence flushed. Matt put a protective arm around her. Mimi looked worried.

'Lunch is ready,' she said. 'Who's hungry?'

★　★　★

Their spirits lifted after lunch, when the rain stopped and Gilles suggested a fishing trip. He took the tackle in the car with Lily and Paf, who had joined them for the afternoon. The others followed on bicycles. The tide was out as they crossed into the park along the sea wall at la Concurrence, and the air was sweet after the rain, the scents of damp earth on their left mingling intoxicatingly with the strong briny smell of exposed rock pools and seaweed on their right. The grey of the sky was streaked with pale sunlight now, and the whole world seemed to shimmer. As Florence cycled slowly through the park, the morning's despondency already forgotten, she felt as if the world were entirely new and she was discovering it for the first time. Very few people were out, and there was something dreamy, almost languorous about the afternoon. It was a pleasant feeling, and for a while she forgot who she was with, and where she was going, and why.

Ben shot past her out of nowhere, causing her to swerve suddenly. She rapped her ankle bone sharply against the frame of her bike and winced with pain. 'Be careful!' she called, but he was gone, already shooting out of the far end of the park on to the white stone of the dyke. *Boys!* thought Florence. *They're all the same.* But she could not shake off a sentiment of disquiet, the feeling that this was not true. Matt and Tom would have stopped for her, would at least have called out to make sure she was all right, given her some warning, some indication that there was no malicious intent. Ben had meant to hurt her.

Gilles was waiting for them by the Résistance monument with Lily and Paf, at the top of one of the flights of stone steps leading down to the tidal rocks, and they began to pick their way carefully towards the distant water. This was not the wild open landscape of the beach at Ré. From here they could see the ancient towers guarding the entrance to the old port on their left, the masts of thousands of sailing boats at Les Minimes, the modern buildings lining the road on the other side of the channel, the cranes at Chef-de-Baie. Even so, down here among the rocks, in full view of the town, they felt completely removed from it.

The ground was covered with brown seaweed. Matt draped some over his head and pretended to chase after Lily, who squealed and ran away, screaming that she hated him. 'Put a crab down his shirt,' yelled Tom. 'Go, Lily, go!'

Ben slipped, put out his hand to stop himself

falling, swore as he cut it on a rock.

'Let me see that,' said Florence — magnanimously, she felt, considering the incident with the bicycle.

Ben snatched his hand away. 'This place is useless,' he said. Tom shrugged at Florence behind his back, as if to say *what did I tell you?* and Florence, feeling discouraged, shrugged back.

She had not fully appreciated before how solitary an exercise fishing was. They stood several metres apart from each other, dark upright figures in the flat opalescent seascape, hooking bait, casting lines and waiting, waiting for a tug. It was, thought Florence, a rather complicated but also rather an agreeable way of doing nothing. She sat on a damp rock and watched the others. Tom was furthest away, jeans rolled up, ankle deep in water. She guessed that he was somehow *intellectually* involved with the whole process, that he was comparing it, perhaps, with literary descriptions of other fishing expeditions. Ben was next in line, and it seemed to Florence that his solitude was more aggressive than the others'. He did not look around, did not wave at Lily and Paf (fishing with Matt, another example of Matt's kindness, she thought), did not get his feet wet, did not move at all but sat on his rock entirely immobile, not even staring out to sea but glaring intently at his line. She noticed that Gilles did not linger with his son, but accorded him if anything less time than he did to the others. When he did approach him, his gestures lost their usual ease,

58

became smaller, more restrained. *He's afraid of him*, thought Florence. *Or rather, he doesn't understand him, and he's afraid of that.*

Lily and Matt yelled. They had a bite, and were reeling it in. Tom and Florence wandered over to watch.

The fish turned out to be a tiddler, too young to know better than to go nosing around hooks, certainly too small for the frying-pan. 'Oh, poor thing!' cried Lily.

'What shall we do with it?' asked Paf.

'Put him in your bucket,' said Gilles. 'We'll have a competition to see who catches the most, and then we'll put them back.'

There were twelve fish at the final count, and Lily and Paf were declared joint winners after Matt — under some pressure — agreed to add his catch to theirs.

'Can we keep them?' begged Lily.

Gilles said no, they couldn't, and so they crouched over the bucket for a last tender goodbye before standing for the release back to the sea. They all felt rather noble at this moment, aware of the irony whereby just a few short hours before they had been hoping for catches large enough to eat, but choosing not to linger on it. Gilles stepped forward with the first bucket and tipped it gently into the water. The little fish continued to swim in dazed circles for a few seconds before darting into the waves and vanishing. Everyone cheered, except for Ben, who still sat apart from them, his own bucket at his feet.

'I'm not putting mine back,' he announced.

They turned towards him, eyes wide with surprise and shock as he plunged his hand into the bucket, grasped the first of his two tiddlers, and smashed its head expertly against a rock. The fish went limp.

'Their mouths were damaged by the hook,' said Ben savagely. 'They were as good as dead anyway.'

He reached into the bucket for the other fish. Lily began to cry.

★   ★   ★

The fishing trip sealed Ben's fate, as far as his cousins were concerned. Lily and Paf lost no time in describing the killing of the fish to anyone who stopped long enough to listen. The incident grew in the telling: Ben stopped them throwing any fish back to sea, he laughed as he killed their entire catch, his hands and arms ran red with blood. The grown-ups did not comment — or rather they commented only with sympathetic nods of the head, murmuring that *they were sure it couldn't have been that bad.* The La Pommeraie cousins, always hungry for drama, lapped up the story. School had been out for over a month, and they were growing bored. Ben provided opportunity for endless gossip and amateur analysis.

The sun had returned the day after his arrival, radiant as before, as if denying it had ever been away. Gilles had excelled himself planning expeditions — digging for clams on Ré at low tide, with full complement of Pommeraie cousins; a bicycle ride out of town into the countryside, ending with a swim on the pebbly beach at L'Houmeau; horse-riding through the salt-marshes; a trip to the Aquarium; an afternoon sailing. Claire, who claimed to be exhausted just at the *thought* of their schedule, had accused her brother of hyperactivity but Florence loved it. She threw herself into each activity with enthusiasm: she was growing physically stronger every day, her skin, which would never be as dark as her cousins', was a pretty peachy gold, her appetite was enormous. She adored them all: not just Matt, but also Lily who had adopted her as a big sister, and Tom who presented her with nineteenth-century novels as if she might actually read them, and Mimi, who came into her room every night to talk in whispers so as not to wake Lily. And Claire, and Hector, and the Pommeraie cousins, who had accepted her into their fold, simply and without fuss, after the sailing trip with Amandine. She was happy.

Florence alone among her cousins tried to gloss over the fishing incident and Ben's general rudeness. Rather moved by her own generosity, she sought to share her experience with him, to show him how it was possible here to overcome anger and loneliness. She tried, through simple gestures, to be nice to Ben. She waited for him when the others shot off ahead, she consulted him when a choice needed to be made, about a beach to go to, or food to buy, or a direction to take. She didn't want to give up on him, but in the days following his arrival, as his father organized ever more elaborate outings, Ben only grew more withdrawn and contemptuous. It was impossible to fully enjoy yourself with someone who scowled continuously, and who appeared to despise the very things you loved. 'He is basically just a thoroughly unpleasant little prat,' declared Matt dismissively. The cold indifference which met her efforts eventually wore her down, and she decided that it was simpler to do as the others did, and ignore him.

'The problem is,' she said to Louise and Camille after about a week of this, 'that none of us *wants* to be nice to him any more. We were all really sorry for him at the beginning, because of his red-haired mother and the Italian lake, but nobody knows *what* to do now. And Lily *hates* him.'

Louise nodded wisely. 'Paf does too. Because of the fish. That sounded awful. Mind you, he *is* awful.'

They were sitting at their favourite café on the old harbour. It was a commonly accepted myth among the older members of the family that they abhorred crowds, a myth which went hand in hand with a general contempt for the tourists who flocked to the town every year in greater numbers. As a result, the family rarely visited the harbour in the summer months, which for the three girls out on their own gave it an additional, illicit thrill. It was the complete antithesis of their protected worlds of La Pommeraie and avenue Carnot. The crowds waiting to embark on pleasure-cruises, the hippies selling cheap, pretty jewellery, the penny artists with their water-colours of lighthouses — they all gave the place a gaudy, carnival atmosphere, accentuated by the cobalt blue of the sky, and the sea glinting in the reflected sunlight. The harbour was packed with boats bobbing gently along their jetties in the rising tide, the air full of the scent of frying *gaufres* and seafood which sharpened their appetites as they lingered over their drinks.

'I don't think he's ghastly,' said Camille. 'All that brooding intensity, I think there's something tragic about him, even more tragic than you, Flo.'

'Thanks,' said Florence.

'Don't mind her,' said Louise airily. 'She sees tragedy everywhere. She's actually a bit obsessed. So what's Gilles planning next?'

Florence hesitated before answering. She toyed with the idea of telling Louise and Camille about the row she had overheard between Ben and Gilles that morning. Gilles' latest idea had elicited exuberant enthusiasm from Matt and Tom, a more guarded response from Florence, torrents of tears from Lily who was not allowed to come. Only Ben had shown himself coldly indifferent to the whole plan. When Gilles — who was finding it more and more difficult to control the irritation caused by his son's attitude — tried to force the issue, Ben had suddenly burst out that he couldn't give a *shit* what they did, that he didn't *want* to be here anyway, that *nobody* wanted him, and what the *fuck* did it matter what he thought about Gilles' *stupid* plans since whatever he thought they'd do it anyway. Then he had burst into tears and locked himself in the bathroom, yelling that he hated everybody and especially his father.

All the others had been out when the row took place, and nobody but Florence had heard Ben's outburst. Gilles had thundered down the stairs and stormed out through the front door, not seeing Florence who was cowering by the door to the garage. She had crept up to the bathroom and was going to knock when she heard Gilles return. She had bolted for her bedroom instead. Gilles had stormed back upstairs and hammered on the door, demanding to be allowed in. After that there had been more tears — she was sure she had heard Gilles crying — and a long muffled conversation, followed by the sound of the bathroom taps running. She felt that she owed it to Ben to tell the others, and at the same time she knew that to do so would be a betrayal of his privacy. *How complicated it is*, she thought, with a surge of annoyance against her difficult cousin. It was easier, far easier, to dislike Ben snapping and snarling and being obnoxious, than to dislike Ben crying alone in the bathroom.

'Camping,' she said simply in answer to Louise's question. 'We're going camping on l'Île d'Aix.'

'Too unfair!' cried Camille. 'I'm *longing* to go camping, but *papa* says we can't.'

'He says there are too many of us,' added Louise. 'He says he'd have to spend his whole time counting us, and it isn't his idea of a holiday.'

64

'So is Ben OK with it now?' asked Camille.

'What do you think?' said Florence. 'Obviously not.'

★   ★   ★

In fact, contrary to all expectations, Ben loved Aix.

They arrived in the late afternoon, when the light had mellowed and the heat abated and the whole island seemed to be shaking itself awake. Cars were not allowed on the island, and they wheeled their bicycles on to the dusty quayside, with Matt pulling the camping material on a luggage trolley.

They passed through a stone archway and along the edge of a wide meadow which they would later discover was the village's main square, before turning sharply left on to a wooden bridge over a moat and into a narrow cobbled street. The small campsite was situated in the ruins of an eighteenth-century fort and dominated by two lighthouses. Gilles had booked a pitch apart from the others, just beneath the low remains of the old fortifications. Climbing over the wall at the back of the pitch, they saw that on the other side a grassy verge sloped gently away from them to fall, a few metres further, straight towards the moat. 'No wonder Gilles wouldn't let Lily come,' whistled Matt, and Florence gulped, suddenly overcome with vertigo.

A warm breeze was blowing off the sea, mingling the tang of iodine with the sweet land smells of grass and sun-baked earth. Directly opposite them lay the island of Oléron. To their right, in the distance, they could see the cranes of La Pallice and the elegant curve of the bridge to Ré.

'What's that?' asked Ben, pointing to a solid stone structure rising straight out of the sea.

'Another fort. Fort Boyard,' said Gilles. Florence turned away, embarrassed by the look on her uncle's face as he turned to his son, hopeful and somehow vulnerable. The atmosphere between them had changed, she thought. Both seemed to be tiptoeing around each other now, aware that they could not continue as they had before their recent row, but uncertain as to what they *should* do next. 'Begun by Napoleon in 1801, finished in 1857 to keep out the English. Now host to a TV games show. *Ainsi va la vie*. Now,' he went on, with a return to his usual heartiness, 'is anyone going to help me, or do I have to put this tent up on my own?'

The village, where they went once the tent was pitched, consisted of a cluster of neatly laid out streets. The houses, as on Ré, were low and and whitewashed, with shutters painted green or pale blue. The only notable exceptions were the hotel and the museum both named Napoléon, and both, at two storeys high, towering almost grandly over the rest of the village. The absence of cars and the super-abundance of blowsy, windblown hollyhocks gave a timeless, picture-book quality to the whole place.

'I don't get it,' said Matt as they made their way back to the campsite, laden with provisions.

66

'This island is what, tiny . . . '

'Seven kilometres long, and barely 500 metres wide,' murmured Tom. 'I read it in a guidebook.'

'Like I *said*, tiny. So what's with the forts, and the whole Napoleon thing? The hotel, the museum . . . even the main street's the rue Bonaparte. And as for the place d'Austerlitz . . . '

'Aha!' said Gilles. They had arrived back at the tent and he was starting to unpack. He pulled a bottle of red wine out of his rucksack with a flourish. 'Time for a drink.'

'*Papa!*' said Ben sharply. 'Napoleon?'

He was frowning, but not with his usual truculence. He looked younger, simpler. Like an impatient child, asking questions. Gilles' expression became almost tender. For a second, Florence thought Gilles was actually going to ruffle his hair, and she mentally willed him not to. *Bad, bad idea*, she told him fervently in her head. *Don't do it!* Gilles smiled.

'All in good time,' he said briskly. 'First, there's work to do. Then I'll tell you everything you want to know. Flo, I seem, unbelievably, not to have packed a corkscrew. Go and smile at that group of young people over there, they're bound to be getting drunk. Tom, get frying the sausages. Ben, I've a feeling we can buy *frites* at the café down there, go and tell them we'll need some in vast quantities in about half an hour. Matt, start chopping tomatoes.' Gilles lit a cigarette and inhaled deeply. 'Fantastic,' he murmured. 'Delegation. Nothing like it.'

When the sausages had been fried, and the tomato salad made, the bread torn into large chunks and smothered with mustard, the chips brought and the ketchup opened, and they all sat cross-legged on a rug licking their fingers, Gilles waved his arm vaguely behind him, presumably to indicate the world beyond Aix.

'Look out there,' he said. 'What do you see?'

'Well, if I stand up and look straight ahead, I can see the lights on Oléron,' said Matt. 'Though I only *know* it's Oléron because Tom told me so.'

'And we can see the bridge, and Fort whatever-it's-called,' added Florence.

'And a few gulls,' said Tom.

'And the sea,' said Ben.

'Yes!' cried Gilles. 'At last, a sensible answer!' Ben looked gratified but tried to hide it. 'The sea. Or to be more specific, the Atlantic, not a sea but a mighty ocean. The reason a glorified rock like Aix can boast two forts — there's one on the other side of the island as well — and an *hôtel Napoléon* etc., etc. Did you know — no of course you didn't, but I'm telling you now — that this was where he set sail from, on 15 July 1815, to surrender to the English? Imagine it. That great man, who rebuilt France after the Revolution, whose *code juridique* we still use today, whose armies conquered most of Europe, who had visions of such ambition and greatness ... He was here, on this island. Maybe he walked along these very ramparts, looking out on to Oléron, as he pondered the wisdom of handing himself over to the English. He admired the English tremendously, you know. He believed they would play fair with him, that they would treat

68

him as a great military leader. He certainly didn't anticipate St Helena. Pesky, those English. Never trust 'em.'

'Dad says Napoloeon was a tyrant,' said Florence. 'That he deserved what he got. That he inspired Hitler.'

'Yes, well,' said Gilles, looking hurt. 'That's one interpretation.'

Ben's eyes were shining. 'Napoleon, right here! That's so cool. What else?' he demanded. Florence, Matt and Tom exchanged surreptitious glances behind his back. 'It's him,' muttered Tom under his breath, 'but not as we know him.'

'What else?' repeated Gilles. He sounded worried. 'Well, that's about all I can tell you about the big man. Relevant to Aix, that is.' Ben looked mutinous, and Gilles hurried on. 'But you know about the treasure, of course.'

'Treasure?' Four pairs of eyes turned on him expectantly. 'What treasure?'

'The treasure belonging to the cousins of the Empress Josephine, before she was Empress of course, which is supposed to be buried in the grounds of La Pommeraie . . . No? Then let me tell you . . . '

Night was falling fast now. Gilles' bottle of wine was almost empty, dinner was finished and a large bar of chocolate lay between them on the rug. Florence had made tea — 'that *pesky English* drink,' she teased her uncle — and steam rose from their tumblers, adding atmosphere as they huddled around the gas-lamp Gilles *had* remembered to bring. Like most of the family, he knew almost nothing of what was actually buried at La Pommeraie. But he was feeling particularly expansive, and the night lent itself to tales of mystery and secrets. Gilles was good at telling stories. He spoke about the Revolution and the Terror, about homes abandoned in panic, about magnificent jewels, diamonds and rubies and emeralds buried in haste in the garden of an old house, which at the time was not La Pommeraie but an earlier house built on the same site, destroyed (and they guessed that this part was completely made up) in a fire caused by a husband jealous of his wife's lover. He told them about the siege of 1627 which pitched the Protestant city against the Catholic crown, about the Duke of Wellington on Ré and about Cardinal Richelieu, about townspeople eating rats and about British blockades. And then he told them about the last siege of La Rochelle, during the dying months of the Second World War, when the town formed one of the few pockets of German resistance right until the end, when peace was declared in May 1945. 'And all because of that,' he said, waving towards the sea again, and this time they did not have to ask what he meant. 'These little islands with their big strategical position. These Atlantic seaports facing America.'

Tom, who knew much of this already, could have told him that his history was confused, but the storyteller was too good. He brought the narrative closer to home, and told how for generations people had tried to find the Empress' cousins' jewels, to no avail. Rémy, he said, had once been so convinced of his calculations that he had insisted on pulling up the floorboards in the dining room, certain that the treasure would be in the ground directly beneath.

'And?' asked Ben eagerly, leaning forward. Again his cousins exchanged loaded glances behind his back.

'And nothing,' sighed Gilles. 'Not a button, not a pin. It's the same for the tunnels.'

'Oh my God, there are tunnels too,' drawled Matt, but he was clearly as riveted as the others.

Gilles nodded. 'There are tunnels everywhere under La Rochelle. Some date back to Viking times, and extend far out into the *marais*. They were a way of giving warning as well as an escape route from invaders. Others were built during the sieges. Legend has it one runs under La Pommeraie, and that it was used as recently as the last war to hide *résistants*, but nobody knows where it is.'

Tom, who had managed to hold back his scepticism over the Vikings, could control himself no longer. 'Surely if an underground tunnel was used during the war, Mimi or Tante France would know about it,' he reasoned.

Gilles was up-ending the wine bottle hopefully over his tumbler. 'I think that one's wrung dry,' murmured Matt, and Gilles shrugged sadly before turning back to Tom.

'You would think so, wouldn't you?' he said. 'But France was away for most of the war, and Mimi left as soon as it was over. It's perfectly possible that my grandfather was involved in the

Résistance but never told them a thing about it. People did that, you know. To protect themselves, each other. I heard the rumours from the old priest at La Pommeraie, a *résistant* himself, but he didn't say much. There was a radio, I know, and guns hidden above the choir stalls in the church. There are stories of my grandparents receiving coded messages from my uncle Louis in England, but I don't know how many, or even how.'

'Great-uncle Louis, the one who died?' asked Florence, though they all knew that there had only ever been one Great-uncle Louis.

'The very one.'

'I'm going to ask Mimi about it,' declared Ben. 'I'm going to ask her to tell me everything she knows, and then I'm going to find the tunnel, *and* the treasure.'

'Best not, if you don't mind,' said Gilles. 'She won't talk about it. Too many memories, she says. It'll only upset her.' He stood up and stretched his massive frame. 'Come on, you lazybones! The moon is bright, and the tide is high, and still no one's done the washing-up. To work! To work, all of you!'

★   ★   ★

Florence walked back from the shower block across the grassed-over ramparts. The wind that whipped her hair over her face was stronger than before, but still warm and slightly damp. She licked her lips, and tasted salt. It was one of those moments, she thought, like on the dunes

72

on Ré, when simply being alive felt like an extraordinary, exhilarating adventure.

She almost stumbled over Ben before she saw him. He sat on the western point of the campsite, staring out at the open ocean between the tips of Oléron and Ré. Every few seconds the view was illuminated by the lighthouse's sweeping beam. She watched him curiously for a while before he noticed her. In the intermittent light, he no longer seemed small or sullen. In fact, there was something almost sensual about his profile, with its straight classical nose and full lower lip. She had not noticed this before.

Later she never could explain to herself why she acted as she did. It had something to do, she recognized hazily, with remembering the sound of his crying in the bathroom, but also with the night, the breeze, the salt, and the feeling that here was a moment outside time, which as such commanded behaviour out of the ordinary.

There was nothing dramatic. No argument, no recriminations, no great pronouncement either. Simply Florence who, instead of slipping past in the shadows, chose instead to join Ben where he sat watching the light playing on the water. He looked up at her as she arrived, and he too must have recognized the moment for what it was, for instead of shrugging her away as she almost expected, he indicated by a slight shuffle, a vague tapping of the ground beside him, that she was welcome.

They were not accustomed to talking together, and so for a while they sat in silence. Ben spoke first, surprising them both.

'You heard us, didn't you? Me and my dad, yesterday. I think you must have, because I heard someone, and later I realized that everyone had been out except for you. You heard us arguing.'

'Yes,' she said.

'And afterwards, you heard, you heard what happened afterwards?'

'Yes.' There was a long silence, in which he made as if to speak, but stopped. 'I won't tell anyone,' said Florence. 'If that's what you're worried about. I haven't, and I won't.'

'I'm not worried,' he said quickly.

'Because I cry all the time,' she went on rapidly. 'Since the twins were born. Mum thinks I'm jealous, but I'm not. And Dad tells her I'm just being a teenager, and maybe that's right, except actually I'm not a teenager yet, and I didn't use to cry *before* the twins.' She stopped for breath. 'Actually, I don't think they know I cry. They just think I'm angry.'

Neither of them looked at the other for a time.

'It's cool, this island,' said Ben eventually, and she agreed. 'I liked Dad's stories, too,' he added. Florence giggled, and he shot her a look unfamiliar on his sullen features, half-amused. 'What, didn't you believe him?'

'*I* don't know! Not all of it, I don't think. I'm sure the bit about Napoleon was true, but I'm not sure about the treasure . . . It *would* be fun to look for it, though.'

'Yeah, it would.'

He had found a stick and was digging a small hole in the ground in front of him, carefully, methodically, almost as if he expected to discover something, then and there, just beneath the surface. 'I'm interested in the past,' he said. 'I *like* the past. I think — it feels to me — that it's more real than the present. Do you know what I mean?'

She thought about it. Until very recently, since the birth of the twins, the past had seemed infinitely *preferable* to the present, but distant, and belonging to a different life altogether. And she had enjoyed Gilles' stories, but the events he described belonged to a romanticized, celluloid world which felt as though it had never actually existed. No, the past did not seem real to her. The present was all there was, fleeting and intense.

'Not *really*,' she said. 'Explain.'

He put down his stick, and leaned back on his elbows. 'My parents are nutters,' he said. 'It's bad enough Mum crying all the time, but now Dad's at it too. They say *I'm* difficult, but at least I'm a fucking teenager, I'm meant to be. And Séverine was a psycho, she wouldn't let Dad see me. Not that he tried very hard.'

'I'm sure he wanted to,' murmured Florence.

Ben poked the earth savagely. The stick broke. 'I hate school. Every subject, except history. The way the past is there, just out of reach, but waiting to touch us. Voices that can't speak any more, but that we can hear . . . I don't know. It just feels real. Better, really. More interesting. Than my life.' He went back to digging his hole, and they sat in silence for a while. She was still trying to think of a suitable response when he spoke again.

'I've been a prat, haven't I?'

'What do you mean?'

'You know. Since I got here. I've been a total prat. I'm not surprised you all hate me.'

'We don't hate you!' Florence found it hard to lie effectively. 'I don't, anyway,' she corrected herself.

His rueful laugh startled her. 'It would just help, you know, if you *talked* more,' she said.

'I don't really like talking.'

'We kind of noticed.'

'I just . . . ' He paused before carrying on in a rush. 'Sometimes I just feel like there are too many words. D'you know what I mean? People talking talking talking, and all these words spilling out of their mouths and into the air and into other people's brains . . . It does my head in. D'you know what I mean?'

'I think so,' she said hesitantly.

'Kind of like all the people in the world, going about their business like they're so important whereas in fact they're like little ants, all the same.'

'Yeah.' It seemed important to agree, though in truth she found it hard to understand what this had to do with anything. She racked her brain for something to say that might make him feel better.

'We're going to cycle round the island tomorrow,' she offered as they stood up to go back to the tent. 'Your dad says there are some lovely places to swim, off some rocks. He says we have to be careful, because of the man-eating oysters' — she rolled her eyes, and Ben's laugh this time was frank and open — 'but that other than that it's lovely. You will come, won't you? We would all so love it if you would,' she added, instantly embarrassed because she realized she sounded like an over-anxious grown-up.

'Yeah,' he smiled. 'That sounds cool.'

Later, Florence would tell herself that none of what happened subsequently could have taken place if that evening had been different — if Gilles had not spoken so enticingly, or if she had not stopped with Ben. A few plans made on a balmy night, the promise of a bicycle ride and a swim, and yet . . . No, nothing dramatic happened. Just the meeting of two minds previously wandering separately, the tentative forging of a new friendship, the innocent extension of a hand. Neither Florence nor Ben, that evening, could possibly foresee what was to come. But as they turned their back on the lighthouse and followed the dark contours of the old battlements back to their pitch, they both knew that a new bond had been formed between them, and that it was likely to grow stronger.

Back at the camp, Gilles greeted them with relief. 'There you are! We were beginning to worry. What kept you?'

'Nothing,' said Ben.

'We were talking,' said Florence at the same time. They looked at each other and laughed. 'We were looking at the sea, and talking about buried treasure, and families, and man-eating oysters,' she added.

'Don't mock the molluscs,' said Tom. 'I heard someone talking about them. They're razor sharp, and prolific. Apparently that's all the island doctor does all summer, sew up tourists who get too close.'

'Just so,' said Gilles. He pulled a face in Ben and Florence's direction. 'Well, I'm glad you had a nice time while we considered dragging the moat to find you. Let us know, next time you go wandering off — ' He broke off as Florence threw her arms around his shoulders, pressing her face into his neck. 'I'm sorry, Oncle Gilles!' She pretended to sob. 'I'm sorry, it's my fault, I'm sorry!'

'Mad child.' He pushed her gruffly aside, but she could tell he was enjoying himself. 'Go to bed,' he said.

* * *

She climbed over the wall for one last look at the sea before turning in. Matt came up to join her.

'So what did you really talk about, you and psycho?' he asked lightly.

'I told you. Treasure, and families, and dangerous oysters.' She frowned. 'You shouldn't call him that, you know. He's OK, he's just a bit mixed up.'

'Yeah, right.' Matt picked up a pebble, and threw it towards the moat. It landed short, bounced, then rolled over the edge. Florence strained her ear, but did not hear it hit the water. When she turned towards Matt, she was surprised to see that he looked sombre.

'I'm sorry,' she said, not knowing what she was apologizing for, but feeling that it was the right thing to say. He smiled at her, and leaped to his feet.

'Don't be silly.' He pulled her up, and for a moment, so short that afterwards she wondered if she might not have imagined it, he held her close. She felt the warmth of his body, his sharp, well-defined muscles, heard his breath, quick and shallow. He helped her down from the wall, and she thought that he might kiss her, except that of course he couldn't, not with Gilles and Tom and Ben so close by in the tent.

'Goodnight,' he whispered.

She wanted to stay awake, to relive that brief moment in his arms, but somehow it didn't happen. She rested her head on a bundle made of her folded clothes, closed her eyes and, a wide smile playing on her lips, fell instantly asleep.

★ ★ ★

Ben, to quote Tom, did not *change* after that night, but he did improve. He remained solitary and secretive, but somehow managed to be solitary and secretive in a more sociable way, no longer sneering at the joyous cacophony which was family life at avenue Carnot and La Pommeraie. The vulnerability which Florence had glimpsed in the course of their conversation on Aix became more clearly apparent. Having seen it once, she was quick to recognize it again, and pointed out its symptoms to her more sceptical cousins. Couldn't they see that when he turned away from them, it was through fear of rejection? Did they not understand that the

79

smallest gesture on their part would be enough to tame him?

'We've made gestures before,' pointed out Tom. 'And all he did was snap.' He made a small grudging effort for her sake, however, which resulted in the discovery of what was to become a passion which lasted throughout his teenage years. Walking back towards the car from the beach one day, he asked Ben what he liked to read, and was introduced to reams of authors of heroic fantasy of whose existence he had previously been ignorant. From then on, Tom developed almost schizophrenic reading habits. He was working his way methodically through the great classic works of European literature, but his enjoyment of these paled in comparison with the breathless, urgent way he devoured the huge novels recommended by his cousin. The first pursuit was precociously intellectual, a task he had set himself as a challenge but for which he really lacked the necessary maturity. The other demanded his full emotional involvement, and he agonized and triumphed with his heroes, as they confronted adversity and overcame the powers of evil, again and again, despite the terrible odds stacked against them. His relationship with Ben did not extend much beyond the limits of their shared enjoyment of these books, but this in itself was enough for them to become friends of sorts.

Matt was more difficult to convince, but Florence — who was secretly, thrillingly aware that he was jealous of her own friendship with Ben — bullied him gently until he rather ungraciously suggested that the two of them cycle together to the furthest tip of Ré. Ben accepted equally glumly. They set off early in the morning under a light drizzle, barely talking to each other but by their return they were on cordial terms, Matt laughing about the soaking they'd had, Ben making sardonic remarks about suing him if he caught pneumonia, slapping each other on the back and calling each other *mec* in a way Florence found bizarre, but endearing. They both shot her looks from time to time, as if to say 'Look at us, see how well we are getting on,' and she could not help but feel complacently virtuous. The fact that both Matt and Ben seemed to consider they had a special bond with her did not displease her either. She still adored Matt, but there was something about the way Ben looked at her, a mixture of humility and covert admiration, which gave her an unfamiliar and rather exciting sense of power.

Ben gradually became assimilated into family life. The La Pommeraie cousins as a body eventually came round to Camille's opinion that Ben was more tragic than ghastly, and took him — inasmuch as he allowed himself to be taken — under their collective wing. He ceased to be an object of conversation for his cousins, and if he occasionally struck them as more surly than shy, they simply shrugged as if to say 'That's Ben,' and thought no more about it. The only ones not to be converted were Lily and Paf, who staunchly refused to forget about the *poor, murdered fish*. But they were six years old and prone to melodrama, and their opinions were ignored.

★ ★ ★

The cousins did try to find out more about the tunnels and treasure described by Gilles in his stories. Mindful of his request not to question Mimi, they addressed themselves, with conspicuous discretion, to their grandfather.

Hector was teaching Tom to play chess. They played in the evenings at the little card table under the eaves of Hector and Mimi's converted attic bedroom, Hector stiff and straight in a hard upright chair, Tom perched on the edge of the deep leather sofa. It was a relatively new ritual but nobody, not even Mimi, ever interrupted it until the evening after their return from Aix when Ben, Florence and Matt, under the pretext of wanting to learn too, crowded round to watch.

Their questioning revealed nothing they did not already know. Hector himself had been a medical officer in the British Merchant Navy. He had met Mimi in Paris after the war, when he was not yet demobilized and she was working as a waitress in a café he liked. Their great-aunt had spent much of the Occupation in Montpellier while Mimi had stayed in La Rochelle and their Great-uncle Louis escaped to England to fly with the RAF. His father-in-law may have been involved in the *Résistance* but Hector had never met him to ask. He could tell them about his own war, though. He leaned back in his uncomfortable chair, and grew quite excited as he told them of how his ship had been torpedoed on two separate occasions. They listened politely and with genuine interest as he expanded on his memories of the ensuing drama, but were left knowing just as little about the tunnels and their potential treasure. Hector, when pressed by Ben, admitted that he had heard the usual rumours, but that he had never seen any evidence of their actual existence, and he asked them, with a mildness which did not fool them, not to question their grandmother on the subject of the war. It would upset her. It would bring back memories of her brother, whom she had loved dearly, who had been killed over the North Sea and whose body had never been recovered. There were reasons why people chose not to speak of these things, reasons which had to be respected. The cousins were unconvinced, but obedient. They speculated amongst themselves for a short while as to why the ancestors, as they called them, were so ill informed, or if not ill informed, so unwilling to talk. But then Matt decided to do a windsurfing course, and the others naturally followed suit. They soon forgot about Gilles' stories. Ben, whilst feigning an interest in prevailing winds and tidal currents, still pondered on the mysteries hidden beneath La Pommeraie but kept his preoccupations mostly to himself.

London, 2005

Cassandra is rather irritated by the additional complication of Ben's growing role in Florence's story. She had been so certain of her earlier diagnostic, but it does not seem unreasonable to suppose that Ben — utterly charmless to her mind's eye, whatever Florence might say, but no more trustworthy than Matt — might also be a potential father to baby Zélie. She is annoyed by the questions this throws on her neat solution to the mystery of Florence's solitude, but reminds herself fatalistically that solutions are rarely as tidy as one could hope.

'So what happened next?' she asks. Florence yawns and stretches.

'Oh, I don't know!' she says. Cassandra recognizes one of those sudden changes of mood which come over the young woman after she has spoken for a long time, a disconcertingly quick switch from the passionately engaged reverie of her reminiscences to a sort of bored flippancy aimed at discouraging further confidences.

Cassandra is not easily discouraged, but as she prepares to launch her fresh attack — 'What happened next? Did you find the treasure? How is this relevant to you, now, to your baby?' — the door opens and Florence's room is suddenly full of people.

The doctor, a prominent obstetrician in his mid-fifties, whose cloud of flyaway grey hair frames a surprisingly youthful face, beams at her with the special smile he reserves for his private patients.

'Ms Peabody!' he exclaims genially.

'Professor Carlisle,' answers Florence shortly.

'And this is . . . '

'Zélie.'

'Unusual.'

'French.' The manner in which Florence makes her final pronouncement makes it quite clear she has no wish to discuss Zélie's name, or Frenchness, any further. She has no great affection for this man, whose manner she finds patronizing, but he does not seem remotely troubled by her attitude.

'Excellent!' He rubs his hands. 'Well, as you see, I brought quite a party. You don't mind a few students, do you? With any luck, we'll be sending you home today!'

Florence bites her lip as Carlisle examines her Caesarean scar, explaining the conditions of Zélie's emergency delivery — a long labour, primigravida, right occiput posterior — to two bored-looking students. She answers his questions in truthful monosyllables, all the time trying to fight the tide of panic rising in her chest. *Home*, she thinks. She will have to call her parents — she can't very well keep putting it off. She can hear Catherine wailing, *why didn't you tell us before?* Why, indeed. She will have to think of a good reason.

She wills herself to concentrate on Professor Carlisle, who appears quite unaccountably to be talking to her about sex.

'You have the body of a seventy-year-old woman,' he tells her.

'Thanks.'

'Sexually speaking, I mean. It's to do with the hormones.' He smiles kindly. 'Don't be surprised if your libido is low for a while.'

'I'll bear that in mind.'

The paediatrician, a small round Indian man with enormous glasses and an equally enormous smile, is examining Zélie. All traces of her post-birth jaundice have vanished, she is the requisite weight, her hips, reactions, stools, feeding are all in order. 'There is nothing wrong with this baby!' he pronounces in the tone of someone who has made a great, even miraculous, discovery, and Cassandra beams as if the credit for Zélie's good health is hers alone.

The decision is unanimous. Florence and Zélie can be discharged. The paediatrician tickles Zélie and beams. Carlisle smiles benignly, wishes Florence well and drifts blithely out of her life. The others all file out behind him, and Florence, Cassandra and the baby are left alone.

Be professional, thinks Cassandra sternly. *Another day, another baby. There'll be more along tomorrow.*

'What happens now?' asks Florence in a very small voice. She is out of bed, staring hopelessly at the few clothes she brought with her when she came in alone five days ago. Cassandra thinks of more usual circumstances, of husbands or boyfriends carrying car-seats, of flowers left behind, of tearful new grandparents following with luggage.

'Can I call someone to fetch you?' she asks solicitously, though she knows what the answer will be.

'NO!' Florence's response is as sharp as Cassandra had predicted. 'I told you already. No one.'

'A taxi, then?'

'Oh Cassandra!' Florence's lovely face crumples, her tears turning her very suddenly into an almost ugly little girl. Cassandra throws her new professionalism to the winds and catches Florence as she sinks towards the bed, she holds her in her arms, cradles her, croons to her softly, a lullaby learned from her own mother, sung to hundreds of other women's babies. Florence sobs into the shoulder of this woman who until a few days ago was a stranger, and yet who now knows so much about the life she has tried to forget. When her crying subsides, Cassandra at last hears quite clearly the words which until now have been incomprehensible. 'I don't want to go home,' Florence is saying. Over and over again.

★   ★   ★

Florence makes Cassandra a business proposition before she leaves. Wrapped in a long brown cashmere coat thrown carelessly over sweatpants now far too big for her, carrying Zélie bundled into a crimson pashmina, she turns to the large, comfortable midwife following just behind with her bag.

87

'Won't you come with me?' she asks. 'I'll pay you. Can't you tell your agency you have another booking?'

Cassandra is tempted. Just for once, she would like to take her work beyond the hospital doors, but at the last minute something stops her — the knowledge that to leave her post now would compromise her with the agency, the worry of the unknown, the fear maybe of growing too attached to this lonely young woman and her unusually named baby.

'I can't,' she says. They walk out of the hospital. A light rain is falling today, and the young woman turns her face up towards the sky to feel it before addressing Cassandra one last time.

'You wanted to know what happened,' she says. She seems to have grown smaller, drawn into her own core. Her arms tighten around her baby, her shoulders sag. She looks sadly at the midwife as she gives her answer. 'We grew up,' she says.

She gives Cassandra an awkward one-armed hug and, taking care not to jolt her sleeping child, climbs carefully into the taxi.

PART II

London, 2005

Florence's flat is on the top floor of a Victorian conversion in North Kensington. It has two small bedrooms looking out over the treetops of a large communal garden, stripped wooden floors, a minuscule bathroom, and a disproportionately large bay window at the front with a wooden seat running beneath it. This window looks over streets and rooftops, back gardens and allotments. Snaking through the picture less than a mile away is the Westway, that great motorway linking the heart of London to the promise of the Chilterns. Florence needed a place from which to reclaim London, and she loved the flat from the moment she saw it. She was twenty-one years old, ten days back from New York, and only seven weeks pregnant. She barely noticed the eight flights of stairs.

The rent was reasonable. She had done well in New York, and put by enough money to see her through the next couple of years. She took the flat on the spot, and the first thing she did on moving in was to turn the large leather sofa, which had previously faced the television, towards the window. She took down the curtains — heavy red velvet drapes which she found oppressive — and kept the windows as they were, bare and unadorned but for the new red and gold Indian print cushions on the wooden seat, which she ordered from a Polish seamstress on Westbourne Grove along with cushions for the sofa to match. She had brought nothing with her but her clothes and a battered volume of Baudelaire's poetry, and she was not interested in setting up home. The flat was basically furnished, and she added to it only as need, whim and opportunity arose, acquiring, as well as the new cushion covers, a set of prints of old New York, pots of geraniums, and a Russian tea-service which reminded her, though she didn't know why, of Mimi. It was a cosy, airy, unusual flat. Few people came to see it. Her parents had left London at the same time as her and moved to Kent, to a big house with a large garden for the benefit of the twins. They made excuses to come to London in order to visit her, puzzled and well-meaning as usual, bringing home-cooked meals which languished in her tiny freezer and news of the wider family which she did not want to hear. The twins came too, ten years old now and rather in awe of their big sister, and her neighbour, Greta Sabinsky, an elderly Danish lady who had come to Britain during the war, and was forever stopping by to borrow things.

Florence enjoys chatting to Greta, who reminds her of a charming, more scatty version of France and who fusses over her benevolently, dropping in with home-made cakes and soups, pretending that she made too much to eat herself.

'You need to go out more,' she said reprovingly on one of her visits. 'You need to see more people, people your own age, not always old fogies like me.'

'I do see people,' protested Florence. 'I go to antenatal classes. I catch up with old friends. And anyway — ' dropping a kiss on the old lady's thin snowy white hair — 'I like old fogies.' She did not add that the antenatal classes, with their preponderance of middle-class women each happily involved with her baby's father, made her lonelier than ever. Nor that she had little in common anymore with the school-friends she occasionally saw, who for the most part had by then been through university and were embarking on careers as lawyers and accountants.

'It's not enough,' said Greta firmly.

'And I walk,' added Florence. 'I walk all the time. Through the parks, and along the river. I see people. I walk, I see people, and I write.'

'Aha!' Greta was triumphant after this admission. 'I knew it! A writer makes sense. A writer *needs* solitude. And a writer needs food! I will bake you a cake, *yndling*.'

Greta, attempting discretion, regularly asks after Florence's book in hushed tones, and Florence tries to intimate, without actually lying, that it is going well. But she is not writing a novel, as Greta imagines. What she writes are letters, letters she does not send. She writes to Mimi and Hector, to Matt and Ben, to Lily and Tom. She writes to Claire and to Gilles, to Tante France. She writes to Pierre, page after page. She often cries as she writes, though she is barely aware of this fact, and when she has finished writing she crawls into bed, or on to her newly

upholstered sofa in front of her wide uncur-
tained windows, and she sleeps.

★ ★ ★

The flat feels empty and strangely unfamiliar as
she crosses over the threshold on her return from
the hospital. Perhaps too much has happened
over the past five days. Perhaps she herself has
been so marked by these events that she is in
need of new landmarks. The cab driver, an
eastern European of indeterminate origin,
alarming physiognomy and tender disposition,
has carried her bag up, and placed it in the
middle of the room. He refuses a tip but after a
moment's hesitation steps forward to touch her
arm in a gesture which she takes to mean that he
is wishing her well. He strokes Zélie's cheek and
leaves, dewy-eyed. She is reminded painfully of
her uncle Gilles.

The light on her answerphone is flashing
furiously. Her parents, obviously. She will listen
to them presently. First she must settle Zélie,
who is stirring in her arms, still bundled in her
scarlet pashmina. She sinks on to the sofa
without removing her coat, lies on her side
holding the baby carefully in her arms, and it is
uncertain at this stage whether she is seeking or
giving comfort. Her gaze turns to the view
outside her window. The cars on the Westway
have put on their lights. She sees them, a trail of
white coming into town, red tail-lights heading
west. Tom is somewhere at the end of that road,
ensconced as they always knew he would be in a

university library, working on his Ph.D. in English literature at Oxford. In her imagination, she follows the stream of red lights with Zélie in her arms. A normal thing to do, to visit your family to show off your new baby. She pulls herself abruptly out of her daydream. She will not go to Oxford. She's had enough of academics.

New York, 2004

Florence met Pierre one crisp March morning in Bryant Park, when romance or sex or emotional attachments of any kind could not have been further from her mind. All around her, the new spring gave extravagant witness to its recent arrival. The sycamores, after months of winter starkness, had unfurled their leaves of tender green. Flowers bloomed in the beds beneath them, tulips red and gold. Overhead, wispy cirri streaked a pale blue sky. On Fifth and Sixth Avenues and along 42nd Street, New Yorkers hurried to work as usual, except that while their collars and scarves were turned against the biting northerly breeze, their faces were raised smiling towards the sun.

★   ★   ★

It is in fact a morning for romance, but Florence, dressed in a strapless pale green evening dress and very little else, sits on a cold stone bench and glowers. She pays no attention to the other occupant of the bench, save to note in a vague corner of her mind that he is male, that his upper body is almost completely hidden from view by the *New York Times*, and that he is dressed appropriately for the season, which is to say that despite flowers, sunshine and newly opened buds he is dressed warmly.

A small, nervous-looking man with curiously simian features is busying around her.

'Max, let me get my coat,' she pleads.

Max is the artistic director's assistant, Puerto Rican by birth but New Yorker by life as he likes to say. He is dressed in black from head to foot in emulation of his boss, the divine Pieter, except of course that he wears a blend where Pieter's cashmere is pure. For his part, Max is only too aware of the man on the bench. Pieter's vision for this shoot is decadently sylvan, or sylvanically — if the word exists, and who is Max to say it doesn't — decadent. The models, in their evening wear, are to recline on stone benches beneath the trees. In the background, Manhattan will go about her daily business. The girls, carefully tousled, will look appealingly lost, leftovers from the previous evening's revels. Possibly their setting, between city and woods, and their ethereal attire, will bring to mind the concept of urban fairies. Max, who is *devoted* to Pieter, thinks the whole idea deliciously ironic. He also feels that the man on the bench is superfluous. Superfluous, and unaesthetic. The bench upon which he sits will not be used for the shoot — another has been secured for the purpose — but to Max's mind it is an integral part of the morning's proceedings. Here the models will sit, he will sit, Pieter may sit (though the great man rarely rests). Max politely asked the man on the bench to move on, when they first arrived earlier. But there is absolutely no law, save perhaps that of common courtesy, which states that he should move. And he is stubborn, Max has learned. When asked if he wouldn't care to sit elsewhere, he answered with quiet yet final authority that he always read his morning paper on this bench, but that Max was not to worry. They — Max, the models, the photographer — would not disturb him. And then he smiled, in a bland, kindly, utterly dismissive way, unfolded his paper, and began to read. Max, torn between profound irritation and quite inappropriate desire, flounced off to other duties, returning periodically to stand always a little too close or shout a little too loud, hoping to dislodge the man, hoping also to catch another glimpse of that calm air of command he had secretly found so thrilling.

'No coat,' he snaps bossily in answer to Florence's question. Max doesn't like models, and he particularly mistrusts Florence. He thinks she gives herself airs, and that she lacks respect. 'Pieter says you wear your coat, it spoils your dress. You spoil the dress, everything's ruined. You can have a wrap. A light wrap.'

'Yeah well if *Saint* Pieter was sitting here *butt-naked* . . . ' retorts Florence. The man on the bench gives a loud snort of suppressed laughter. Max stares, scandalized. Florence backtracks. 'C'mon Max, just get me a coffee then,' she coaxes.

'Pieter says no coffee,' answers Max with satisfaction. 'No coffee, or didn't you hear about Rebecca last week? The *incident* with the caramel mochaccino and the Masalucci wedding dress? No coffee, no tea, no food, no nothing. Not even water.'

He flounces off again, still hopelessly aware of the man on the bench, wondering if he has impressed him with his own authority.

'OK, a wrap then!' Florence pleads as he trots away. He ignores her, and she hunches forward, hugging herself in an attempt to keep warm. Next to her, the man on the bench lowers his newspaper a fraction, just enough to peer over the top.

'I have coffee,' he announces.

She turns towards him, and as she prepares to answer, she begins to take in the physical details of his appearance, beyond his maleness, his newspaper and his seasonally appropriate clothes. Brown hair, tanned face — at this time of year? — generally pleasant appearance.

'Excuse me?'

'I have coffee,' he repeats. 'I haven't touched it yet. It was too hot. I hate it when it's too hot. You can have it, if you like.'

Eyes the colour of coffee. No, of chocolate. Eyes like melted chocolate. And not pleasant, no not *pleasant* at all. Gorgeous, actually.

'I . . . I can't,' she falters. 'Pieter . . . there's this model . . . '

'Ah,' he says. 'Rebecca. And the wedding dress.' He raises an eyebrow — just one — at her look of surprise, and she thinks *I've always wanted to be able to do that.* 'Take it,' he says. He holds out the coffee, flips his newspaper up again, and whispers loudly from behind an advertisement for haircream and an article about fighting dogs, 'I promise I won't tell.'

His hands are large, with a few dark hairs on

the knuckles, well cut nails, surprisingly delicate
fingers. She drags her eyes away from them and
takes the coffee. Not to do so, she decides, would
be churlish.

'Thank you,' she says. 'Mind you don't.'

She takes a tentative sip. The coffee is no
longer hot, but warm, just the way she likes it.
She remembers now that she skipped breakfast
again this morning. The first sip leads to a
second, and the second leads to a gulp. The man
on the bench next to her continues to read his
paper. Before she knows it, and quite uninten-
tionally, Florence has drained the cup.

'That was delicious,' she says gratefully.

Down comes the newspaper again. His smile is
kind, his mouth generous, his teeth even.

'Are you feeling less cold now?'

'A little. Thank you.'

'You're still shivering.' He stands up. *Oh don't
go!* she thinks, and is surprised by the thought.
'Here, take this.'

His jacket is soft brown leather, good quality
but battered. It smells faintly of tobacco and of
vetiver cologne, and it is warm, with the warmth
of his body. Without it, she sees that he is slim
but powerfully built, his broad shoulders shown
off by a close-fitting dark grey polo neck sweater.
He wraps the jacket around her, pulls the lapels
together, pats the shoulders lightly.

'There,' he says softly.

'I'll get into trouble,' whispers Florence. She
tries to smile, but finds that she can't.

'To hell with that.'

They are staring at each other. She should say

something, but what? What should she say? What *can* she say?

A few feet away, they hear Pieter suddenly bellowing to Rebecca, who despite her recent misfortune with the wedding dress has been poured into a gown of white organza tulle. She sports a garland of white flowers and ivy in her waist-length chestnut hair.

'Ophelia!' Pieter is screaming. 'I want you to think of Ophelia. Pre-Raphaelite, romantic, tragic. Why can't you do that?'

'Ophelia? Didn't she, like, *drown*?'

'Drown shmown,' says Pieter. 'Who cares, she looked good.'

Florence and the man on the bench — who is no longer on the bench, in fact, but still standing rather unnervingly in front of her — catch each other's eyes. She gives a suppressed little giggle, which grows louder in response to his outright laughter. He tips his head back when he laughs, she notices. And he hasn't shaved.

'You must think this is all very ridiculous,' she says.

'Not in the least. I think it's fascinating. I've been taking mental notes.'

'Taking notes?' What is he? A film-maker, a writer? A journalist?

'I'm an anthropologist,' he says, smiling. 'I've just got back from a year in the Orinoco delta, now I'm at NYU.'

'Oh,' she says. She is rather lost for words again. 'I see.'

'Have dinner with me tonight,' he says.

'I . . . ' Oh God, what can she say, what should

she say? I don't want to? I don't date? I don't eat?

They remain like this, Florence and this stranger, in the middle of a photo shoot in the middle of Manhattan, staring at each other, and she has the curious, absurd feeling that somehow she has known him all her life. They remain like this, not speaking, just watching, knowing that they are on the brink of something huge, that their lives may never be the same again, until Max bustles up, takes in the jacket, the coffee cup. The situation. 'You're on,' he says jealously. The man on the bench — the standing man, now — does not budge, does not take his eyes off Florence to acknowledge Max's presence. He does, however, speak.

'Not now,' he says pleasantly.

'Excuse me?'

'We're kind of in the middle of something?'

'No,' says Florence quickly. 'I'm going. And the answer's no. Thank you . . . for everything, but the answer's no. I have work to do. So, goodbye.'

'C'mon, c'mon!' Max hurries off, not before shooting a final lingering, triumphant glance at the troublesome man who has so thoughtlessly gatecrashed Pieter's shoot. Florence rises to follow him. The man puts out his hand, touches her arm.

'Lunch, then. Tomorrow? Please?'

Now that she knows it, she cannot escape that smell, the warm woody smell of vetiver and tobacco. She somehow knows that she will always, whatever happens, associate it with him.

'You've drunk my coffee, you've even worn my clothes. Surely we can have lunch?'

He pulls a face, woebegone, suddenly so comical that she laughs again. 'All right,' she says. 'All right. Lunch, tomorrow. Now go! I have to work.'

'Madison Square Park, twelve-thirty,' he says. He makes no attempt to hide his grin.

'Twelve-thirty, Madison Square Park. Now go, *go*!'

* * *

She was still laughing when a sudden thought occurred to her, and she called him back.

'I'm Florence,' she said. 'In case you were wondering.'

His grin grew wider still.

'Hello, Florence,' he replied. 'I'm Pierre. My name is Pierre.'

London, 2005

Night has fallen outside by the time Florence wakes. For a moment, she is at a loss to know where, even who, she is. She stretches out, and her scar tugs painfully. Zélie sighs. Florence remembers.

She eases herself carefully into a sitting position, yawns, and looks around the flat. The red light of the answer-phone is blinking even harder in the darkness, angry and reproachful. She cannot ignore it any longer. She will take one of the painkillers Cassandra gave her before she left hospital, then listen to her messages.

They are entirely predictable.

'Florence, *chérie, c'est maman, appelle-moi.*'

'*Chérie*, it's me again. Your father and I were wondering how you are. How the baby is. Call us!'

'Florence, *chérie*, I'm starting to worry . . . '

Finally her father, Robert, trying to sound authoritative, clearly uncomfortable in the role, especially with Catherine interrupting.

'Florence, it's your father. Your mother's worried sick. So am I. I mean I know you like your independence, but this is pushing . . . *What? No, let me deal with this . . . oh, all right* . . . Florence, if you don't call us back by the end of the day, we're coming to London. It's Thursday. Er . . . lots of love, Dad.'

She smiles despite herself, as she holds down the delete button. Robert's rambling answer-phone messages are something of a trademark.

She picks up the handset to call him back, but the phone rings before she has the chance to dial. Her parents' number flashes up.

'Hello?'

'Oh, thank God!' exclaims Catherine. 'Robert! She's there! Where have you been?' she asks. 'Didn't you get my messages? We've been worried sick, we were going to drive down tonight if we didn't hear from you. My bag is packed and everything. Why didn't you call?'

'I've been busy.'

'Busy? You don't mean . . . '

Zélie, alone on the sofa, lets out a sudden, piercing howl of hunger.

'Oh my God. Oh my God, you've had the baby. Oh my God, Robert, she's had the baby.' Catherine bursts into tears. At the other end of the line, as if in sympathy with her unknown grandmother, Zélie sets up an unrelenting cry. Robert comes to the phone.

'Flo! Is this true?'

'It's true.' Florence laughs, a little wickedly. 'Listen.' She holds the phone up. 'You can hear them in stereo,' she says.

Robert chuckles. Catherine takes the phone from him.

'What is it? And when?'

'A girl.' Florence winces. 'Five days ago.'

'Five days! Five days, and you didn't say!'

'It was difficult, I couldn't use my mobile.'

'There's always a way,' says Catherine shortly. 'We're coming to see you.'

'What, now? Mum, it's nearly eight o'clock.'

'This is my first grandchild. At this stage, they change every day.'

All traces of smile fade from Florence's face, as a familiar feeling of panic resurges. She could not explain it, if you asked her to. If you asked her why she feels like this, all she could say would be that she does not want them, her parents, her brothers, or any other member of her family. That she wants only to be left alone with her baby.

'Mum, I'm so tired.'

'Then we'll help you. I'll help you. I'll look after the baby.'

'Mum, please . . . '

'We're coming.'

'Tomorrow. Come tomorrow. Please? I'm going to bed now, we're both going to bed. You wouldn't get here till gone ten, it's too late. *S'il te plaît, maman.*'

Catherine relents. They will come tomorrow, at first light. More tears are shed and protestations of love uttered by Catherine; apologies are clumsily offered by Florence. By the time she turns to Zélie — red and damp from crying — Florence is exhausted again.

'Come on then, little lady,' she says gently, lifting her off the sofa and carrying her to the bedroom. 'Tomorrow, let them come. Tonight it's just you and me.'

*   *   *

Greta comes early the following morning, twittering with excitement, bearing milk, apples and a packet of custard creams in her crocheted shopping bag. 'I heard the baby crying in the night,' she beams. 'And I thought, knowing her, she will not have any food. The little darling! May I hold her?' She sits on the sofa, no bigger than a child herself, her tiny bird frame swallowed by the vast cushions, and she sings softly in Danish as she cradles Zélie. 'I brought you another present,' she says, when her song is finished. 'Look in my bag.'

The shawl, though unevenly knitted, is beautiful, soft and lacy and surprisingly warm. Greta nods with satisfaction. 'Months,' she sighs. 'It has taken me months.' She holds up her hands, the joints swollen with arthritis. 'Not easy. But I did it!'

'You certainly did.' Florence leans over and kisses the old lady on the cheek. She smells of lavender and powder and very faintly of pee.

Greta leaves, flushed with pleasure, reminiscing about her own three boys, exhorting Florence to make the most of her daughter's fleeting childhood, and promising to return later with a batch of muffins. Florence watches her go with something like regret, and it occurs to her that she does not, perhaps, crave solitude as much as she would like to think. She thinks of Cassandra, of her warm, comfortable presence, and the ease with which she talked and the midwife listened. *Up to a point*, she reminds herself. She only revealed herself up to a point.

The intercom rings, announcing the arrival of her family. They troop in, sucking up the flat's sense of space and order, discarding coats and scarves, putting down bags and a small suitcase — a suitcase! — crowding round an oblivious Zélie who snores softly as she sleeps, arms thrown back behind her head, snugly wrapped in Greta Sabinsky's frothy white shawl. Florence sighs inwardly, braces herself against the tidal wave of emotion she knows is coming. Sure enough, Catherine cries as soon as she sees the baby, but when she turns to Florence, and takes her in her arms, she is gentle. For a moment, Florence allows herself to be held. She leans her head on her mother's shoulder, and it feels as if no time has passed since she was a child herself. The feel of Catherine's embrace — the height of her shoulders, the curve of her arm, the softness of her chest — is imprinted on her daughter's memory. Florence shuts her eyes and for the space of a few seconds — a few seconds which last a long time — she feels safe again. Perhaps this is why she allows herself to be guided unprotesting to the sofa, and wrapped in blankets, and told not to move while Catherine unpacks the shopping she has brought, heats up soup and bread, opens packets of cheese, puts a large fruit cake — 'I made it last night, I couldn't sleep!' — out on to a plate. Zélie wakes up, and the twins squabble over who should hold her.

'I'll take her head, and you take her feet,' says Sam, but Luke does not agree.

'You take her feet,' he says. 'I'll hold her head.'

'No, I —'

'Why don't you take it in turn to hold her?' intervenes Catherine, and they turn to her as one body, four great long-lashed brown eyes glaring.

'We like our way best,' announces Sam, and Luke agrees.

'You can hold her head first,' he says. 'Then we'll swap.'

Florence watches anxiously, but Catherine is hovering, making sure Zélie does not come to any harm. When she starts to cry, she sweeps her up, takes her into the bedroom to change her nappy, brings her proudly back to Florence to be fed. Florence, who had been ready to resist, who had braced herself to prove that she did not need help, finds to her surprise that it is easy to let herself be carried. She opens the gifts they have brought, clothes from her parents, a soft toy each from the twins, and she kisses them all to thank them. She eats the food Catherine has prepared, she drinks hot camomile tea, she accepts a hot-water bottle and the offer to mind the baby while she goes to bed after lunch.

She had expected recriminations, but there are none. Robert and the twins leave after tea, but Catherine stays. The suitcase is hers. She has packed for several days and she has no intention of leaving with the others.

'You can't manage on your own,' she says firmly. 'Those stairs. Your scar. I'll stay till you're better.'

'But I'm fine,' protests Florence weakly.

'Of course you are. And how do you intend to shop for food, while you are in this state?'

'Internet?'

'*Chérie*, please don't be stubborn.'

Florence finds that she is too weak to resist.

The long labour, the emergency Caesarean, the succession of broken nights have taken their toll. Over the next few days, she allows herself to be mothered. She spends her time drifting from bed to sofa in her pyjamas, feeding her baby, being fed by her mother. The days and the nights roll together, a succession of deep sleeps and light dozes punctuated by endless breast-feeding. Her scar tightens, itches, heals. Zélie's little body uncurls, grows fatter and stronger. Catherine and Florence tend to her together. Now would be a good time, perhaps, to talk about the past, but neither of them mentions it. Their conversation is restricted to the here and now, to nappies and babygros, feeds and sleeping patterns. A nurse comes to visit, and when she has gone they talk about vaccinations and baby clinics, and whether or not Florence should take Zélie to baby-massage classes.

Florence does not dream again. She tells herself that she is free, that talking to Cassandra has liberated her from the clutches of her past, even though she has told Cassandra so little.

She tells herself that the hours spent between sleeping and waking, when daydreams and reminiscences are at their most lifelike and real, when she lies in her bed overlooking the trees of the communal garden and can almost feel Pierre next to her, when she can almost believe that if she stretches out her hand she will be able to touch him, when she can pretend that the warmth of the duvet wrapped around her is actually the warmth of his body, and the smell of vetiver on her pillow comes from him and not from the small bottle she keeps by her bed ... she tells herself that these hours do not count.

New York, 2004

It took her all morning to prepare for their first date. She pulled on jeans, then miniskirts, sweaters, blazers, shirts. She wore her hair up, then down, swept over her face, pinned back. She put on foundation and powder and lipgloss and eye-liner, then scrubbed it all off in favour of a few touches of mascara. By the time she settled on an outfit — bootleg jeans, Converse sneakers, short fitted jacket, embroidered pashmina and Coccinelle tote, Miss Dior at her throat and Carmex on her lips — every square inch of the pristine studio apartment she rented on the Upper East Side seemed to be covered in clothes, and she decided not to go but to stay home and tidy up instead. Then she remembered how serious Pierre had looked when he asked her to lunch, and his grin when she agreed, and she decided to go after all. Then she reminded herself that she didn't know him, and changed her mind again.

★   ★   ★

She is nearly half an hour late when the taxi drops her off at the corner of West 23rd and Fifth. She looks round the park. It is a beautiful day again, warmer than yesterday. Parents are out with their children, couples lounge on the lawn, squirrels chase each other frantically over

112

railings and around the trunks of trees. She catches sight of him at last, seated near the hamburger kiosk. He is engrossed in a book and does not see her walk up.

'You're always on a bench,' she says. 'And you're always reading.'

He looks up. 'You're here!' he smiles.

'Did you think I wouldn't come?'

'I didn't know what to think.' He stands quickly, tucking the paperback into his jacket pocket. She feels suddenly awkward. How should she greet him? With a handshake, a kiss? The first feels too formal, the second . . . well. He solves the problem by offering her his arm. 'I'm starving,' he announces. 'Shall we?'

They walk over to the line of people queuing outside the kiosk.

'We're staying here?' asks Florence, surprised.

'They do the best burgers,' he says mildly. 'And it's such a beautiful day, I thought it would be nice to have a picnic.' He seems genuine, but something in his tone tells her that he is teasing her. *Well two can play at that game*, she thinks.

'You know,' she says seriously, 'most people, if they wanted to impress with alfresco dining, would have gone for the Boathouse.'

'Maybe I'm not trying to impress.'

'Charming.'

He looks suddenly uncertain. 'Of course we can go somewhere else if you'd prefer,' he says. 'It's just that actually I thought . . . '

'What?'

'I thought that actually you would be more impressed if I *didn't* try too hard. I thought we

113

could eat, have a coffee maybe here, maybe somewhere else, take a walk, play it by ear . . . Was I wrong?' He is looking straight at her, and though he smiles quite disarmingly, his eyes of melted chocolate are serious. She has to tear her eyes away.

'No,' she says. 'No, not wrong at all.'

The burgers — which come with fries for him, salad and no bun for her — are indeed delicious, though whether this is a quality inherent in them or the influence of their surroundings is unclear. The sun warms them as they eat. Children run amongst the metal café tables, dogs on leashes lie hopefully beneath them. Florence, who actually hates sitting still at a table to eat, stretches out with her feet up on a chair. She feels happily, comfortably, completely at ease and somewhere at the back of her mind she acknowledges that Pierre's choice of eatery — the term restaurant would be stretching it — is absolutely perfect.

★ ★ ★

As they eat, they play a game which Pierre describes as a variant of twenty questions, the best way, he says, of learning about each other fast.

'Why does it have to be fast?'

'Because I'm impatient.'

'What for?'

'To get to know you. You're wasting questions, by the way. That's two already. You might as well start.'

'Twenty's an awful lot of questions.' He glares

114

at her, and she laughs. 'OK, I'm wasting time. Umm . . . How old are you?'

'Thirty-one.'

'You sound American, and not American. Where are you from?'

'I was born in Aberdeen.'

'Interesting,' she says, 'but you *really* don't sound Scottish. Where did you grow up?'

'Scotland, Egypt, Russia, Brazil, finally the US.'

'How long have you lived in New York?'

'I've been based here all of my adult life.'

'Your parents . . . '

'My dad's English. My mother's American.'

'And you travelled because . . . '

'My dad worked for Shell, we moved every five years.'

'And now they live in . . . '

'Miami.'

'How often do you see them?'

'Whenever I can.' He shifts impatiently. 'Hey, this is supposed to be about me. The last four questions were about them.'

She frowns, a severe, schoolmarmy look. 'I can't really be expected to understand you without knowing about them.'

'And do you want to?'

'What?'

'Understand me.' His tone is light, but Florence rushes on.

'What does an anthropologist do?'

'That's way too big a question for now. I was hoping to tell you over dinner.'

She ignores him.

'Favourite colour, favourite food, favourite book, favourite place . . . '

'Depends on my mood but probably red, depends on my mood but probably oysters, impossible to say but probably *War and Peace*, anywhere near the sea but the fewer people around the better.'

Anywhere near the sea . . . Florence feels her playfulness begin to leave her. She has a sudden mental image of Pierre walking along the beach with her on Ré, and she is surprised by the longing contained in that image. Her next question comes from nowhere, practically asks itself.

'Why are you called Pierre?'

'I had a French grandmother.'

She definitely doesn't want to play any more. Her mood change must be palpable, because Pierre does not push her for more questions, or claim his turn at asking. He stretches, yawns, shakes his head then smiles, a quick, uncomplicated smile, neither lingering nor teasing. 'How about that walk then?'

★   ★   ★

They spent the whole afternoon together. Pierre did ask his questions, but unobtrusively, gently coaxing answers out of her, though she kept some things back. She told him that she was born in London, that she had twin brothers twelve years younger than herself, that she had fallen into modelling when she left school, literally picked out by a talent scout as she

116

walked down the street. That she had gone along to the initial go-see 'just for something to do,' and found that she was good at it. That she had come to New York by chance on a shoot, and stayed because she found the city suited her. She told him that she liked cities by the sea, that she would quite like to study one day but that for the time being she liked earning good money and being independent. She did not tell him that she hardly ever spoke to her family, that coming to New York had been like running away, that although she had always been a good student she couldn't bear the thought of carrying on studying because that was what she had always done and for life to continue as it always had was suffocating. She did not tell him which other cities by the sea she loved, nor which city in particular she had in mind. She told him her favourite poet was Baudelaire, and her favourite poem was 'L'Invitation au voyage,' and when he commented on her accent when she recited the first verse at his request, she did not tell him that she too had a grandmother who was French.

'I love it partly because it's so different from the rest of the collection,' she said when he asked her. 'The woman he is addressing isn't a sexual object, to be possessed or feared. He calls her his child, his sister. He de-sexualizes her, she becomes a soulmate, an equal. He paints a picture of the place where they can go and live together, and it's a misty place, full of beautiful, comfortable objects, golden, but above all peaceful. It's a place I want to go.'

They were standing on the southernmost tip

of Manhattan, and as she looked over the shimmering sea in the soft light of late afternoon at the tail end of a perfect spring day, she fancied she caught a glimpse of the land the poet had described. She turned back to Pierre. 'I'm sorry,' she said. 'I guess you just have to read it.'

'I know the poem.' His eyes again serious and playful. She could stand there for ever, between New York and the Atlantic Ocean, with the Statue of Liberty and the Staten Island ferry on one side and Battery Park on the other, just looking at those eyes.

'I have to go,' she said abruptly, because suddenly to stay seemed too terrifying.

He did not try to hold her back, but walked with her until they found a cab. As it pulled away, he thrust something through its half-open window. A packet of cigarettes, still half full, a telephone number hastily scribbled on the back.

She stared at the number all the way home, and wished that she had stayed.

* * *

She told herself she should wait before calling him. *He won't want to see me. He won't care whether I call or not. He doesn't actually like me. He just feels sorry for me. Possibly I remind him of his sister, if he has one. Or if he doesn't, he thinks that if he did she'd be like me . . .* It took her three days to pluck up the courage to call him, and when she dialled his number, her hands were shaking. When he answered, relief that he seemed pleased to hear from her flooded

118

her, obliterating everything. She heard his voice rather than what he was saying, and having agreed to all his suggestions had to ask him to repeat them.

They met on a Thursday evening in Union Square to go to the movies. Spring had already beat a sulky retreat, and it was cold and raining. Florence wore boots, a long coat, a scarf, a hat. She carried an umbrella. He almost didn't recognize her. When he did, this time it was he who was not sure how to greet her and she who, standing on tiptoe, broke the impasse by kissing him quickly on the cheek before slipping her arm through his. He felt warm, and solid.

'It's good to see you.' He was smiling.

'You too.' So was she.

They never did go to see the film. They started talking in the line for tickets, and realized that neither of them wanted to go in. Instead they sloped off to an Italian restaurant in SoHo, where they ate carpaccio with truffles followed by *spaghetti alla puttanesca*, and drank copious amounts of sangiovese.

'One notch up from hamburgers,' said Pierre.

'Don't knock the hamburgers,' she said. 'I liked them. Tell me about your work.'

'So dull.'

'Surely not.'

He filled their glasses again, and sat back. 'Anthropology. From the Greek, *anthros*. The study of man. More precisely, the study of man, and his place within society. Typically the study of man in so-called *primitive* societies, though many disapprove of the word 'primitive.' I've spent the last three years split between my NYU lectureship and Venezuela's Orinoco delta, studying the lives of indigenous Indian tribes. I basically go there on extended field trips, I live with them, eat with them. I talk with them. I return to New York, I teach, I collate my notes, I prepare my forthcoming book on the subject, etc., etc. Eventually — and this is something of a well-known secret — I would like to leave academia, and make film documentaries based on my research. I spend much of my non-existent spare time trying to get that off the ground.'

'By which you mean?'

'Trying to get funding.'

'Ah.'

'Ah indeed.' He raised his glass. 'I sound flippant, but actually I love what I do. Sometimes, I even love my fellow academics, the whole scheming, over-ambitious lot of them.' The wine was making him expansive. 'The thing I really love is being in the field. Flying in to Caracas from New York, driving across this huge country to get a boat downriver, arriving in a tiny village of mud huts and half-naked people and calling it home . . . The first time I went, I stayed with an old man in one of the larger huts. He had a garden, and when I walked there in the morning the ground was covered with passion-fruits which had fallen in the night. The smell as I stepped on them was incredible. Later that day, I sat by the river and watched the village children swimming. You had to listen very carefully — every now and then you heard a splash in the distance, actually more of a plop, and you knew another cayman was in the water with them. A child had been killed by one a few weeks before, but they didn't seem too bothered. And then I met the priests, the Marist brothers who have set up a mission there. I stay with them now. They've taught me to play poker.'

'It sounds like a mad place,' said Florence. The wine was making her light-headed.

'Once, when the delta flooded, I paddled across a field in a canoe and a cow waded by, up to her breast in water and nonchalant as cows are. Nobody thought this was funny, or even odd. Nobody else even noticed. It's surreal.' Surreal, and wonderful, and a privilege, really to live there.'

'And when are you going back?' asked Florence.

'Not sure. I've got contractual obligations here. And strictly speaking I've gathered enough material for my book, but like I said, the film, the series . . . It *would* be great.' He takes a long sip, hesitates before going on. 'I feel responsible for them, somehow. Theirs is such a fragile environment, so easily disturbed. Tourism, climate change . . . If I can play a part in protecting them, I'll be pleased.'

'Protecting them? How?'

'By bringing them to the public eye. Except of course that that would mean more change.' He rubbed the bridge of his nose ruefully. She had noticed this mannerism before. She liked it. 'It's a complicated balance,' he admitted. But possibly no one will see my film, if it ever gets made. Certainly no one is going to read my book, outside the small handful of unfortunate undergraduates I feed it to.'

She laughed. 'I'm sure your film will happen, and people will love it. But perhaps you don't need to protect them. People evolve. Perhaps we attach too much importance to the part we play in their lives. Perhaps we should accept that our own impact, however great we may think it, is minimal.'

'I think on the contrary we *underestimate* our influence on other people. We have to take some responsibility for our actions, surely?'

His gaze is frank and open. She cannot meet it. 'Of course,' she says. 'I just mean that change happens. It's not all your fault.' She looks up, smiles quickly. 'I don't really know *what* I'm trying to say.'

He smiles back, brushes aside her comment, the barely perceptible shadow cast over the evening. 'And you?' he asks. 'What about you, do you love what you do?'

'Aspects of it,' she says. 'I like the clothes. The end products, the photographs. The feeling that I have been recreated, that I can be, or seem to be, somebody different.'

He frowns. He is clearly puzzled by this statement, but he does not comment, for which she is grateful. She does not want to explain why she should want to be recreated or anything other than what she is.

She leaves the restaurant on his arm, leaning into him. She is not used to drinking, and feels giddy with the red wine and his proximity.

Outside, hiccuping gently, she puts up her umbrella and stands back while he tries to hail a cab.

'Here you go!' he calls. She hurries over. 'Florence, what *are* you doing?'

'Why?'

'The umbrella.' He reaches out, and tugs gently at one of the open spokes. 'It's not actually raining.'

She puts her hand out. 'So it isn't.' She giggles, but cannot take her eyes off him as he pulls her gently towards him.

'You muppet,' he says, and kisses her.

The umbrella, abandoned, falls to the ground. Florence's arms creep up to Pierre's neck. He kisses her lips, her eyes, her cheeks. She closes her eyes, and sees stars. She opens them, and sees his face.

'Hey, lady!' An exhausted-looking business-man, raincoat open over a crumpled suit, slips between Florence and Pierre and the taxi. 'You gonna take this cab?'

She blinks. Slowly, the swirling images in the background behind Pierre come back into focus and rearrange themselves into the streets of Manhattan. 'Well,' he asks, his forehead against hers. 'Are you?'

'Aw, for Chrissakes!' The man leaps into the cab. 'Take me to Brooklyn.'

She laughs. 'Not that one, no.' He kisses her again, and again Manhattan disappears. She pulls gently away. 'But the next one,' she says. She cups his face gently in her hands. 'I'll call you,' she says.

'Give me your number.'

'I don't have a pen.'

'I have. Here, write it on my hand.'

'Like a *teenager*,' she teases, and is silenced by his mouth on hers.

'Making out in the street,' he says. '*That's* what teenagers do.'

I seem to always be driving away from him, she thinks, as her taxi swings north. *Always driving away, and always wanting to stay.*

★   ★   ★

On their third date, he cooked for her. She was apprehensive about this at first. It worried her, leaving the security of the New York streets, the knowledge that at any moment she could step into the crowds and disappear, even though she had thought about Pierre almost constantly over the two days since she last saw him. Their kiss, his mouth on hers, the strange dual feeling that she was losing herself completely and yet that she had never been more herself, that this was the sort of moment she had come to think of as her 'dune on Ré' moment, when she was somehow both separate from the world and a fundamental part of its existence . . . She savoured the memory of that kiss, his arms strong around her, his lips soft but firm, the warmth of his body. She tried to remember every detail of it — had she touched his hair as she imagined she had, stroked the back of his neck, *kissed* his neck? Had she told him she loved him, or was this too something she only dreamed of?

124

Because she *did* love him. Florence had fallen in love with Pierre with a violence and suddenness which left her quite literally breathless, and this was not what was meant to happen at all. Contrary to most women her age, contrary in fact to most women, and most men too probably, she had not gone looking for love. What Florence prized above all else, what she had achieved in New York, was anonymity. Here she had acquaintances, but none that she was close to, a profession in which she was tied to no one, neither team, nor boss, nor even specific location, a profession in which, as she said to Pierre, she herself could be recreated according to whim. No one knew her, she knew no one. She had perfectly achieved her goal.

Falling in love had not been a part of the plan, which was why she worried about this next step, this going-to-his-place-for-dinner step, this who-knows-what-might-happen-next? Yet as she stood outside the door to Pierre's Lower Fifth Avenue apartment, she was aware that one of the emotions which caused her heart to swell so painfully was happiness. Nerves, apprehension, excitement, shyness — all of these played a part in what she was feeling, but they did not surprise her. Happiness, however — unfounded, vague, tenuous but real — did.

The first thing she noticed when he opened the door was that he was barefoot. He wore jeans, as usual, and a loose-fitting jumper over an untucked shirt, but all she noticed were his feet, the fact that they were brown like his face and hands, but with a paler band across the top

125

where presumably he had worn sandals, and in their nakedness they seemed somehow shockingly intimate. He moved forward to kiss her, and she shifted unconsciously to offer him her cheek instead of her mouth. Unperturbed by her sudden reticence, he took her hand and pulled her after him through an open plan living space with a slanting glass ceiling towards a small galley kitchen.

'I'm cooking sea-bass,' he said. 'I can't relax until I know everything's OK.' The fish was laid in a dish on a bed of foil, and as he spoke Pierre rubbed it with olive oil, added slices of fennel and quarters of lemon, sprinkled salt and ground pepper. 'My mum just sort of *wafts* around the kitchen and conjures up feasts, but I have to concentrate.' He deftly folded the foil around the fish and slid the dish into the oven. '*Voilà!* Now on go the potatoes, and we're done. Drink? I bought a bottle of Gewürtztraminer, but we can have martinis if you'd rather.'

'Gewürztraminer would be lovely.'

She wandered back to the living room ahead of him while he got the wine out of the refrigerator. 'I don't understand the glass ceiling,' she said. 'We're not on the top floor, how does that work?'

He came in carrying the bottle and two glasses. 'Used to be a roof terrace. The building gets narrower above this floor. Someone built over it. Nice, huh?'

'Great view.' Outside Manhattan presented its more homely face, not quite brownstone but not skyscrapers either, windows through which people were preparing evening meals, roof gardens just perceptible in the twilight, twinkling lights. 'You can actually see the sky. Stars.'

'Luxury.' He was pouring the drinks, and it only occurred to her now, seeing that his hand was not quite steady, that he might be feeling as nervous as she was. 'The room's nice too,' she said shyly.

'It's a mess,' he replied. 'I tried to tidy up before you came. The trouble is that I sublet the apartment from a friend. He's been posted to Tokyo, but we have an arrangement that the other bedroom is his, so I work in here.'

'I like it.' It was the radical opposite of her own meticulously kept apartment, but she meant it. She noticed with amusement that Pierre's idea of tidying up seemed to be to make piles of the books and papers which overflowed everywhere, and to hide them beneath armchairs and in corners, where she also spotted a squash racket and a pair of boxing gloves. But she also noticed that the small table beneath the glass roof was set with candles, that the flowers on the glass-topped coffee table were fresh, and that the cushions on the brown leather sofa on which they sat a little distance from each other had been plumped. She was touched by these details. The apartment reminded her a little of the boys' room in her grandparents' house in La Rochelle, where Mimi's housekeeping efforts clashed head on with her cousins' pathological messiness. The recollection, rather than causing her pain, actually made her smile. 'Really,' she said. 'I like it.'

He turned back to the coffee table to refill his glass. 'You know,' he said, not looking at her, 'I lied. To your friend Max.'

'Max is so not my friend!' she laughed. 'What did you say?'

'I said I sat on that bench every morning to read my paper. It's not true. I just happened to be going to the public library that day, and because it was a nice morning I stopped to have a coffee on the bench. I wasn't intending to stay for more than a few minutes.'

'And?'

'And then I saw you.' He looked up again, and as she met his gaze she lost track of time and place again, was aware of nothing but her heart beating in her throat. And then Pierre reached and brushed the tips of her fingers with his.

* * *

In the end they ordered out for Chinese. They never heard the timer on the oven ping, never noticed the acrid smell of burnt potatoes or the smoke that billowed out of the oven until the alarm on the smoke detector began to ring and Pierre ran naked out of the bedroom to switch it off while Florence laughed helplessly from the bed. They didn't think about food until much, much later, after Pierre had come back to bed and murmured *now where were we*, and Florence had reached up and pulled him down on top of her, whispering *we were just about here* and he disagreed, trailing his lips gently down her body to close on one of her breasts

128

saying *actually I think it was here*, and then they stopped talking altogether and made love again, until Florence's lips were bruised from his kissing and her whole body sang with the knowledge of his.

They ate by candlelight on the sofa, straight from the cartons, sitting cross-legged in front of each other wrapped in bedclothes, and Florence thought that nothing, not even the distant picnics of her childhood, had ever tasted better. She watched him, this man she hardly knew and whom somehow she had always known, sitting in his boxer shorts at two o'clock in the morning after making love to her three times, eating Singapore noodles and laughing, and she felt overwhelmed by the love she already felt for him.

'What are you thinking?' he asked, catching her watching.

'That I love you. And that I can't understand how that can be, since I hardly know you.' There seemed no point in hiding the truth. Florence had little experience of love or relationships, but even if she had, she would not have been able to conceal her feelings at this moment.

Pierre put down his chopsticks and the carton he was holding. He pushed the remains of their meal out of the way, picked up the bottle of wine and their empty glasses from the floor, and then he gathered Florence to him, duvet and all, and held her tightly against his chest.

'That's good,' he whispered softly against her ear. 'That's very good. Because I was thinking exactly the same thing.'

Florence didn't go home for the rest of the weekend. And two weeks later, she left her pristine apartment on the Upper East Side and moved in with Pierre.

London, 2005

On the sixth day of her visit, Catherine casually suggests that they call Mimi.

Florence is sitting on the sofa, tickling Zélie's feet to stop her from dozing off at the breast. She has no thought for anything beyond this immediate moment: the comfort of her sofa and its bird's-eye view, the solid warmth of her baby, the way her toes curl when she runs her finger beneath them. She does this again and again, fascinated by the reflex, and laughs softly each time it happens. She is, she realizes, quite in love again.

'*Chérie*, I said we should call Mimi,' repeats Catherine. Her voice is quavering but defiant.

Florence freezes. Her finger comes to rest in the arch of Zélie's foot. She presses hard against it without realizing. The white London sky turns grey, the cool air grows cold.

'No,' she says, and her voice is low, much lower than usual.

'She's dying to speak to you.'

'You know this, do you? You've spoken to her?'

'*Chérie*, Zélie is her first great-grandchild! Of course I've spoken to her.'

'While you've been here?'

'Yes. From my mobile,' adds Catherine, as if this makes all the difference.

'Then she knows everything she needs to know,' says Florence. She turns back to Zélie.

But Catherine will not let the matter drop. Florence tries not to listen, tries to shut down her ears, her mind, so that her mother's words wash over dully, stripped of meaning, rolled together like pebbles by the tide. *How long are you going to keep this up you are so hard your family love you you can't turn your back for ever you have always been so stubborn so stubborn we've all been hurt and we pick ourselves up it's not by locking yourself away that things get better you're being ridiculous . . . ridiculous . . . ridiculous.* Ridiculous. This word stands out from the others, the solid boulder on the beach, unmoving as the pebbles are tossed this way and that. Ridiculous, the wave of pain which engulfs her, the sense of drowning in sorrow, the choking tears, the chasm of loss.

'I want you to leave,' she says, and now her voice is so low it is barely audible.

'What? Oh now you're being . . . '

'Ridiculous. You said. I want you to leave.'

'*Chérie*, can't we talk about this?' More words, more pebbles, more crashing waves. Something inside Florence snaps.

'Get out,' she says. She is trembling. 'Get out. Get out. Get out!' Her voice has risen by several octaves.

'*Ma petite Florence* . . . '

'Go!' She is shrieking now, standing with Zélie in one arm while the other points towards the door.

'I'm not leaving,' says Catherine bravely. 'I'm not leaving you alone with a baby while you're like this, it's not safe.'

Florence glares at her. 'Fine,' says her mother. 'I'll leave. But on your head be it, young lady. I've done what I can, so on your head be it.'

She is gone within the hour. Florence watches her gather her things silently. She knows her mother well enough to realize that her tight-lipped silence signifies that she is fighting tears. A part of Florence hates herself for what she's doing. It would take so little, an apology, an embrace, but she can barely bring herself to respond when Catherine hesitantly kisses her goodbye. *If there's anything you need,* she hears her say from a great distance, *you know where to find us.* And then she is gone.

Florence stands by the window to watch as Catherine climbs into her waiting minicab. When the car has disappeared around the corner into Ladbroke Grove, she turns towards her bedroom. She places the baby carefully in her cot, then goes into the bathroom. She feels cold. Her jaw is clenched, her stomach tight. She starts to run a bath, as hot as she can stand it, and while it is running she stares at herself in the mirror. Her reflection gazes balefully back. Her rich mane of hair looks wilder than ever, her eyes are huge, the bags beneath them still very present despite Catherine's care. Tears come now, coursing down her face. Her nose begins to run, but she does not wipe it. She continues to stare, and as she stares she thinks that she looks quite, quite mad. Her bath run, she lies back so that only her nose and mouth show above the surface, and she stays there until the water grows cold.

That night, her nightmares return. And three days later, the first letter arrives.

★ ★ ★

The first letter is quite thin. The envelope is white, oblong, of thick, good-quality paper. The writing is a careful copperplate, the ink black and heavy. As if the familiar stationery and the handwriting were not sufficient clues, the envelope bears a French stamp, and the postmark of Charente-Maritime, La Rochelle's *département*. And when Florence turns the envelope, Mimi's name and address are written on the back, as she knew they would be.

The second letter is identical to the first, but fatter. The third appears to be the same length, the fourth also. She cannot be certain, for Florence, the writer of letters she does not send, has now become the recipient of letters she does not read. She keeps them, though. The letters arrive at regular weekly intervals, and she places each one carefully on her small mantelpiece, stacking them up behind a heavy silver candlestick acquired from a stall on Portobello Road in the last month of her pregnancy. There they sit, quietly gathering dust. She tells herself that to really leave the past behind, she should throw them away. But she can't do it, and this annoys her.

When Zélie is four weeks old, Florence takes up her walks again. She has taken the baby out before, pushing her in her pram down to the local shops or round the local park, but now she

134

ventures further. Sometimes she takes her out of the pram and carries her in a sling. She walks down to the market, then through the streets towards Holland Park, occasionally venturing as far as Kensington Gardens. Sometimes she stops to feed Zélie, having identified the places — Italian, usually — where she will not be frowned upon for doing so. As long as she is out, she does not think. At the end of the day she returns home, either by taxi or by bus, tired, her back aching from carrying or pushing the baby all day.

Zélie sleeps remarkably well. Florence is exhausted by her walks. Each night she tells herself that this is the night when finally she too will sleep, but each night in the small hours her dreams return. She is haunted by them now, afraid of going to sleep, and at the same time afraid of not sleeping, so tired that she thinks she is going to go mad.

★ ★ ★

Returning from one of her walks, one evening in early March, she finds Cassandra on her doorstep.

Out of uniform and out of context, the midwife looks different. Smaller, somehow. More subject to the vagaries of the world. Then Cassandra smiles, and the full strength of her personality shines through.

'You don't recognize me!' she chides, laughing. Florence, taken by surprise, laughs back. Cassandra's cheerfulness, after these weeks alone, is a relief.

'Just for a minute,' she says. 'It's the uniform. Or rather, the lack of it. What are you doing here?'

'I was in the neighbourhood.' This is true, but Cassandra chooses to hide for now the fact that she knows the nurse who still comes to see Florence and Zélie once a week, and who has confided in her, very indiscreetly, that she is worried about her. 'I thought, I'll drop in on that nice young lady and ask her for a cup of tea.'

'Yes! Come up, come up.' Florence fumbles for her key, then frowns. 'How did you get my address?' she asks.

'It was in your notes,' says Cassandra blithely. She hopes that Florence will not ask more questions. She knows that she should probably not be here, that she shouldn't have taken the address or questioned the nurse, but there, Cassandra is curious, and Florence has touched her, and she is between jobs at the moment and in need of work.

Florence does not ask questions. She has opened the door into the hall and stepped inside. The post has arrived since she went out and on the mat, nestled between the brown envelopes of bills and the bright advertisements for pizza deliveries, lies the sixth letter. Her heart skips a beat. As she lowers herself carefully to pick it up, holding the baby's head, she does not notice Cassandra's sharp eyes watching her.

* * *

Back in the flat, Cassandra makes tea and searches the kitchen for something to eat while

Florence, ensconced once more in the sofa, feeds a ravenous Zélie.

'I came to see how you are,' says Cassandra when she joins them. 'And to ask you if maybe you still want some help, like you offered before.'

'Help?'

'With the baby. With everything.'

'I don't need help,' says Florence quickly. 'I'm fine.'

'Sure you are, darling.' The nurse has warned Cassandra about this. *She's always fine. She's thin as a rail, she doesn't eat, she sees no one, she always looks like she's been crying. The baby sleeps, but she doesn't. And she's always fine.* Cassandra reaches out, lays her warm black hand on Florence's arm. 'But we can all do with a bit of help, sometimes. Why don't I come see you maybe a couple of hours every day? Just for a bit, to give you a break.'

Her hand on Florence's arm has cut through the weeks of steely resolve against the horrors of the night, through the stubborn resolution to manage alone and the hardening of her heart to creeping loneliness. She wants to lay her head on Cassandra's plump shoulder and feel the midwife's arms close around her in a hug. She wants to talk to her again, as she did in hospital, and lay at her feet the images which haunt her, and she doesn't want to be alone when she wakes crying in the night.

'No,' she says. 'No, not a couple of hours. I mean that would be great and everything but . . . Cassandra, can't you come and stay?'

137

Florence's dreams are changing, the sense of loss which previously haunted her replaced by a feeling of terror. Until now, her dreams have had a strong visual element, she has seen places and people she recognizes, and she has woken weeping with longing and nostalgia for what once was and can never be again. But on Cassandra's first night in the flat, the day after her serendipitous appearance on Florence's doorstep, she awakens not crying but screaming. Even Greta hears her, sleeping fretfully as she always does in the flat next door. Zélie is startled awake by her mother's cry, and Cassandra rushes into her bedroom.

Florence is sitting up in bed, eyes wide and staring, shaking. Cassandra soothes the crying baby, sits with her in her comfortable lap on the edge of Florence's bed, stroking the young woman's hand. 'There now,' she says. 'It's all right, darling. There now.'

She calms down gradually. Her trembling grows less, her eyes focus, her breathing returns to normal. She leans back into her pillows and attempts a faint, unconvincing smile.

'You want to tell me what the dream was about?' asks the midwife.

'Nothing,' says Florence. Cassandra suppresses a sigh. *Patience*, she thinks. This is no less than she expects. Florence is not going to suddenly open up to her, spill her heart out, confide her innermost secrets. And why should she? Cassandra is not a mother, nor even a friend. *Remember why you are here*, she chides herself. *To help her look after the baby. To make her feel better. And something more*, chimes a little voice in her head. *This isn't just a job for you, is it? This is about you too, about wanting to see one of your cases out, about finding out what happens beyond the hospital door. Enough!* thinks Cassandra, and the little voice is silent.

Florence sees the frustration in the midwife's eyes. She understands that Cassandra wants only good for her, that she is here to help, but she cannot tell her about the dream.

Nothing. This really is what she dreamed, inasmuch as a dream *can* be about nothing. Nothing, and darkness. The sort of darkness you can only get underground, pitch black, not a ray or a hope of light. Except that there was light. A tiny candle, like those on a birthday cake, flickering just out of reach, dancing ever further away, mocking her. Florence, the dreamer, tried to tell Florence in the dream. *Look!* she cried silently. *Can't you see? There, in front of you!* But however hard she tried, she could not make herself heard, until the light grew smaller and disappeared completely and the two Florences and their terrified scream merged into one.

Florence knows what this dream is about. But to tell Cassandra would be to reveal far too much.

★   ★   ★

139

Florence wakes late after these dreams. A week after Cassandra's arrival, she wanders sleepily into the living room to find Cassandra playing with Zélie, who coos softly in response. The room looks even tidier than usual, a breeze blows through the half-open window, and the smell of fresh coffee wafts in from the kitchen.

'Your neighbour came by,' says Cassandra. 'Nice lady. She brought pastries, she made them herself.'

'Greta,' smiles Florence. 'She does that. She worries I don't eat enough.'

'They're good,' says the midwife. 'You'd better hurry before I eat them all.'

Florence takes a pastry, a cinnamon roll, one of Greta's specialities. She pours herself a mug of coffee, comes back out into the living room and sits cross-legged on the sofa in her old rose dressing-gown. 'This is nice,' she says. 'I could get used to this.'

Cassandra shoots her a sideways look, pleased and sly. 'Ah, it's good to be spoilt sometimes,' she says. 'Isn't it, little one? Isn't it?' She holds both the baby's legs and pedals them energetically like a bicycle. Zélie's coos escalate to squeaks.

'I thought maybe later I would take her to the park,' says Cassandra. 'If that's all right with you, of course?'

Is it all right? Florence isn't sure. In Zélie's six weeks of life, she has never been further from her mother than the next room. 'I'll come with you,' she says.

'You should rest.'

'I want to come.'

Cassandra may be formidable, but she has more than met her match in Florence. They eye each other firmly, until Cassandra admits defeat, by a nod of her head and a conciliatory smile which show that she understands her place in this relationship and that she does not seek to defy Florence's authority. Yet.

★　★　★

In the park, they sit on a bench under oak trees shimmering with new buds, by a lawn of dazzling green dotted with crocuses and a family of baby rabbits. A couple of toddlers waddle importantly nearby, watched anxiously by their mothers, each of whom rocks a pram containing, presumably, a baby brother or sister. Squirrels dart about in trees. Birds sing. Peacocks call in the distance.

'I often feel, when I come to this park, that I am living in some sort of picture book,' says Florence. 'Like I've slipped into this parallel universe in which central London is actually a sort of bucolic paradise designed specifically for toddlers. It's nice. Weird, but nice.'

'Good for the soul,' assents Cassandra.

'Exactly.'

'I'm curious to know more about your cousins,' says Cassandra. 'About what happened next, when you grew up.' Eyes closed, face tipped up towards the sunshine, she looks anything but curious, but Florence is not fooled. She has always known that this moment would come, that Cassandra would ask questions. Just

141

as she knows that her main reason for wanting Cassandra nearby is so that she can answer them. But where to begin?

She stands up from the bench. The wind is cold, and the morning's blue sky is clouding over. She shivers with tiredness and cold, and pulls her large cashmere coat closer around her. She will talk — she has to talk — but she cannot do so sitting down.

'Come on,' she says. 'Let's walk.'

★ ★ ★

'I was,' says Florence, 'a model teenager. I studied hard, I hardly did drugs or got drunk, at the weekends I played tennis and went to dance classes and hung out with my girlfriends. I wasn't into boys, apart from the occasional snog to see what it was like.'

'Because of your cousin.'

'Because of Matt. No one else interested me, frankly. So there I am, this on the whole I think pretty good kid, except that I think my mum's secretly worried I'm emotionally warped or a lesbian or something because I'm not interested in boys, and my dad keeps giving me lectures because he thinks I'm not interested enough in the twins, whereas we all know that what really bothers them is that I'm just not that interested in *them*, either. Because basically since the twins were born, and since the summer I told you about when I was in hospital, they no longer felt like my real family.'

'Excuse me?'

'They no longer felt like my real family. I lived with them eleven months of the year, they did everything for me — I do realize that — but somehow, after the twins were born we never quite got back to where we were before. I could see it hurt them, and I didn't like it myself. But by then I had another family.'

'In France.'

'In France. Cousins who were more like brothers and sisters, uncles and aunts who accepted me just as I was, who never asked more of me, who never seemed disappointed in me. And Mimi . . . '

'And Mimi,' echoes Cassandra. And then she asks her question again. 'So, darling. Where are they now?'

La Rochelle, 1999

For the past two years, Florence had done the whole journey from London by train, catching the Eurostar to Paris, then a taxi from the Gare du Nord to Montparnasse and the TGV to La Rochelle. Robert and Catherine usually came out later than her with the twins. She left with them at the end of the summer, squashed into the back of the car with the two booster seats, barely noticing her discomfort through the veil of glumness which descended on her because the holidays were over. But on the way out she could hardly manage to keep in her seat, and she spent much of the journey prowling to and from the bar, where she bought endless cups of coffee and bars of chocolate and struck up conversation with a succession of other travellers. The first time she had done this journey, as the TGV sped through the flat marshlands surrounding La Rochelle she had gathered her belongings feverishly, anxious not to leave anything behind, her palms suddenly clammy, her mouth dry, overwhelmed by a sort of nervous excitement which had her eyeing the toilets as she wondered whether she had time for one last pee before they arrived. Since then, however, she had become something of a veteran. She sat with her feet in their wedge-heeled lace-up espadrilles up on the seat next to her, engrossed in a book, ignoring the admiring looks of a group of teenage boys with practised indifference. It was the last week of July. Florence had already spent ten days in Cornwall with her friend Jess's family, and she looked and felt fantastic. Her hair, now hanging half-way down her back, was bleached white, her green dress showed off the optimum gold of her limbs, more rounded and muscular than four years previously. She was happy. With every passing year, the feeling intensified that in returning to La Rochelle she was coming home. Life in London, for all its richness, could never compare to life here. Here she felt completely free, loved without question, entirely herself. Here life was sunshine and rain, intoxicating fresh air and cosseting interiors, minor squabbles but major friendships. It did not occur to her that perhaps life here was held in delightful but artificial parenthesis, not just for herself but for all the others too, including Mimi and Hector who for one month every summer had their routine disrupted, their house turned upside down, who saw none of their usual friends and pursued none of their usual activities. Nor did it occur to her that in fact her real life, and the real Florence, was the one she left behind, and that one day she would be forced to accept this.

The focus of the holidays had shifted over time. For the past two years Matt had had a part-time job at one of the bars on the port, which had meant a lot of free drinks and ice-creams until the manager noticed, and a lot of sitting around one drink for as long as possible afterwards. The girls spent more time in town while Tom read and Ben did his own thing, and they all congregated at the bar at the end of Matt's shifts. Afterwards, if the weather and the mood and the tide were all right, they drifted to the town beach and swam and sunbathed there, or sometimes — if they weren't feeling too lazy — they cycled up to the tennis club. There were still picnics on Ré to be had as well though, and big lunches under the trees at La Pommeraie, and rainy days playing Monopoly with Lily, and every year without fail there was Oncle Gilles' camping trip to Aix — some things were immovable. This summer promised to be especially good, thought Florence, stretching out her long legs to the obvious enjoyment of the watching teenagers. This summer Catherine and the twins — whom she did love, but who rather cramped her style — were only to join her for a short fortnight at the end of August. This summer Matt could drive, and had promised that when he wasn't working they would take off on their own (he hadn't specified if by *on their own* he meant without the grown-ups, or just the two of them, and she hadn't dared ask). This summer she had passed her GCSEs and though she didn't have her results yet she knew she had done well, and this summer she felt that she had finally shed the diffidence of childhood, and that the world lay at her pretty brown feet. This summer, she was sure of it, would be the one when she and Matt finally got together.

* * *

As the train pulled into the station, she pressed her nose up against the glass to catch her first glimpse of her grandfather. Ever since that first summer when she had travelled alone, Hector had come to fetch her at the station. They never spoke much — Hector just didn't — but that moment, when she stepped out of the air-conditioned train into the warm air of the old grey platform and into his diffident embrace, was an important part of the ritual of summer.

She pressed her nose up against the glass now as the train pulled in. One of the boys who had been eyeing her up offered to help with her luggage, but she swung her rucksack up on to her shoulder with a look of supreme disdain and jumped lightly down on to the platform. She hadn't seen Hector yet. He would be waiting further down, by the station doors. She started to walk towards them.

Once the platform had cleared, small children in lollipop colours swept up by loving grandparents, teenagers with huge backpacks swallowed by the island buses, townspeople melted into the city, she had to accept the truth. A cold, irrational dread filled Florence's heart. Hector, for the first time in four years, had not come.

* * *

147

'He was tired,' explained a flustered Mimi, hurrying into the station a few minutes later. She kissed Florence distractedly. 'I'm sorry, *chérie*, I couldn't park. Every year, it gets worse, and they keep changing the one-way system. I've actually left the car in the bus lane. Have you been waiting long?'

'Is Grampy all right?' Mimi must have detected the slight quaver in her voice, because she stopped rushing and gave her a proper hug.

'He's fine,' she said. 'Really, he's very well, all things considered. He just gets tired. You know, since his stroke.'

'Grampy had a stroke?' Florence, too shocked to move, stood rooted to the spot. 'When?'

'March. Darling, you knew . . . '

'Nobody told me.'

'They must have. Unless . . . oh.' Mimi looked confused for a moment. 'I forgot. We did agree not to tell you.'

'Me?'

'The grandchildren.'

'Why?'

'So as not to upset you. It was only a *little* stroke. Nothing to worry about.'

'Then why didn't you tell me? If it was nothing to worry about?'

Mimi looked helpless. 'We thought it was for the best.'

'I can't believe . . . '

'*Chérie*, the car, the bus lane, really, we must go.'

Since when did Mimi worry about parking?

And since when, for that matter, did she look confused or helpless? Florence followed her out, frowning. Outside, as if belying what had just happened, Mimi leaped nimbly behind the steering wheel of the silver Golf, just ahead of two angry bus drivers and a traffic warden. 'Get in!' she cried. 'Yes!' she shouted, as the car took off with screeching tyres. She actually punched the air, a gesture she had learned from her grandsons.

'I can't believe you didn't tell me about Grampy,' repeated Florence stubbornly. Mimi's elation evaporated.

'Not my idea,' she said flatly.

'Whose?' Mimi didn't answer. '*Mum's?* Mum's,' she repeated, when Mimi still did not reply. 'Do the others know?'

'No.'

'How *could* they hide something like that from us? Treat us like children, it's so unfair!'

Mimi pursed her lips the way she always did when she was annoyed but trying to be patient. 'The point is,' she said, 'that he is well. He grows tired more easily, and his headaches are more frequent, but he is well. We even went to Ré earlier this month, before the tourists arrived, and he swam. And that is the important thing,' she finished fiercely. '*Not* who told what to whom.'

Florence opened her mouth to speak, then closed it again. Mimi's eyes, fixed hard on the road, were glistening suspiciously. Feeling chastised and a little ashamed of herself, she remained silent, and tried not to linger too

149

despondently on the worry that the unthinkable was happening, and the unchangeable changing.

★ ★ ★

Matters did not improve back at the house.

'I thought you could have the green room,' said Mimi.

'But that's Claire and James's room,' said Florence. 'I can't have that, where will they sleep?'

'Sweet child, they must have told you!'

'Told me what?'

'That they're not coming. I can't believe they didn't tell you.'

'I can,' said Florence crossly. She felt sick with incomprehension and disappointment. 'Why? I mean, how can they not be coming? I thought they were arriving on Saturday.'

'Actually, they're coming later. Tom's on crutches, didn't you know? He had a crash on his bicycle and twisted his ankle. They're staying in Devon a little longer. They'll be here in a fortnight or so.'

'But Matt . . . his job . . . '

Now Mimi was looking downright uncomfortable. 'Matt received a last-minute invitation to go to Greece with some friends. Sailing . . . I thought he might have told you.'

'Clearly no one ever tells me *anything*. And anyway, he's crap about keeping in touch, I haven't heard from him for months.'

'Well,' Mimi reached out to stroke her cheek, 'none of you are great at keeping in touch. But

150

he'll be here later. You *do* know about your Pommeraie cousins, don't you?'

Florence nodded glumly. She had been pleased when Catherine told her Camille and Louise would not be in La Rochelle for the first part of the holidays. More time with Matt, she had thought. No sharing. More opportunities to be alone with him. She had actually laughed when Catherine told her what they were doing. Ever since Amandine had dropped out of university to live with a much older man whose occupation she loosely described as *professional poker player*, Agnès had tightened the reins on her girls. Camille and Louise had been bundled off to a strictly Catholic holiday camp for a month. Florence had already received letters from each of them, complaining bitterly about their mother, the camp, their exile, the possibility that life would never be fun again and the general unfairness of existence. From being pleased to see the back of them, she suddenly wished that they could be here.

'Yes,' she said. 'I did know about that. So when are *they* coming?'

'Hopefully for France's party on the *quinze août*. Poor darling. She misses them terribly, and she says Paf and Marie-Jo are wandering around like little lost souls.'

'And Ben — '

' . . . is with Gilles, in Corrèze.'

Not even Ben.

'Here's your grandfather.'

'Darling Flo!' Hector walked in, smiling shyly. 'I heard the car.'

151

Florence temporarily forgot her own grievances and felt her eyes well up at the sight of her grandfather. This was *well?* How must he have looked before? She had always thought of Hector as old — his headaches, his white hair, his idiosyncrasies — but she realized at this moment that until now he had merely *seemed* old to her in contrast with her own youth. This new frailty of his as he shuffled into the room, this thin body, this transparent, papery quality to his skin . . . He gripped her shoulders with surprising strength as she went to kiss him, and she had to force herself not to cry out, and to give him her customary warm, first-day-of-the-holiday hug.

'Got you all to ourselves, eh?' he said. 'Won't be bored?'

'Of course not!' said Florence, then felt instantly guilty for lying.

Mimi slipped over to Hector and took his hand, and at that moment Florence saw that Mimi also looked older. Her fluster at the station, worrying about the car, the tears she had hidden driving back . . . Hector's illness had taken its toll on her too, and she looked tired. 'We'll make sure you have a lovely time until the others get here,' said Mimi, and Florence threw her arms around her grandmother in a spontaneous and entirely sincere embrace.

★ ★ ★

In the event, she wasn't to be alone for long. Gilles rang that very night, as Mimi and Hector and Florence prepared to attack an enormous *mouclade*. Florence answered the telephone.

'How's Corrèze?' she asked.

'Hot. Green. Quiet. Can I speak to Mimi?'

'Sure.' She handed the phone to her grandmother, and slid back into her seat feeling disgruntled. 'Nobody speaks to *me*,' she complained to Hector.

'I do,' he said.

'Not much.'

'That's because I *don't* speak much. I speak more to you than to most people. Have some wine.'

'I don't really drink wine.'

Hector poured a glass, ignoring her. 'Trust me,' he said. 'It's perfect with the *moules*.'

She drank, and found that he was right. Hector raised his glass and she tipped hers back, and turned to listen to Mimi.

'I do understand, *chéri*,' Mimi was saying. 'I can only imagine how difficult it must be to write a detective novel. A detective *series* . . . *Very* lucrative, darling. I know, you did say . . . oh, I see.'

Hector leaned over to Florence and whispered, 'This is the bit when Gilles asks us if Ben can come here for the summer.' He winked. 'You mark my words. We were running a bet on it, your grandmother and I. I said he wouldn't last a week, Mimi gave him three.'

'No, of course we don't mind,' Mimi was saying now. Hector smirked triumphantly and Mimi glared at him. 'I can quite imagine how bored he must be. No, Florence is here, it'll be nice for her to have company, with the others not coming until later. Oh Gilles, I *told* you about that!'

'Bet she didn't,' muttered Florence.

'The day after tomorrow. Fine. We'll fetch him at the station.' Mimi talked a few minutes more before hanging up. 'There's no need to look so pleased with yourself, Hector,' she snapped as she sat down. 'We only bet we would cook each other dinner, and I don't think I could stand another one of your omelettes. Poor Ben . . . '

'So Ben's coming now, is he?' Florence hiccuped gently.

'Ben is coming,' said Mimi grimly. 'Your uncle has it in his head that he is going to make his fortune writing a series of blockbusting detective novels. The plan for Corrèze was that he would hide away and write. He rather overlooked the fact that Ben might have other needs.' She sounded depressed. Hector gestured to Florence to pour out more wine.

'He'll be better off here then,' he said brightly. 'And company for Flo, as you said.'

'I personally think it would be nice for Gilles and Ben to spend some time together,' sighed Mimi. 'But yes, it's all worked out. Flo, you have a playmate. Are you happier now?'

'I was happy before,' said Florence. She took another sip of wine. *I could grow to like this*, she thought a little hazily. Easier to focus on this, at any rate, on the crisp Muscadet and the garlic-infused mussels, on the bread she used to mop her plate and the smell of the plum tart wafting through from the kitchen, than on

154

the disturbing thought of Ben's presence, undiluted by the cheerful cacophony of her other cousins.

★ ★ ★

It was no great surprise that Florence's feelings towards Ben should be complicated. Everybody's feelings towards Ben were complicated. Ben was complicated.

Over the years, Karen had developed a taste for holidays in the Italian lakes. As a result Ben's visits to La Rochelle had increased, but his relationship with his cousins had evolved little. He continued to talk fantasy novels with Tom, to high-five Matt with forced joviality, to ignore Lily who ignored him right back, to maintain an amiable distance from the Pommeraie girls. The only person he really opened up to was Florence, which she regarded as a mixed blessing. It was touching and rather gratifying to be chosen as a confidante and he was, she had to admit, easier to talk to than any of her other cousins, who all had stories of their own to tell, who were always interrupting or waiting for her to finish so that they could speak about whatever was close to *their* hearts. Ben confided in her at length, about hating school and his father's lack of interest and his mother's odious boyfriend, but he did listen when Florence responded with confidences of her own. He listened and he *understood* when she talked about her own parents and their obsession with the twins, or about her plans for the future which involved law or drama school, she wasn't sure which.

She knew that there was more to Ben than met the eye, more than the secretive, taciturn boy he still appeared to be despite being, in Tom's words, *much improved.* But — the other side of the coin, of which she was a little ashamed — she did grow weary of him. She liked him — she *did* like him — but he was not an easy companion, and after time spent with him she found herself longing once more for the light, silly banter of her Pommeraie cousins, for Matt's flirting or Tom's philosophizing, even for the bossy demands of the younger children. The intensity Ben had shown at thirteen had grown stronger. His view of the world was of a dark and brooding place, ruled by disappointment and mistrust. And Florence, for all her grumblings, wanted to be happy. So she sometimes found herself slipping away, inventing tennis lessons and errands to get away from him. She knew that he did not believe her excuses, but she also knew, with the instinct of self-preservation, that too much time alone with Ben would drag her down.

She never asked him to accompany her on her jaunts about town, and he did not ask to join her. Long after the others had forgotten about them, he remained fascinated by the stories of treasure buried beneath La Pommeraie, and he spent much of his holidays looking for it. In deference to Mimi, he concealed his search behind a feigned interest in building tree-houses and dens, a pursuit which allowed him to spend hours roaming the grounds of the old house, and which endeared him slightly — but only slightly — to Paf, Lily and Marie-Jo, who appropriated his creations for their games. At first, Ben reported back on his findings — or lack of findings — to Florence, Matt and Tom. In time, faced at first with their teasing and eventually with their indifference, he stopped. He conducted his searches alone, and to the others these became an undisputable part of him, in the same way as his dark moods and occasional radiant smiles and mutinous outbursts of temper.

★ ★ ★

At the station, Mimi stayed in the car, hunched over the steering wheel, silently daring parking officials to ask her to move on.

'I can't bear another fine,' she said. 'The last one ended in a court summons, and it upset Hector terribly. But I will not buy a ticket. Not in my own town. I pay my taxes. At least, Hector does. I'll wait here.'

Florence almost didn't recognize Ben when he stepped off the train. She scanned the crowds for a small thin figure with badly cut hair uncomfortably dressed in shorts and polo shirt. Instead, as the crowds cleared, she saw a boy, taller than herself, closely cropped hair revealing huge brown eyes and a wide generous mouth, casually dressed in loose-fitting jeans, battered sneakers and a black rock band T-shirt. Florence stared, dumbstruck. Ben, it appeared, was growing up.

'Hey, Flo,' he said as he loped up to her. 'What's up?'

'Excuse me?'

'What's up, what's happening? What is occurring?'

'You *have* changed,' she said.

Even his walk was different. He strode off towards the exit, and she trotted behind to catch up. 'Nah,' he said, and was he actually smirking? 'I've been like this all along. You just didn't notice.'

'You *have*,' she said firmly. 'You've had a haircut. And your clothes are different. You look almost . . . cool.'

'You needn't sound so surprised.'

'You know what I mean. So how'd it happen?' She had caught up with him now and was walking beside him, grinning slyly. 'D'you have any help? With your makeover?'

He glared at her and she smiled back innocently. 'Not that I'm prying.'

'It was Séverine,' he said shortly. 'If you really want to know.'

'Séverine? As in . . . '

'My ex-stepmother. I think she did it to piss Mum off. Not that it worked, because Mum barely noticed. Too wrapped up in bloody Jerome and whether or not he'll propose.'

'That's so weird.'

'About Mum?'

'About Séverine.'

'Yeah, well. Welcome to my world.'

A hint of bitterness had crept into his voice and he looked more like the old Ben, the one

158

who walked alone and confided only in her, who mistrusted the world around him and was angered by it. She slipped her arm through his and quickly kissed his cheek. 'You look great,' she said. 'Really. I'm going to have to keep an eye on you.'

★ ★ ★

It rained almost continuously for the first few days after Ben's arrival, and the household at avenue Carnot slipped into an easy, lazy routine. They all slept late, even Hector, traditionally an early riser. Someone — usually Florence, rubber boots and raincoat pulled on over her pyjamas — went for bread and croissants, and they ate breakfast. Later on Mimi went to market, occasionally accompanied by one of her grandchildren, and when they felt hungry they ate lunch. In the afternoons Florence and Ben went out on the bikes for long damp rambles through the parks to the pleasure-harbour at Les Minimes, where they drank hot chocolate in front of rows of sodden yachts before cycling home to change into dry clothes and settle into an evening of watching DVDs, sprawled out over the living room's cherry-wood boat bed and tall blue armchairs, sometimes with Mimi and Hector, sometimes without. Give or take the occasional bitter remark, Ben's change of look appeared to have ushered in a lightening of his personality too, and he was a good companion. He laughed more readily than before: at funny films, at the sight of Florence in a cagoule with her hair plastered over her ears, at Mimi's attempts to teach him to cook.

Florence let the days carry her, enjoyable and unremarkable. In time, Matt would arrive, and the sun would come out again. The Pommeraie cousins would return, and life in La Rochelle would resume as it always had, joyous and noisy and full of tantalizing hope. For now though, the cosy cocoon of their little world was enough.

And then Ben spoiled it.

On what turned out to be the last night of the rainy weather, and the end also of their companionable late evening DVD sessions, the easy atmosphere between them was destroyed with just a couple of short sentences.

'This is cool, isn't it?' asked Ben.

'What?' Florence, in pyjamas and wrapped in a duvet, lay half asleep on the boat bed, only just focusing on the screen, where humanoid aliens were attempting to capture a screaming silver-clad blonde.

'This. Being here, just the two of us. Without the others. Kind of . . . easier.'

Florence rolled over to look at him, but he was staring at the television. 'It's probably more relaxed,' she admitted. 'Less shouting and arguing. It'll be nice when they get here though, don't you think?'

'I sort of like having you to myself.'

Florence had very little experience of boys, but even her innocent ear picked up on his layers of subtext. Ben did not make casual remarks. Everything he said carried weight. His words — his few words — brought other incidents to her mind, incidents she had tried to ignore, of Ben squeezing a little too close to pass her in the kitchen, or holding her arm a little too long and too protectively when they crossed the road.

She had no idea how to respond. On screen, the aliens were preparing to eat the silver-clad blonde, who was thrashing about with wild abandon. 'This movie is gross,' said Florence.

Ben sighed. 'Her boyfriend zaps them.'

'Tomorrow can we get something, like, gentler?'

'Whatever.' He glared gloomily at the TV as an improbably handsome hero, also wearing silver, burst in on the aliens. Florence pulled the duvet closer around her shoulders and stared straight ahead at the screen until she could bear it no longer.

'I can't watch any more of this,' she said with an exaggerated yawn. 'I'm going to bed.' She stood up, duvet wrapped round her shoulders like an oversize shawl. ' 'Night.'

' 'Night.'

She thought about dropping a kiss on the top of his head as she passed, then decided against it. Suppressing a sigh, she trudged upstairs to the green room. Her last thought before falling asleep was that life, so pleasant in its simplicity, could be about to get complicated.

★   ★   ★

She had hoped that would be the end of it, but it got worse the following day.

She woke earlier than usual, conscious that something was different, and it took her a while

161

to understand that it was the light streaming in through the slats in the shutters.

She jumped out of bed and threw open the window. Hector and Mimi were eating breakfast in the garden. 'It's stopped raining!' she called down.

'Rapunzel, Rapunzel, let down your hair!' chuckled Hector. She blew him a kiss, and ran downstairs.

'Blue sky. Not a cloud. And hot!' She chattered away excitedly, tearing off pieces of croissant and dunking them in a pot of fig jam. 'Can we go to the beach?'

Mimi gently but pointedly moved the jam, and handed her a plate. 'Not we,' she said. 'Your grandfather has a hospital appointment. But if you drag Ben out of bed, the two of you could still make a day of it.'

'I can go on my own — ' began a protesting Hector, but Mimi put her finger over his mouth and would not let him speak.

★   ★   ★

Florence and Ben cycled down to the old harbour to catch the boat to Aix. She would have been just as happy to cycle over the bridge to one of the closer beaches on Ré, but Ben had a hankering for Aix, and she wanted to make him happy, worried that she had upset him the previous evening. And as they leaned side by side against the railings of the old boat, and he laughed at her because she had a large dollop of sunblock on her nose, and she laughed back when the wind caught his baseball cap and carried it overboard, and there was no trace of tension from the night before, she told herself that she had imagined the whole thing and that yesterday's remark had meant nothing after all.

Once ashore, they set off out of the *bourg*, with Ben in the lead and Florence following just behind. It was windier here than on the mainland but the wind, cocking a snook at the weather of the previous few days, was warm. As she cycled easily over the stone path, Florence thought of nothing but how very pleasant it was not to have to wear a sweater, and of the breeze caressing her bare legs, and of the smells of salt and damp earth and plants opening up to the warm embrace of the sun. She grinned at Ben cycling next to her, and he grinned happily back. 'Let's press on to the dyke on the northern coast,' he said. 'The tide's coming in, swimming should be good.'

'Cool.'

The rocks where they swam were deserted. People rarely came to this corner of the island. There was barely any beach, and the swimming was made too dangerous by the rocks covered with razor-sharp wild oysters. It didn't do to swim when the water was too low, or without a mask or protective footwear, though properly equipped and at the right time it was a paradise of white sand and turquoise water bordering patches of dark shadow teeming with marine life which provided hours of fascinated exploring for the boys.

'I saw three crabs,' said Ben, flopping down next to Florence on the tiny patch of beach.

'That's nothing,' murmured Florence, her face concealed beneath a straw hat. 'I saw a conger eel.'

'You're kidding!'

'Yes,' she said. 'I am kidding. Since when do I go poking around those little dark rocks? Three crabs. You win.'

They lay for a while in silence. Florence dozed, then grew too hot, and flipped over on to her front.

'Amazing, the heat, after yesterday,' she said. 'I hope Grampy'll be OK.'

'Course he will. He's fine. It's just a check-up.'

'Don't you think he looks old? I think he looks old. How does that happen? We saw him at Christmas, and he didn't look old then. How can a person look perfectly normal one day, and then suddenly be *old*? Mimi too. Not so much, but still. How can a few months make such a difference?'

'That's how people change. Suddenly. You were shocked by how I'd changed in a year.'

'Yeah but that's just like your *clothes*. Well, and your hair, and your voice and things. You're still the same, really.'

'Well so are they. So are you, and yet you look different.'

'I do not.'

'Yes you do.' He turned on to his front as well, and the movement brought him closer to her. She shuffled imperceptibly away. 'You move differently. Last year you were still running

164

around like a kid. Now you glide.'

'Glide!' scoffed Florence. She was irritated to find her eyes suddenly pricking with tears, and she blinked furiously. She hated change as much at sixteen as she had at twelve.

'I know you're crying under that hat.'

'Like fuck I am. I don't *glide*.'

'Well, you move differently to before, and there's probably a reason for it. Grampy looks old because he's been ill; Mimi looks tired because she's been worried. I dress differently because my bitch of an ex-stepmother wanted to piss off my cow of a mother. The point is, I don't think our appearance changes gradually. There are catalysts.'

'Ooh, *catalysts*,' said Florence, sitting up. 'I've switched from ballet to modern jazz. Would that explain it? My *gliding*?'

'Maybe. I don't know anything about dance.'

It was probably unwise, suspecting what she did about Ben's feelings. It was probably even unkind. But Florence was sixteen years old, and she was growing restless lying in the hot sand. Their tiny beach was still deserted. There was nobody to see her, and even if there had been their presence would probably not have stopped her. She leaped to her feet and assumed first position.

'This,' she said solemnly, raising her arms above her head and lifting her left leg gracefully, 'is ballet.' She did a gentle pirouette, and curtsied. 'And *this* is jazz!' She spun round in the air, landing in a lunge, arms thrown out behind her, head flung back. 'Ballet . . . ' — another dainty step — 'jazz' — a leap, followed by a kick.

Florence loved to dance. She giggled self-consciously at first, but as her steps gathered momentum and she concentrated on remembering a complicated routine, the last one she had practised before class broke up for the summer, she forgot about Ben, about the lack of music. Wet sand clung to her legs, the breeze coming off the sea whipped her body in its scanty olive-green bikini, lifted the mane of tawny hair loosely gathered at the back of her neck. Florence ceased to think about anything at all, exulted only in the elements against her skin and the agility of her body obeying her subconscious orders.

She spun into her final position and laughed uproariously, aware, now that it was over, of the absurdity of the moment. 'Do you think that's why I glide?'

She turned to face Ben, and stopped laughing. Her cousin still lay on the sand, and was looking at her through the lens of a camera.

'What the fuck are you doing?' she asked.

'Filming you,' he grinned. She snatched up her T-shirt and pulled it on.

'Well don't,' she snapped, and marched off towards her bicycle.

They argued all the way back to the ferry, and cycled back from the harbour in stony silence. Later on, anxious to restore the peace, she apologized. 'I'm sorry I lost it on the beach,' she offered. 'You just kind of freaked me out. I don't like being photographed.'

'Sure.' Ben shrugged, and flicked on the

television. Florence waited.

'Aren't you going to say anything else?' she asked eventually.

He looked up. 'What d'you want me to say? I thought you looked cool, I filmed you, you went ape. No big deal. I won't do it again.'

'Right.'

She had the feeling he was watching her as she swept — *glided* — out of the room. Part of her wanted to go back, to run up behind him and hug him as she would Tom or Lily after a row. That part knew that he wanted her to, sensed that she only had to give him an opening, pretend that she hadn't understood the wider implications of the camera, just as she had pretended not to understand last night's remark. She knew intuitively that Ben would forgive her more easily if his pride were intact and she claimed all the responsibility for their argument.

'Goodnight,' she called back from the foot of the stairs. Ben grunted and switched channels.

The other part of Florence — the part angered by Ben, the part that didn't see why she *should* take all the blame — won out, and she went to bed angry.

★ ★ ★

Agnès called for her the following morning. 'I've got a favour to ask you,' she said. 'Christophe and I are going away for a few days, and I was wondering if you would help *maman* with the children? I was thinking maybe every afternoon for a few hours, to give her a break.'

'Will she pay you?' asked Hector when Florence told him.

'Five euros an hour.'

'You should have asked for ten,' he sniffed, at which point Mimi said piously that family was family and Florence should be pleased to be paid at all.

Ben went with her that first time. *Why?* she wanted to yell at him, as they set off again in cold silence. *Why bother, if you're going to be so fucking moody?* At the house, Paf and Marie-Jo ran to meet her. They pulled up short when they saw Ben and he made no effort to greet them but followed a few paces behind, kicking stones, setting the pattern for the rest of the afternoon. The children dragged Florence first to the old gardener's cottage to see a litter of newly born kittens, then to the kitchen for a snack — '*maman* always lets us eat the whole packet,' said Marie-Jo innocently, sinking her teeth into a chocolate biscuit, and Florence pretended to believe her. Afterwards, high on sugar, they went back outside to fill up the paddling pool, and then on to the woods to build a den. Ben stuck with them at all times, silent and morose.

'You might as well help us,' hissed Florence at last. 'You're the expert at this sort of thing.'

'I need to talk to you,' he mumbled. 'Away from the kids.'

'Marie-Jo's annoying me!' complained Paf. 'Can't I have my own shelter?'

'It's not true! He started it, Flo, he said he was going to spy on me and cut off all my hair when I wasn't looking!'

'I did not!'

'You did!'

'Jesus!' sighed Ben. 'Do you really think we care?'

'Ben!' Florence, who had been thinking much the same thing, sprang to her young cousins' defence.

'Well it's true,' he sulked. He stepped up to her and tried to draw her aside. 'There's something I want to show you.'

'Not *now*,' she answered, in a voice of steel which rather impressed her. 'I'm looking after the children,' she went on. 'I'm being *paid* to look after the children. So grow up and stop sulking or bugger off.'

'Fine!' he snapped. 'If that's the way you want it.'

'It is.'

'I'll go, then.'

'Fine.'

'See you later.'

'Whatever.'

He went. Florence felt irritated, then sad. She watched him stride furiously away, and she wanted to call him back and hug his skinny body with his trendy new clothes, and tease him and make him laugh and tell him to stop being an idiot. But he was gone before she could quite swallow her pride. The children, jubilant and united in their dislike of him, pounced on her and claimed her for themselves, and she spent the rest of the afternoon helping them to furnish their den.

He sulked at her for the next few days. It

wasn't in Florence's nature to bear a grudge, but his behaviour exasperated her, and she could be just as stubborn as him. They were studiously pleasant to each other in front of their grandparents, but the rest of the time they either avoided each other completely, or warred in silence, as if goading each other to speak. And then before they had a chance to make up they heard that Claire's lot were due in a couple of days' time, and the excitement of this news put everything else from her mind.

★   ★   ★

Looking back for years afterwards, Florence told herself that the die had been cast well before the start of that short, turbulent summer. The events that followed and the part she played in them were easier to accept that way. *Instruments of fate*, she would think. That is what they were. Instruments of fate, playing to a tune written for them long ago.

Claire's lot arrived in the afternoon, before she came home from La Pommeraie. She had not expected them until later, and so she had dawdled, taking the long way home, cycling back into town and along the Concurrence, stopping for a quick swim at the beach. By the time she reached avenue Carnot, the familiar Mercedes estate, more battered than ever, already sat in the front courtyard. A jumble of cases and surfboards and fishing equipment and tennis rackets seemed to have exploded over the pristine living room floor, and she heard them all laughing in the garden long before she saw them.

She ran out to meet them, greeting them one by one, deliberately leaving Matt till last. She kissed Claire and James first, then Lily, then Tom, stopping to sympathize over his bandaged foot and admiring his new, very serious, surprisingly trendy horn-rimmed glasses. And only *then*, heart beating, did she shyly turn to Matt. Golden haired, bronze skinned, sapphire eyed, he had jumped up from his chair as soon as she appeared, but he too waited for her to greet the others before claiming his kiss.

'Heyyy,' he laughed, both hands on her waist. 'Look who grew up!'

She blushed, suddenly acutely aware of her long long legs and her very short shorts, of the way her skimpy green vest clung to her body, of her cute little John Lennon sun-glasses and the toe-ring she had bought at a market stall that morning, of her hair curling damp and tangled down her back as if she had just stepped out of the shower. As his eyes appraised her good-humouredly, she was conscious of every inch of her body.

'I haven't changed that much,' she protested feebly. Her casual laugh came out as a croak.

'Ben, mate.' Matt turned to the garden door, where Ben was leaning, watching them. She knew that although her exchange with Matt had lasted only seconds, Ben would have caught and understood every moment. He was smiling, a look she knew well — the tight, enigmatic smile which gave away nothing of his emotions. She

171

turned away, annoyed.

'Matt.' The hand-clasp, the slap on the back. Turning to Tom. Ignoring Lily's glare, politely kissing Claire, shaking James' hand — James had never learned the French habit of kissing other men. Hector joining them, bearing champagne, Mimi following with a tray and glasses. Lily's arms laced adoringly around Florence, plans being made for the following day. Matt smiling at her, summoning her over to sit next to him. Leaning in to him, Lily leaning against *her*, somebody calling for a camera, *the cousins reunited*. His hand on the bare skin of her arm, goose-pimples along her spine. Wondering if maybe, just maybe, this summer might be the One after all.

★   ★   ★

'You might have told me you were going to Greece.'

Florence sat with Matt on the terrace of the café at the Concurrence, at the end of a nearly perfect day. In a completely perfect day, she would have had him to herself. Claire and James would have given him the car keys, and Florence would have driven off with him to Ré and not come home till late and . . . she was not entirely sure what, but it *would* have been perfect. In real life of course Claire had needed the car to do a supermarket run, and Lily had clung adoringly to Florence's side, and Tom turned out not to be as handicapped by his foot as she thought he would be, and Ben had reverted to hanging around her moodily, and they were all starting to get on each other's nerves when she announced that she had to go to La Pommeraie to look after Paf and Marie-Jo. At which point Claire suggested Lily go too, and Matt offered to take them, and they all agreed to meet up at the beach later, the others joining them on bicycles at high tide in the early evening. Not quite the romantic escapade she had nebulously day-dreamed about, but at least she had been with him for the entire afternoon, even if their conversations at La Pommeraie and on the beach had been continually interrupted by children asking for food or drink or attention, or by France stopping to chat, or by Rémy pontificating about the new breed of chicken he was planning to acquire. And now this stolen moment at the café terrace, sipping a *menthe à l'eau*, alone with him at last while the children played on the swings and carousel behind them.

'Can I have some more money?' Lily, breathless, flung herself at their table. 'We want another go.'

'I thought you were too old for the toys here,' teased Matt as he dug into his pocket.

'It's not for me, it's for Paf,' she retorted.

'I remember loving those rides as a kid,' said Matt. 'And I remember *you* still having a go on those swings when Catherine was pregnant with the twins.'

He had ignored her question about Greece. Undeterred, Florence was preparing to ask it again when Tom and Ben appeared.

'So weird, cycling with a bandaged foot,' said

Tom, sinking into the chair next to hers and putting his leg up on the seat in front. 'I can move my leg up and down but I can't flex my ankle. I never realized before how much you use your actual ankle when you ride a bike.'

'Drink?' said Matt. 'Ben?'

'Whatever.'

Ben, Florence noticed curiously, appeared to have grown smaller since Matt's arrival. Smaller, and darker. Perhaps it was inevitable, perhaps he was bound to be relegated to the shadows by the radiance of Matt's assurance. He sat opposite her, blocking her view of the sea, and she felt a sudden weariness in the face of his mutinous surliness. The time for forcing confidences from Matt was clearly over. She stood up. 'I've had enough of this place,' she said. 'Let's go and swim.'

The water was warm, the beach beginning to empty. It was Florence's favourite time of day. She swam a long way out that evening, cutting through the water with her strong, steady crawl, then turned to watch the others. Ben had swum out too, further than her, on the other side of the bay. Tom was lying on the sand, and Matt was playing with the children along the shoreline. She felt a sudden fierce stab of love — not just for him, but for all of them, for this place, this light, the feel of golden wavelets breaking against her face and shoulders. *Tomorrow*, she thought, *I will get him to myself. Tomorrow, it — whatever it is — can start.*

For today, nearly perfect was enough.

Matt, however, proved elusive.

Claire's lot erupted into their quiet lives, spreading their mess and chaos, their babble and chatter, into every corner. Evenings watching DVDs were replaced by long loud dinners, solitary cycle rides by mass outings to Ré. Agnès and Christophe returned, Paf, Marie-Jo and Lily were enrolled on a sailing course, James hired a boat to take them fishing, Mimi's daily trips to the market grew into major expeditions. There was always some forgotten item to be got from the shops, or children to be dropped off or fetched, someone shouting that they were late. Everywhere Florence went, there was somebody else — Tom reading in the garden, Lily spread over the tiny bedroom they were sharing again, Claire absent-mindedly tidying up after her family, sweeping up their belongings from one place only to dump them somewhere else. Florence tried, unsuccessfully, to draw Matt aside. Suggested games of tennis, which seemed to turn into doubles; offered to accompany him on errands, only to end up going in his place; tried to corner him subtly in the garden, only to find herself involved in a complicated ball game. *Almost as if he were avoiding me*, she thought, discouraged. And always, setting her nerves on edge, Ben watching from the shadows.

Florence was nothing if not tenacious. When Matt, about a week after his arrival, announced that he was going over to La Pommeraie, she pounced. Hector was resting, Mimi was tired,

Claire had to go into town with Lily, Tom was buried in a new book, James was in the garage happily tidying fish-hooks, Ben had temporarily vanished. She could at least cycle over to La Pommeraie with Matt, even if she had to share him when she got there.

'I'm only going to help Paf with his bike,' he said. 'You'll get bored.'

'I'm bored anyway,' she said. 'I might as well come.'

Helping Paf with his bike involved taking it apart screw by screw, bolt by bolt, and laying the whole thing out on an old sheet in one of La Pommeraie's numerous dusty old hangars before proceeding to lovingly clean every part of it. It was, thought a dispirited Florence watching from a broken stool by the door, mind-bendingly dull.

'What was wrong with it before?' She yawned.

'It's a *girl's* bike,' said Paf fiercely.

'It'll still be a girl's bike when you put it back together,' she pointed out. 'Just it probably won't work any more.'

'Ignore her,' said Matt. 'O she of little faith. I told her she'd get bored.'

'No, really,' she assured him. 'I'm fascinated.'

'We're going to paint it red,' said Paf. 'And change the saddle. And put in more gears.'

'Right,' said Florence. She leaned forward on her knees with her chin on her hands and sighed as she looked out towards the woods, so cool, so inviting, so absolutely made for walking in *à deux*. 'Oh bloody hell,' she said.

'What now?' asked Matt mildly.

'Ben's here.'

'What's got into you two this summer? Have you had a row?'

'He pissed her off,' said Paf. Matt laughed.

'Hey Ben,' he said.

'What are *you* doing here?' asked Florence. Ben shrugged.

'Just hanging. I'm allowed, aren't I? And I've got news.'

'What news?'

'I just saw Agnès. She's in a right state. The girls are coming back.'

* * *

'Expelled!' crowed Tom when they told the others later that afternoon. 'Excellent!'

Matt pursed his lips and assumed their aunt's *hautebourgeoisie* falsetto trill. 'Expelled!' he exclaimed. 'From a holiday camp, a church camp! For smoking, the shame of it! And not just smoking . . . trading! Selling cigarettes, extorting money, running a racket . . . the disgrace!'

'You're kind of overdoing it,' said Florence drily, but everybody was laughing, even Ben.

'Honestly, she was going mental,' said Matt, lapsing back into his normal voice.

'I'm not surprised,' said Mimi, wiping tears of laughter from her eyes. 'I could never quite see the camp idea working, somehow. When are they coming home?'

'This very evening,' said Matt. 'So watch out, La Rochelle! I've a feeling things are going to liven up around here!'

177

⋆   ⋆   ⋆

Florence remembered this comment a few days later, as she sat on the sea wall along the Concurrence late one evening watching Camille and Louise pour rum straight out of the bottle into Matt's upturned mouth. *Things have livened up all right*, she thought glumly. *Things have livened up no end.*

She had never been the *leader* of the little gang of cousins, but over the years she had grown used to being one of its shining lights. She was the one with the edge, the cool one with the funky clothes, who travelled alone where the Pommeraie cousins moved as a pack dressed in hand-me-downs chosen by their mother. She had drawn confidence from this perception of herself. But now — getting expelled from God-camp for running an illegal smoking ring, that wasn't just cool. That was spectacular. Camille and Louise had returned to La Rochelle two weeks ahead of schedule in triumphant disgrace, and any hope their mother entertained that they would prove more biddable than their older sister was dashed. The old demure dresses were out, replaced by micro-shorts and skinny vests and strappy sundresses out of which they spilled exuberantly. The rebellious streak which Amandine had carried off with such panache found a wilder expression in them. Amandine had been almost elegant in her revolt, with a genuine lack of concern for other people's opinions. Her younger sisters, in contrast, were self-consciously loud. Loud when they laughed, loud on the beach, loud when they drank. And they drank a lot.

Florence was developing a taste for the wine Hector served every evening at dinner, but she had no stomach for cheap rum, even diluted with warm Coke. They had been meeting after dinner like this ever since the girls got back from camp, with Matt, Louise and Camille matching each other shot for shot, until they were all reduced to helpless giggling wrecks. Ben kept up with them, quiet and resolute, though the drinking had a different effect on him, making him more and more withdrawn. He watched them all silently through bloodshot eyes, Matt and the girls raucous and loud, Tom coolly refusing to drink, sitting calmly to one side smoking neat little joints which he shared with Florence, who had given up trying to compete with her exuberant cousins. She sat huddled up next to Tom, wishing the dope would soothe the edges of her jealousy, trying and failing to look like she hadn't a care in the world.

Really bloody lively, she sighed to herself as Tom gently sprawled out on the cool white stone of the ramparts and fell asleep. Behind him, Ben lay on a park bench, snoring gently. *Party on.*

A great commotion further down the ramparts roused her interest. Camille and Louise had climbed down the steep steps leading to the sea, and were darting about among the rocks and pools. 'We're going shrimping!' shrieked Camille. 'Here, shrimpy shrimpy shrimpy!' She collapsed, giggling,

179

against her sister, and the two of them sank to the ground.

Matt sat alone now, his legs dangling over the edge of the wall as she walked towards him. Florence doggedly seized her moment.

'I hardly ever see you these days,' she said as she sat down next to him. She tried to make her tone as light as possible, but the words felt heavy on her tongue. *Furry*, she thought, in the more stoned recesses of her mind.

'You're slurring your speech,' he smiled.

'I am not,' she retorted indignantly.

'Yes you are.' Matt slid a companionable arm around her shoulders and held her close. 'Little Flo. Little Flo, getting stoned.'

'I'm not so little,' she pouted.

'No,' he said, and his eyes on her face were mesmerizing. 'No, you're not.' There was a screech from down below, and she dragged her eyes away from his towards the rocks where Louise, her jeans round her ankles, squatted to pee over a rock pool. 'The crab is going to pinch my fanny!' she screamed. 'I'm going to catch crabs!'

'Nice,' said Matt.

'They're such a laugh,' said Florence. *Rule number one*, a girlfriend had once told her. *Never show you're jealous.*

'They're drunk,' said Matt dismissively. Something in his tone made her curious.

'I thought you liked getting drunk with them,' she said.

'Yeah.' He looked uncomfortable suddenly. Shy. *Oh my God*, thought Florence, awareness

180

cutting through her drug-hazed brain. *Something's going to happen!*

'Flo, can we go somewhere tomorrow? Just me and you?'

'Without the others?' she asked stupidly. *Oh my God, Oh my God, Oh my God.*

'Yeah. There's something . . . I really need to talk to you.'

'I thought you'd been avoiding me,' she whispered.

'I have, sort of,' he whispered back. His hand was warm against her bare skin, his thumb rubbing her shoulder. 'I've been kind of scared.'

Me too, she wanted to say, except the words wouldn't come out. *Oh, me too.*

That was the night before *it* happened, the night before the whole chain of events that was to change their lives was set in motion. Florence could feel the future, tantalizingly close, just out of reach of her eager fingers. *Tomorrow.* The word echoed through her mind, full of promise. On the night before *it* happened, Florence sat close to her cousin Matt, watching the new moon ride high over the silver sea, and she hardly dared to breathe.

And then they met Jean-Marc.

* * *

It was all the fault of the Pommeraie cousins, Florence told herself later when she was looking for someone to blame. If Matt hadn't been helping Paf with that stupid bicycle, he wouldn't have had a can of red paint in his pocket. And if it hadn't been for Paf's sisters, Matt might not have been so drunk. If they had not encouraged him, he would not have sprayed the image of a giant penis over the wall of the millionaire's villa in the *rue de l'Hôpital*, the one built like a Swiss chalet, with the pointed roof and all the balconies and the massive garden full of pink hydrangeas. And if they had not screamed quite so loudly, they would not have attracted the attention of the gendarme, wobbling wearily homewards on his bicycle after another night patrolling the streets surrounding the old port, on the look-out for English tourists making a nuisance of themselves.

The gendarme took a dim view of painting revolutionary slogans on the walls of million-aires' houses.

'It's not an obscenity!' Camille shrieked. 'It's a work of art!'

Which did little to help their case.

The gendarme was in a quandary. On the one hand, Matt had committed a criminal offence, and should be arrested. On the other, it was the end of his shift, he was tired, and he had to get up early in the morning to drive his wife to her aunt's in Saint Jean-d'Angély. He was making a great show of taking down Matt's details while pondering on the best possible course of action, when the gate to the millionaire's house swung open and a young man walked out.

Jean-Marc was the most beautiful person Florence had ever seen. His eyes were dark with heavy lids, his mouth full and sensual, his cheekbones chiselled, his jaw square and strong. His closely cropped hair revealed a wide intelligent forehead, his tight-fitting T-shirt a lean, well-muscled torso, his legs were interminable in his Diesel jeans. They all gaped at him. The girls, the boys, even the gendarme. Smiling, smoking, perfectly at ease, his appearance stunned them all into silence, and he had to ask them what was going on twice before anybody answered him.

'Well that's easy,' he said, when the gendarme, shaking himself back into officialdom, explained the facts as he had witnessed them. 'No need to press charges. This young man will just have to come back tomorrow — when he's sobered up — and clean up the mess he's made. It *was* just you?' he asked Matt. Matt nodded. 'Well then. Do I have your word? You'll come tomorrow?'

'Yes.'

'Then that's sorted.' Jean-Marc's gaze flickered, amused, over the discomfited Matt. 'Until tomorrow, then.'

'Thanks,' mumbled Matt.

'You're welcome.' The young man turned to go back to the house. 'Goodnight, children. Be good, now!'

Matt had gathered himself together by the time they crossed over the railway bridge.

'Shit, I really thought I was going to spend the night behind bars!' he laughed. 'I don't know what the fuck got into my head.'

'We're still on for tomorrow though, right?' asked Florence anxiously.

'Course we are. I'll get there early, and be

183

done by lunchtime.'

But lunchtime came the following day, and there was no sign of Matt.

★   ★   ★

'It took longer than I thought it would,' he said when he came home late the following afternoon. 'You didn't wait for me?'

'God, no!' said Florence, because what was the point of telling him she had lied to Claire about having a headache, and stayed in all afternoon in the hope that he would come back? 'Claire told me you'd been delayed.'

'I have to go back tomorrow.'

'Bummer.'

'We'll have our day out soon though, I promise. The day after tomorrow, when the painting's finished. I'll ask for the car, and we'll go to Ré and eat crêpes at the Café du Commerce.'

'Sure. Whatever.'

'You're not pissed off?'

'Don't be daft.' She kept her voice light, her tone insouciant. 'It's not your fault.'

He left early the following morning, and this time he didn't come home to eat.

'They've invited him for dinner,' said Claire.

'Who are they, these people?' asked James.

'The family made a lot of money in shipping,' said Mimi. 'I used to see the mother sometimes at the tennis club. They live in Paris most of the year now, I think they only come back for the summer.'

'And the boy?' asked Claire.

'I've never met him.'

'Ah, well,' sighed Claire. 'It's nice for him to make friends.' She turned to the others. 'What will you lot do? Will you go out again?'

But there wasn't much appetite for going out without Matt. It was gone three when Florence heard him come in. *So much for going to Ré together tomorrow*, she thought. *At this rate, he won't surface until lunchtime.*

She got up early anyway, just in case. Claire was simultaneously eating breakfast and piling beach stuff into the car. 'My turn to take the kids sailing,' she yawned. 'We're going to make a day of it, eat there. Wanna come?'

'Did Matt mention going to Ré?' she asked.

Claire shook her head. 'I haven't seen him since he went out yesterday morning. Why?'

'It doesn't matter,' said Florence.

The morning dragged. Claire left with Lily and James. Mimi and Hector drove into town. Tom shuffled down, ate breakfast, and shuffled back to his room, and Ben went out on his bike. Florence sat with a book on the cherrywood boat bed, and waited.

It was gone twelve when he came down, already dressed and showered. Her heart leaped at the sight of him.

'Claire took the car,' she said.

'Where'd she go?'

'She's taken the children sailing. Going to make a day of it, she said.'

'Cool.'

'So we can't go to Ré.'

185

His hand froze as he reached out to the fruit bowl to grab a peach. 'Oh fuck, Flo, I'm sorry. I completely forgot.'

'Thought you might have.' She wanted to sound like she couldn't care less, but her voice sounded very small to her ears.

'The thing is, I sort of said I'd go back there today. They've got another job for me to do.'

'It doesn't matter.'

'I tell you what, let's do something this evening. We'll go out for a drink. See if the others want to come too.'

'Great.'

*   *   *

'You look about as cheerful as the avenue Carnot on a rainy afternoon in November,' said Mimi later that evening. She had come up to her room to write a letter. Florence had followed her, sighing heavily, and was slumped in a corner of the cream leather sofa by the window. 'What's up?'

'It's Matt,' said Florence mutinously. 'He keeps promising things, and then breaking his promise. Like tonight.'

'What happened tonight?'

'We were meant to go out. We were meant to go to Ré today — actually, we were meant to go to Ré the day before yesterday, then yesterday, then today, then that turned into a drink tonight, and he's *still* not bloody home.'

'He called to say they'd asked him to dinner again.'

186

'I KNOW!' cried Florence. 'But he *promised*!'

'It's hard,' said Mimi. 'But it's good for him to have friends. To grow up, to spread his wings. You're all going to have to do it, sooner or later.'

'I'm not,' growled Florence. 'I don't want to spread my wings, *ever*. I want to stay here, and for nothing to change, and for us all to be together, *always*.'

Mimi laughed. 'My darling Florence,' she said. 'My big independent granddaughter.'

There was profound sympathy in her eyes, despite her teasing tone. Florence felt a sudden urge to throw herself into her grandmother's arms and hide there, warm and cosy as a little girl tucked up in bed, safe from the pain of her first love and the cruelty of disappointment.

A motorbike pulled up outside, and Florence leaned forward to look out of the window. 'That'll be him now,' said Mimi without getting up. 'The same bike woke me up last night.'

★ ★ ★

Florence is standing now, about to knock on the window, to call out and wave, ready to forgive Matt, ready to grab her bag and run down and assume that their original plan is still on, but something stops her.

Matt has not moved. Surely by now he should have slapped Jean-Marc on the back, should be letting himself in, should be calling out from the garage to announce that he is home. Surely he should not be standing there, standing too close to this man he has only just met, who still sits

187

straddling his motorbike with his helmet on his lap and his hand softly clasping the back of Matt's neck. Even as Matt leans in to him, even as Jean-Marc slides off the bike and in one almost brutal, powerful movement pushes Matt against the wall, even as their mouths meet and their bodies cling together, chest to chest, hip to hip, legs entwined, even then she thinks that she can hear him running up the stairs, expects to see his head appearing round the door of Mimi's bedroom. Down in the street, Matt and Jean-Marc break away from each other, and Florence's confused mind tells her that she has imagined the whole thing. Matt raises his hand to Jean-Marc's, drops it, walks towards the door. *It is over*, thinks Florence. *Whatever it was*. But just as Matt reaches the door, when Florence has to press her forehead right up against the window because he is standing directly underneath her, Jean-Marc pulls him back. Florence lets out a little cry, a small involuntary *oh*, a single tiny syllable which somehow carries all of her pain. Mimi looks up sharply.

'What is it?'

'Nothing. Nothing at all.'

But Mimi has already joined her by the window. And as Jean-Marc folds Matt into his arms and seeks his mouth again, Florence buries her face in her grandmother's shoulder, and sobs.

London, 2005

'And that's it?' asks Cassandra. 'Your big secret? That your cousin is gay?'

They are back in the flat now. Dusk is slowly gathering outside the darkening bay window. It was drizzling when they returned from the park, and now the rain has gathered momentum, driving and steady. Florence sits on the sofa, feeding Zélie. Cassandra, sunk low in an armchair opposite, looks disappointed.

'There's no *big secret*,' says Florence tersely. 'I'm just telling you . . . stuff.'

'Stuff,' sniffs Cassandra. 'Darling, I can tell a secret when I see one. You're telling me all this cousins grandma auntie stuff but I've been here a whole week and there's been no sign of any of them. And now you're telling me it's because your cousin is *gay*?'

'I didn't say that!'

'Then what is it? What's the problem?'

'There *is* no *problem*! We just . . . lost touch.'

'Lost touch.'

'Yes.' Florence gently prises Zélie off the breast to burp her. She buries her face in the baby's neck, inhaling her sweet milk and biscuits smell. If she stays like this long enough, perhaps Cassandra will stop this line of questioning and go into the kitchen to make tea, or switch on the TV or the radio, or do something, anything, to leave her alone.

'One whole week!' repeats Cassandra. 'And nothing from your family but those letters you don't read.'

'That's enough,' mutters Florence into Zélie's neck, but Cassandra is warming to her theme.

'*Why* won't you read them? *Why* don't you throw them away? What are you waiting for? Darling, you have to face *reality*. Something has happened, I'm sure of it. Something has happened and you have to deal with it.'

Waves crashing on sand, thinks Florence. Just like Mum. She shuts her eyes, leans back against the sofa cushions, Zélie nestled against her shoulder, and she tries to let Cassandra's words wash over her. Soon she will stop. Soon it will be over.

'Child, are you even listening to me?'

Florence opens her eyes. 'I am not your child,' she says wearily. 'You are not my mother.'

Cassandra eyes her with extreme weariness. 'You see!' she announces. 'This is typical.'

'Typical of what?'

'Of you. You cry on my shoulder, you tell me all these stories, and yet you tell me nothing. You have to let people *close*, darling. You have to read letters when people write to you. You have to open your heart.'

'Oh excuse me,' says Florence defensively. 'Is it written in, like, some sort of new mother's charter, *thou shalt tell your midwife your innermost secrets?*'

'So you do have secrets!'

'You're so bloody *nosy*, Cassandra.'

She regrets the words as soon as she has

190

spoken them. The midwife's face darkens, and her eyes close to dangerous slits. Her ample frame grows stiff with offended dignity.

'That was unkind,' she says.

And then the doorbell rings.

'Expecting someone?' asks Cassandra acidly.

Florence is not used to people dropping by. 'It must be Greta,' she says. 'She must have forgotten her keys.'

'You'll never know unless you answer.'

'No.' Florence stares from Cassandra to the intercom and back again, puzzled. 'It's just that it's never happened before.'

'No one's ever rung your doorbell?'

'That's not what I mean.'

Florence puts the sleeping baby down carefully on the sofa, and walks slowly towards the intercom receiver by the front door. She is filled with foreboding and yet somewhere deep within her a little spark has ignited at the sound of the doorbell. Is it, can it be, could it be him? Has he found her? Her heart beats faster as she picks up the receiver, willing the moment to last, the moment when she can believe that Pierre is downstairs, that he has come as she has secretly been hoping he would.

'Who is it?' she asks.

'Flo? Flo, it's Matt! Let me in, will you? I'm fucking drowning out here!'

Disappointment, shock, blind irrational terror. She stares at the entrance button for what feels like an eternity, and when she finally pushes it, she thinks that her finger, the hand it is attached to, the action of opening the door, have nothing to do with her.

'So?' If Florence weren't so flustered, she might have noticed something shifty about Cassandra's behaviour. As it is, she sees nothing. 'Who is it?' asks the midwife.

Florence's face as she turns towards her is completely drained of colour. 'It's Matt,' she says uncomprehendingly. She runs up to Cassandra, their squabble forgotten, and clutches her hands. 'He's coming up. What the hell am I going to do?'

'Why, greet him, of course,' says Cassandra.

'Cassandra, you don't understand . . . this is a big deal, this is a really big deal.'

'Oh, I understand,' says the midwife quietly. 'Make no mistake, sweetheart. I understand.'

★   ★   ★

Matt looks different. The fair locks curling down his neck are gone. His hair is cropped close to his head. The new style emphasizes the line of his jaw, squarer and heavier than Florence remembered. In his dark coat, face flushed and eyes shining from the cold, she thinks briefly that he looks like a movie star. Then she thinks that he looks older. Older, and harder. And definitely out of place.

'What are you doing here?' she demands. The shock of his unexpected appearance is receding, and indignation is setting in.

He smiles, the lazy smile of always which she once thought sexy and which now strikes her as arrogant. 'Just passing,' he says. 'I wanted to see the baby.'

'She's asleep.'

'Can't I look?'

'I don't want to wake ... ' Florence finds herself suddenly lost for words as Cassandra carefully picks up Zélie and walks over to Matt.

'Here she is,' she whispers. 'The sleeping beauty.' Something passes between the midwife and the young man at that moment, an understanding. He holds her eye briefly, and takes the baby, his expression suddenly shy, almost reverential. She smiles approvingly. 'Good,' she says. 'Very good.'

'Cassandra!' Florence finally splutters, but Cassandra has swept off towards her bedroom, and does not answer.

'She looks like Mimi,' says Matt.

'She does not,' says Florence hotly. 'She looks like her father.'

'Ah well, I wouldn't know about that.'

'Matt,' she hisses. 'Are you going to tell me what you're bloody well doing here? Because I'm not buying the whole just passing story. I thought you were living in Paris.'

'Shh,' he says. 'You'll wake the baby.' He glances towards the guest bedroom, and Florence is once again conscious of something, some link, between Matt and Cassandra. Sure enough, as she follows his gaze, the door opens and Cassandra emerges, wearing her coat and scarf and pulling her small suitcase.

'What ... where are you going?'

'Now darling, don't be cross.' Cassandra walks

193

up to her, and hugs her. 'Only it's time I was going.'

'You said you would help me!'

'And so I did, sweetheart. So I did.' Cassandra lets her go, steps over to Matt and gently brushes Zélie's forehead with her lips. 'I'll miss my princess. Let me know how you get on. I left my bill on the little table.' She presses Matt's arm briefly. 'It's been nice meeting you,' she says.

'But Cassandra,' pleads Florence as the midwife makes for the door. 'I need you!'

'No, darling. No you don't. Not me.'

And then she is gone.

★ ★ ★

'I want to know what's going on,' storms Florence once the door has closed behind the departing Cassandra. She turns back to Matt and sighs impatiently. Shoes kicked off, long legs stretched out, he lies on the sofa cradling Zélie as if he had been doing this since the day she was born. He glances back, catches her looking. 'I'm good with babies,' he says. 'Because of Lily. She's really cute. Whoever she looks like.'

Florence sinks down moodily in the armchair facing him. 'D'you want a drink?' she asks ungraciously. He is clearly not going to go away. 'A cup of tea?'

'Tea would be nice.'

'I only have herbal.'

He pulls a face. 'Got any whisky?'

He is standing by the mantelpiece, looking at her collection of unopened letters and still holding Zélie, when she walks back in from the kitchen.

'No whisky,' she says, placing a bottle of red wine and two glasses on the coffee table.

'Wine is great,' he replies. He takes a sip of the glass she offers him. 'Nuits-St-Georges,' he says. 'Nice.'

'It needs to breathe more. Pass me the baby.'

'I like holding her.'

'It's time for her feed.'

'You're not seriously going to wake her up?'

'Matt, she's *my* baby!'

Zélie awakes, and Florence bears her away to her bedroom to feed her, aware that her own behaviour must appear, at best, childish. But how can she help it, when Matt's arrival, Cassandra's departure, all the unexpected events and revelations of the day have left her feeling as vulnerable and unprotected as a child caught outside the familiar perimeters of a safely ordered world? Why is Matt here? Why did Cassandra leave so suddenly? Florence curls into her pillows, Zélie tucked up against her breast, and the more she ponders the afternoon's events, the more she understands that they must be related. For how else to explain the looks exchanged between the two, the complicit nod, the lack of surprise? And how else, for that matter, could Cassandra have packed so quickly?

'She knew you were coming,' she says when she eventually returns to the living room. Zélie, woken from her slumber, has proved voracious this evening, and Florence has not allowed Matt's presence to compromise the length of her feed. By the time she sits down beside him again, the bottle of wine is half empty. 'You're still drinking too much,' she observes.

'Not really,' he shrugs. 'Of course she knew I was coming. It was her idea.'

'Un-fucking-believable. How the hell did she get your number?'

'She didn't speak to me, she spoke to your mum. Quite regularly, apparently. In secret.' He pauses, reaches out to take her hand. She moves away from him. 'She was worried about you, Flo. We've all been worried about you.'

'I'm fine,' she says automatically.

'Sure you are. Is that why you haven't read Mimi's letters?' Florence stares at him, shocked. 'Because that's why I'm here. Mimi heard you hadn't, and she wanted to make sure you did. Wanted to come over herself, but I persuaded her to let me come instead. I'm glad I've seen the baby like this, when she's this tiny. It'll make it all the more incredible watching her grow up.'

'Oh for God's sake!' A painful lump has risen to her throat. 'You're not going . . . I don't want you to . . . ' She stops as Matt's hand closes on her arm.

'Flo,' he says, but she still won't look at him. 'Believe me, we've *all* been through hell. So shut up.' Florence is biting her lip furiously, unable to respond. 'Flo?' he repeats, and his voice is so soft, so soft, that she wants to throw herself in his arms and howl. 'I'm staying.' He nudges her gently, and she nods dumbly, because what else *can* she do? He puts his arm around her and squeezes her quickly, before jumping to his feet and walking over to the mantelpiece. She looks away as he picks up the letters.

'All right,' she says, finding her voice at last. 'All right, I'll read them. But *I* read them first. You only get to see them if I say so.'

'Deal.'

'And another thing.'

'What's that?'

Hunger, prevarication, or the desire to slow this down, to reduce his explosion back into her life to a steady trickle, to — she will only admit it very secretly — to actually *savour* his presence? 'We eat first,' she smiles faintly.

Over dinner, Matt tells her about Amandine's wedding, recently celebrated in great pomp and circumstance near her parents' home at Versailles.

'There was talk of having it at La Pommeraie,' he says. 'But nobody could quite face it.'

'What did she wear?' asks Florence. Try as she might, she can't imagine Amandine in a traditional wedding gown. 'I can just see her now, traipsing down the aisle in her tennis dress.'

'Oh no,' says Matt through a mouthful of spaghetti. 'Dior, all the way. Though she did have the decency not to wear white. Pale gold, with crimson roses, hair half pinned up. Kind of stunning, actually. Her husband had to keep shifting to hide the bulge in his trousers.'

Florence, pleasantly drunk now, giggles, and Matt tops up her glass. 'Did she marry her poker player?'

'Angel, keep *up*! That was years ago. This guy's an accountant.'

197

'An accountant . . . '

'We can't all be supermodels.'

She pulls a face at him, and he grins. 'Hardly a supermodel,' she says. 'What do you do, anyway? All I heard was that you lived in Paris and were making films.'

'Hardly *making* films,' he counters. 'More assisting assistants of assistants. But it's cool. I like it.' Their plates are clean, the salad bowl empty. 'Are you going to have coffee? Because I'd rather stick to wine. And time's pressing on, so . . . ' He looks meaningfully to the mantelpiece, and Florence sighs.

'I'll stick to wine too,' she says.

★   ★   ★

Psyched as she is, it takes Florence a while to accept that the first letter is no more than a standard congratulations card. '*Pour ma Florence chérie,*' she reads. '*Many congratulations on the birth of Zélie. I do hope I meet her soon, with love from your Mimi.* And she's pinned a cheque to it, a hundred pounds! I didn't know she had a British bank account.'

'She kept it from when they lived in England. I think she only ever used it to order hampers from Harrods.'

'Couldn't she use a credit card?'

'Hardly the point. Open the next one.'

He hands her the second letter, and her hand trembles as she reaches out to take it. 'Why am I so scared?' she asks.

'No idea, angel.'

'Do you know what's in the letters?'

'Not a clue.' He smiles encouragingly. 'Come on, babe. She's only your grandmother. How bad can it be?'

The second letter is quite different.

'*Darling Florence,*' it begins.

I don't know whether you have received my card yet, or if having received it you have even opened it. I spoke to Catherine yesterday, who told me something of the way you parted. Knowing you as I do — as I did — I wonder if this explains your silence. For my part, I am tired of silence. To tell the truth, I am tired full stop. Life, I realize from the vantage point of my great years, is short. Actually, it occurs to me that life grows shorter as it gets longer, if you follow my logic. Whichever way you look at it, there is not much time.

Florence has read the first part of this letter curled up against one arm of the sofa, with Matt dutifully awaiting instruction leaning against the other. 'You might as well come over here,' she says.

In a sense of course, one's past is one's own, and thus one should feel entitled to reveal as little or as much as one pleases. What harm can it do to others? And yet there comes a time when the past, to use a cliché, catches up with you. When it bears so much relation or

199

resemblance to the present that it can no longer be ignored. I want to tell you something of my own past. I hope it will help explain why I acted as I did, that summer six years ago, and that you will forgive my part in the tragedy. I hope that it will help you to understand that tragedy rarely results from one act, but rather that it is generally the unfortunate result of a convergence of circumstance.

'Did you read what comes next?' whispers Florence. Matt nods, and takes her hand. Together, they read on.

My story starts at the beginning of the Occupation. It is a story of love, and betrayal, and it features to no small degree the tunnel beneath the grounds of La Pommeraie.

Antoine Duchesne — Mimi's father — was not a man of half-measures.

Eve, his wife, was fragile and delicate. She loved books, and her children, and her home, and was perfectly happy to slip into the background of her little world. Antoine, in contrast, was always at the fore. He ate like a horse, drank like a fish, entertained on a lavish scale. The wine served at his table — taken from the cellars of the family business — was always the best, and at dinner parties he liked to bring it out in magnums. Outings with Antoine always involved picnics which took the whole morning to assemble, or restaurants forewarned of his arrival and instructed to prepare his favourite dishes. At Christmas, his children always had the largest tower of presents, his wife the most sparkling. When he lost his temper, it felt as if the very foundations of the old family house trembled with his rage. His children never forgot one particular fight with a friend who came to La Pommeraie every Thursday to play cards, who said something — nobody ever found out what — to upset their father. The man had fled with a piece of rump steak over his eye (this last supplied by Germaine, their cook), and Antoine had never spoken to him again.

During the First World War, when Antoine lay wounded in a flooded crater, fully expecting to die, he had been saved by an English captain with a broken leg who spent an entire night holding him and stopping him from becoming unconscious. The English man had been on solid ground, where Antoine was up to his chest in mud, and he had not let go, even when Antoine begged him to. The next day, when their rescue party came, he had heard them mutter that it would be better to shoot him and be done with it, but his saviour had interposed himself again, and stopped them. They had dragged him out and taken him to one of their field hospitals, and he had been cured, and invalided out of the war. He still wrote to the English captain, and spoke of him as a sort of Messiah, and of the whole adventure as an epiphany. Where the rest of his peers returned from the war broken and disillusioned, Antoine declared that this experi-ence was his true legacy, proof of man's essential goodness; he had refused point-blank to go into the family wine and coal business, and had become a teacher instead, determined to drum the concept of lasting universal peace into his startled young charges.

The day after France declared war on Germany, there was another volte-face in Antoine's life. Universal peace went the same way as the friend with the black eye. He never spoke of it again, resigned his job and took over the reins of the family business. And it was entirely in character that when the Germans marched into La Rochelle on 23 June 1940, instead of going into town to watch or cowering at home, he spent the day galvanizing his household into preparing to resist.

★   ★   ★

Mimi spent most of the day the Germans arrived digging in the garden at La Pommeraie.

She had wanted to go into town with her friends, had wanted to be a part of that crowd watching the occupying army. She was excited about today. Not excited in a good way, of course, like when she went sailing with her brother, or at Christmas when she still felt like a little girl before opening her presents. This excitement was more feverish, sprung from the knowledge that a long period of waiting was over and a new era was about to begin.

It seemed to her that there was an inevitability about today, that it was the predestined outcome of the long months since war was first declared.

Her boyfriend Rémy and her brother Louis going off to fight, Rémy based in the East somewhere on the *ligne Maginot*, Louis in Brest, both complaining of boredom and inactivity in letters which had stopped a few weeks before but which were still anxiously awaited every day. Her sister France leaving La Rochelle for Montpellier to stay with Eve's sister, because her teacher at the *lycée* in La Rochelle had been called up (which would not have happened, said Eve crossly, if her daughters had not been so stubborn and flatly refused to attend the private convent school at Chabannes). Going to the station with Eve to help with the refugees, meeting the first influx last September, then the second wave over the last few weeks, bringing some poor fleeing family home, giving them food and shelter for a few hours or a few days before they moved on, further south or further west on any boat they could find that would take them from La Pallice, always in search of the relatives, the town, the country where they might be safe. Eve working herself ragged alongside Germaine, their cook, trying to provide for everybody, never saying what they all knew, that she was doing it not out of human compassion or even duty, but to stop herself thinking about her son, her beloved Louis, her shining first-born conceived in the dying throes of the last war. All of this, all of these moments which she looked back on now almost with nostalgia, had led to today, when a German flag flew above the hôtel de ville, and German soldiers would sleep in *rochelais* beds, and a new future would begin, the daily

203

implications of which they could not foretell. That was why Mimi had wanted to go into town: to mark the divide between before today and after, rather as one stays on a platform until the train taking away a loved one has disappeared from view, or watches night fall over the sea long after the sun has set. But her father had issued his orders, and her mother had begged her not to go, and because she feared the one and pitied the other, she had stayed.

In town, curious crowds had gathered on the place d'Armes. Later they would speak of black uniforms and swastikas and of the terrible sound of boots marching through their streets. A few girls threw flowers, and people argued for a long time about who they were. Children wriggled to the front of the crowds, astonished by the display of military power, the clean uniforms, the discipline in such stark contrast to the ragged spectacle of their own retreating army. A little girl in a red dress, hearing some-one mutter that the occupier *hated the Reds*, ran away crying.

At four o'clock in the afternoon the mayor, Léonce Vieljeux, refused to hoist the German flag above the hôtel de ville. Strong words were exchanged, and the *tricolore* eventually came down, replaced by the black swastika on its red background, but by four-thirty the mayor had already been declared a hero. And by late afternoon, as soldiers in *feldgrau* uniforms wandered freely around town taking photographs, Mimi scattered leaves and twigs over the hole she had finished filling in before standing to examine her work. *Not bad.* Nobody passing would guess that under the earth, at the spot equidistant between two young apple trees, lay a vast chest containing all of her mother's jewellery, the silverware, the best china (Eve had insisted, it had been her own mother's), and every object of real or sentimental value which would not be irreparably damaged by a burial of indeterminate length.

'And even if they *are* damaged,' declared Eve defiantly, 'I'd rather that than see a German eating off *maman's* wedding china.'

While Mimi dug and Eve packed, Antoine drove his beloved DS to a neighbouring farm and hid it at the back of a barn under bales of hay. Back home again, he gathered his hunting rifles and hid them beneath carefully prised up floorboards under Louis' bed, a hiding-place once reserved for banned books and photo-graphs of semi-nude actresses. He concealed his revolver, a relic of the last war, in a secret drawer beneath the tank of splendid tropical fish he kept in his study. Then, satisfied with his morning's work, he turned his attention to the larder.

★   ★   ★

Germaine had been hoarding since the day war had been declared the previous September. Her larder cupboards heaved with the tins of fish and packets of rice and macaroni she had squirrelled away over the months. Its shelves were lined with bottled fruit and vegetables from the *potager*, with jars of plum jam and redcurrant jelly. Hams hung from the ceiling, gifts from her cousins in the country. A seemingly endless supply of *haricots blancs* and potatoes was stacked in large sacks in the darkest corner of the room.

Germaine also remembered 1914–18, and she knew how it felt to go hungry. On the day the Germans came she stood, arms crossed and eyes blazing, defending her domain from an incandescent Antoine.

'Let me pass, woman!' he roared.

'God help me, Monsieur Antoine, I will not!'

'And I will not stand by to watch a horde of filthy Boches eat the contents of my larder. Out of my way, I say!'

Germaine was a small mustachioed woman in her late sixties, but her temper was a match even for Antoine's. 'It is *my* larder, *monsieur*, not *yours*!' she declared. '*I* filled it. *I* managed it out when the Belgians were here!' To Germaine's mind all refugees, regardless of their provenance, were Belgian. 'I DECIDE WHAT HAPPENS TO IT!' she bellowed.

Antoine backed down. 'At least let us hide some of the food in the cellar,' he begged.

'Mice,' sniffed Germaine. 'And damp.'

Antoine spent the rest of the day fixing heavy bolts to the larder door, which he secured with large padlocks, the keys to which he meekly handed over to the old cook.

By four o'clock in the afternoon, as the mayor offered the invading German army the town's first symbolic act of resistance and Mimi finished digging her hole, Antoine looked around his property with quiet satisfaction. Léon, the gardener, had stripped every fruit and vegetable from the *potager*, and they were being bottled even now, ready to go under lock and key. The car was in hiding, the guns safe, the radio concealed in the attic, the family treasure buried. *Let the enemy come*, thought Antoine, rubbing his hands with something like anticipation. *We are prepared.*

But it was to be nearly a year before the enemy showed his face at La Pommeraie.

★　★　★

'Good stuff,' says Matt, pouring another glass of wine. 'D'you remember trying to get information about the war out of Grampy? He never told anything, and I always wondered.'

He falls back against the sofa cushion, pulling her down with him, and she does not resist. She is feeling somewhat mystified by Mimi's letter. 'It's really interesting and everything, but why's she writing to me about this?'

'I'm sure we'll find out,' he says. He nudges her. 'Read on?'

What choice does she have, now that they have started? She fights back her feeling of apprehension and nods. 'Read on,' she says.

I was nineteen years old when war broke out. I wanted so badly to go to Paris to study philosophy, but then Germany invaded Poland and Louis left, and then my sister, and my mother begged me to stay. And so I swapped the boulevard Saint Germain and the smoky cafés I dreamed of for the place de la

Pommeraie and my father's accounts ledgers. I worked in his office every morning, totting up figures and typing out letters, grumbling all the way against the stupid war which had taken away everything — my social life, my future, my boyfriend, my fun. Life had become temporarily more interesting with the refugees, the northerners, the easterners, the Belgians. We even had a few British, still trying to find their way home an awfully long way south of Dunquerque. They parked their tanks on the place d'Armes, and apparently they were full of revolting English food and there was a big debate about whether we should give it to the Belgians, which Germaine thought was ridiculous, because everybody knows the Belgians are genetically incapable of telling good food from bad. But then all of these people moved on, and life returned to normal, except that now normal was a long list of tedious rules and regulations which meant queuing for groceries, and trying to sneak into the larder behind Germaine's back after yet another unsatisfying meal, and being home in time for the curfew, and not being allowed to swim at the beach in case Father found out I had exposed French flesh to German eyes, and not even being able to take one hand off the handlebars of my bicycle for fear of the inevitable, ridiculous 20 franc fine . . .

Mimi came home from work one day in a rare temper. The morning post had brought a letter from Rémy, and Rémy's letters always depressed her, consisting as they did almost exclusively of lists. Lists of things he missed — Mimi, her brother, her sister, their friends, French food, the sea, the beach, the sky above La Rochelle in summer, the sky above La Rochelle after a heavy rain — followed always by lists of things he needed: blankets, socks, sweaters, scarves, food, cigarettes, soap and books. She felt sorry for him, being a prisoner and everything, but she found the tone of his letters unsatisfactory, and struggled to remember why she had given herself to him, that summer afternoon in her bedroom just before he left for the East. Curiosity? Boredom? Patriotic fervour? Until that moment, he had been a friend of her brother's, one of Louis' more successful finds. Louis had a tendency to collect people he found interesting and to bring them home to La Pommeraie, where they either became assimilated into the family or vanished without a trace, and he had found Rémy in a bar. 'He's not actually *interesting*, properly speaking,' explained Louis, whose previous finds had included a communist rabbi, an atheist priest and an artist who painted only in the nude. 'But he is just so very *nice*. Just the type one likes to have around.' The rabbi and the priest, after a couple of lunches, had proved repetitive, and the artist not nearly so interesting in the flesh, as it were, as in theory, but Rémy had stuck and become a lunchtime regular, also joining in their family excursions, into the Poitou countryside to visit relatives, and to Ré to eat oysters in the little restaurant at Saint-Clément. On one memorable occasion — *without* her parents, this — they had even swum naked, the boys running in before the girls under orders not to turn until allowed to do so, the girls sneaking surreptitious looks. And then one day, walking home from the *bal public* on 14 July 1939, he had slipped his arm around her waist and kissed her . . .

'Socks,' she had thought despairingly that morning as she cycled to work. 'Sweaters. What am I supposed to do, knit?' Distracted, she had made mistakes at work, absentmindedly adding revenues from a coal delivery to the wine book, occasioning a fearsome telling-off from Antoine, and she was still furious when she got home. *I hate him*, she thought fiercely as she threw her bicycle down on the lawn. *I hate him, I hate them, I hate the stupid war, I hate everything.* Even the spring weather — the first spring of the Occupation — did nothing to soothe her temper. She stormed into the kitchen, calling out for Germaine, and stopped in her tracks at the sight of the old cook sitting at the kitchen table, cosily drinking coffee with a German officer.

★　★　★

Franz-Emil von Fürst was the only son of an Austrian beauty who sang like an angel, and a German landowner who looked like a pig. His parents had met at the opera in Vienna where Lisbeth, radiant and *décolletée*, was in her element and Franz felt like a fish out of water, and they had baffled everybody by falling instantly in love. The happiness of their marriage

210

continued to astonish all who knew them. The similarities between them were eventually revealed by Hitler's ascent to power and the outbreak of war, when cosmopolitan, urbane Lisbeth and her shy country bumpkin of a husband proved to be equally courageous and determined in the face of everything they despised. Lisbeth had wanted to leave Germany for New York. Franz couldn't bear to go. And so she stayed with him, as both their circles of friends grew narrower, claimed by exile and deportation and the all-consuming Nazi party which they refused to join, and all those who visited them continued to be amazed by the harmony which reigned in their homes on the Bavarian estate and in the little Viennese flat, even though the happiness was more muted now by loss and disillusion and worry for their son.

From his mother, Emil had inherited his hazel eyes and thick dark lashes, generous mouth and love of the arts. His cheerful disposition and practical good sense were his father's legacy. He played three musical instruments, spoke fluent French and English and was universally popular. By the time war broke out, he was two years qualified as an engineer, and already working for the Organization Todt. He stayed within the organization, was given the rank of Lieutenant and in the spring of 1941 was sent to La Rochelle to work on the new submarine base being built at La Pallice.

All of this Mimi was to learn later. For now, she saw only a young man in German military

211

uniform sitting in her parents' house with her parents' cook, who had apparently set aside all notions of patriotic duty and was coyly serving him their preciously rationed coffee. The door to the larder, she noticed, was open.

The young officer leaped to his feet as she came in, and bowed. Germaine nodded approvingly. The smile on his lips as he introduced himself was so joyful, so sincere, that Mimi, still baffled by his presence, could not hold back a fleeting smile in response.

'The lieutenant has been billeted with us,' explained the old cook fondly. 'He's already had some of my rabbit stew.'

Well that explains the mystery of Germaine, thought Mimi. The old cook never could resist a hungry young man. *Just like Louis,* she thought with a sudden pang of misery. News of her brother had finally reached them just before Christmas when a friend of his, a small wiry man who had served with him, had arrived exhausted at La Pommeraie, having cycled all the way from Rochefort to tell them that Louis had escaped to England, and that he was training with the RAF.

Eve had run the whole gamut of emotions after that visit, from elation that her son was alive to fierce pride, to a kind of settled despair from which nothing could shake her. *How will* maman *react,* thought Mimi, *at having another young man in the house?* Better by far to have had an older man, someone who could not be compared to the absent son. She wondered if one could say anything, if it would be possible to swap him for another, older officer. This one was showing her

212

his billet papers, looking annoyingly sympathetic.

'I'm afraid they're all in order,' he said apologetically. 'There's no mistake. But I promise to bother you as little as possible. Strictly speaking, I shouldn't have any meals here. But *madame*' — a little bow here to Germaine, who actually blushed — 'was so insistent, and I was so hungry after my journey.'

No, she was sure they couldn't exchange him. On the whole, the occupiers had proved surprisingly conciliatory, but this didn't stop them arresting people who didn't agree with them. It was unlikely they would consider such a request from her. She looked at the young man with irritation.

'You speak very good French,' she said accusingly.

'Thank you,' he replied. 'My mother. She insisted. I spent several holidays in Paris.'

Paris! Nothing could have made Mimi more ill-disposed towards him. He could have slaughtered half of La Rochelle and she could have forgiven him more easily than for having spent so much time in the city she dreamed of knowing.

'You'll have to wait until *maman* gets back,' she said ungraciously. 'She'll tell you where to sleep.'

He could have told her that as an officer of the Third Reich, he had every right to choose his room himself. But Emil was not made to be a soldier. Lisbeth's impeccable manners, Franz's gruff kindness — consideration of other people's feelings had been ingrained in him from an early age. He did not have to report for duty until the

213

following morning, and so he waited. Mimi received her own portion of rabbit stew, ate it in silence and, having nothing better to do, waited also.

Eve called out as she stepped into the hall.

'*Chérie*, are you in the kitchen? Such a depressing experience in town, I went to Madame Migeon because I'd heard she'd received a shipment of — oh!' She gasped in shock as she entered the room.

Emil had risen, and was bowing again.

'This is Lieutenant von Fürst,' said Mimi frostily. 'He's come to live with us.'

Emil smiled apologetically. Eve burst into tears. A voice thundered behind her, 'What the hell is going on?' and Antoine burst into the room.

Really, thought Mimi as Emil rather warily bowed again, *this is beginning to feel like a very bad opera*.

Eve continued to sob. Germaine scurried off to lock the larder. Emil showed his papers. Antoine scowled as he read them, then looked around the kitchen noting the plates on the draining board, the coffee cups on the table.

'He has eaten my food,' he remarked. Mimi nodded. 'And he is to live in my house.'

Antoine's shoulders sagged. Here then was the enemy. His face — open and sympathetic — was not as he had expected. He scrutinized Emil for a long time. At that moment, Mimi imagined him to be struggling with his old beliefs. Universal peace, or total war — which was it to be?

'I will not speak to him,' said Antoine coldly, and having spoken he turned on his heels and stalked out of the room. Eve followed him, still crying.

Mimi sighed again, and pushed back her chair. 'Come on then,' she said, not looking at Emil. 'I'd better find you a room after all.'

★ ★ ★

'I foresee trouble from the young German officer,' says Matt.

'Shut up,' replies Florence. 'Mimi wouldn't do that, she's far too sensible.'

''Course she is,' says Matt, his voice heavy with irony. 'I was just saying. D'you have any more wine, before we move on to letter three?'

'You'd be better off with my herbal tea. But yes, go for it. It's in the kitchen.'

'Don't go on without me.'

But Florence is already reading by the time he weaves back with the opened bottle. 'You do have a good supply,' he hiccups appreciatively. 'Flo?' he questions, when she fails to answer. 'You OK?'

She looks up, troubled. 'I think we're getting to the bit about the tunnel,' she says.

True to his word, my father did not once speak to the German officer. Emil stayed with us until the early days of the siege, and in that time they had not one conversation. Emil tried in the beginning — tipping his hat, saluting, *bonjour monsieur comment va madame*, that

215

sort of thing, but he soon gave up. *Maman* and Germaine tried to make up for it a bit — especially Germaine, but then she rather liked him. Because of Father, I was polite, I answered if he talked to me — hardly arduous, he never said more than a few words, generally about the weather — but I couldn't stand him, no matter how many gifts of coffee and tea and chocolate-covered marzipan he left out for us. Not his fault, I just didn't want him in the house, especially in view of Father's activities. It was a worrying time. We were all worried.

Given his character, it was inevitable that Antoine should rebel. Organized resistance, the *Résistance* proper, would not come into its own in La Rochelle until the last dark months of the war, but Antoine found plenty to keep him occupied.

Louis had discovered the old tunnel as a child. Somebody had come to date it and vaguely attributed it to the great siege of 1627–28, before declaring it a hazard, and thus depriving the Duchesne children of their favourite playground. Antoine had replaced the old rotting trapdoor and secured the new one with a thick padlock. His anger on the one occasion Louis had succumbed to temptation and taken the key had been so thunderous, and Louis' beating so fierce, that the children had never been near the tunnel again, and the key had remained, one among many, on the row of hooks just outside the scullery door. Now, in the early years of the Occupation, Antoine made clumsy attempts to disguise his activities from his family, but it was impossible not to guess what he was up to when he occasionally wandered out to the garden for a 'last nip of air' after dinner, especially when the nips followed a visit from the priest — the same priest he had spent all of his adult life trying to avoid, and whom everyone knew was now up to his neck in *Résistance* work. In the second year of the war, even after Emil's arrival, Antoine reopened the tunnel, which became a stopping place for refugees — Jews fleeing south, young men evading deportation, Communists on the run.

His behaviour infuriated Mimi, mainly because of the effect it had on her mother, who had grown painfully thin and hardly ever left the house.

'He's killing her,' she hissed, as she raked over potato beds with Germaine, 'with his pathetic little gestures. She's dying of worry for him.'

'It's not your father who's making her sick,' admonished the old cook half-heartedly. In Germaine's view the Germans and their indestructible army were an inescapable fact of life, and it didn't do to try and provoke them with well-meaning heroics. 'It's the war.'

'It's making me sick, too,' grumbled Mimi. 'Sick with boredom. And work.'

The gardener had left them just before Christmas of '41. 'Gone south,' confided the all-knowing Germaine. 'Black market. They were on to him.' He left his nephew behind to take his place, which in practice meant more work for Mimi and Germaine, because Jean, though

young and strong, was also simple. Good-
humoured and gentle, the only tasks he was
good at were gathering kindling and chopping
wood. Other than this, he indulged in his two
passions, which were singing long tuneless ditties
of his own invention and an enthusiastic appetite
for outdoor masturbation. They encouraged the
first, on the grounds that it kept him happy and
did no harm. As for the second, there was not a
lot they could do about it, other than to steer
him away from public places. And so Jean spent
most of his days drifting through the woods,
spreading his seed and occasionally making
himself useful, and his evenings alone in his tiny
cottage on the edge of the property, the only
truly happy member of Antoine's household.

★   ★   ★

'Not so much about the tunnel, then,' says Matt.
'No,' says Florence, relieved. She flicks
through the next pages. 'There's more about the
German officer.'
'I bet there is,' leers Matt.
'Please,' says Florence reprovingly, but she is
beginning to enjoy herself. 'You're talking about
your grandmother.'

★   ★   ★

Emil was true to his word, and in his first year at
La Pommeraie they hardly saw him. He ate all
his meals out, either on the base or in town, and
spent his evenings at the hôtel des Étrangers

with his fellow officers. If he did stay in, he kept to his room, and Germaine could count on the fingers of one hand how many times he asked her for something.

Then, in the spring of 1942, he fell ill. Mimi heard him coughing at night, a dreadful, hacking sound, and one morning when their paths crossed because he was late for work, she noticed that he looked exhausted, with huge dark bags under his eyes. *Good!* she thought, and was surprised by the viciousness of her feeling.

When she returned from work that day, an unfamiliar car was parked in the driveway and a German officer was running lightly down the steps of the porch towards it.

'Doctor,' said Germaine. 'Came for the lieutenant. Influenza, doing the rounds at the base, apparently. Been told to stay in bed if he doesn't want to catch pneumonia.' She was laying out a tray with coffee and toast. 'And we've been told to look after him here. Us!' As an afterthought, she added a small dish of plum jam to the tray, picked it up and thrust it at Mimi. 'There you go *chérie*. Up you go.'

'Me?'

'Well I don't have time, do I? I have to make soup and whatnot for the invalid.'

'Soup?'

'Don't worry, it's all taken care of. The Third Reich will provide.' Germaine bustled away to her larder, and Mimi trudged reluctantly up the stairs to Emil's room.

He was lying in bed reading when she walked in, and struggled to sit up when she appeared.

'Mademoiselle Duchesne! I had no idea, I thought Germaine . . . '

'Germaine's busy,' she answered shortly. She raised the tray. 'Where d'you want it?'

'Excuse me?'

'The tray.'

'Oh! Here, by the bed. Is it already time for dinner?'

'Germaine made you coffee.'

He smiled faintly, pleased. 'She's spoiling me.'

'Yes, well . . . ' She fidgeted by the side of his bed as he stirred a spoonful of sugar into his cup. He took a sip, and closed his eyes. 'That's good.'

'Can I go now?'

He opened his eyes again, surprised. 'Of course,' he said. 'Unless you'd like to stay.'

'Why should I want to do that?'

Had she been too rude? It irritated her that this boy was not more loathsome. A more obvious villain would have been easier to hate. She held her breath, waiting for his anger to erupt, for the occupier to assert his authority, but no assertion came, and she left feeling dissatisfied.

The following day, Germaine sent her up again, this time with a lunch tray.

'I thought you worked for your father in the morning,' said Emil.

'I do. I just got back.'

'You work hard.' He sat up and winced. 'I've never felt like this before. Everything hurts.'

She pointedly did not respond, and he sighed wearily. 'But I'm feeling a bit better than yesterday,' he said earnestly. 'Thank you so much for asking.'

She stared at him for a moment before answering. 'Good,' she said finally, and he smiled weakly.

'That's the first nice thing you've said to me,' he said.

'It'll probably be the last,' she assured him. 'Germaine'll come up for the tray later.'

'Will you open the window before you go?' His voice was small, almost plaintive, and she stopped despite herself. He closed his eyes and was silent so long she thought he must have fallen asleep. She was tiptoeing towards the door when he spoke again.

'I noticed that your lilac tree was in bloom. My mother grows lilac trees. My father says it's a waste of time, the flowers have such a short life, but she says that's the whole point. If you open the window, I can pretend to myself that I can smell it. And then I can pretend that I am at home.'

She strode across the room, hardening herself against a creeping sympathy, and threw open the casement. 'Now as you say,' she said, 'I have work to do.'

'In the garden. With only that boy to help you.'

Mimi had known Jean all her life, and was protective of him. 'He's a good worker,' she lied, bristling.

'I never said he wasn't.'

'I suppose if you had your way, he wouldn't be here. I've heard what you do to people like him in your country.'

221

He flushed, and she was suddenly afraid, thinking that she had finally overstepped the mark of his remarkable patience, subconsciously aware that his anger, once roused, must be a terrible thing.

'It is not what *I* do, Mademoiselle Duchesne,' he said forcefully.

'No,' she muttered gruffly. 'I dare say it is not.'

'It is not my choice to be here, an engineer in soldier's uniform. It is not my choice to be separated from my family and a life I love, nor to find myself cared for by strangers who care nothing for me.'

'I dare say it is not,' she repeated, looking at her feet.

'I do understand, you know. For God's sake, I have imagination enough to understand what it must be like for you, for your parents, to have me in the house while their son . . . well, their son. If I try to be polite, to make friendly conversation, it is only to make the experience more bearable for us all. Can people not be friends, even though they come from opposite sides of the divide?'

His French had become stilted and more formal as his passion grew, but there was no mistaking the fervour of his expression. The thought occurred to her, sad and ironic, that if Louis had met Emil von Fürst he would have borne him home as a trophy, crowing over his latest find. They would have been friends, she thought. In different times.

He was still looking at her, his eyes challenging her brightly. 'No,' she said quietly. 'I'm afraid I think that they cannot.'

He looked away then, and she was sorry for her answer — not for what she had said, because it was the truth, but that it had upset him.

'I hope you feel better soon,' she offered as she headed to the door again. 'Really.'

'Mademoiselle Duchesne.' He was still looking away from her, towards the window and a view of treetops, leaves just coming into bud against a pale spring sky.

'Lieutenant?'

'You would do well to warn your father. I am not a monster. I can close my eyes to his activities. But others might not be so amenable, particularly if he continues as recklessly as he has begun.'

He turned to face her with a tired smile, and she thought that he looked older, already, than when he had first arrived. 'Please don't pretend you don't know what I'm talking about,' he said softly. 'I too have a father, *mademoiselle*. Who would do the same as yours, probably with much the same clumsy attempt at dissimulation, in a similar position. For this reason, I say nothing. But please tell him — discretion would be better. For everybody.'

I spoke to my father, hoping that despite his predictable bluster my message had hit home, but of course he took not a blind bit of notice. The conversation with Emil was not reprised, but the next time I took his lunch up I cut a small sprig of lilac from the tree by the front porch and added it to his tray. A sort of peace offering, I suppose. A small gesture, to acknowledge his humanity. And so there we were, not friendly exactly but with a better understanding. And there matters could have lain, without the catalyst of two quite separate events — my brother's death in combat, and the arrival at La Pommeraie of Captain Heinrich Spätzer, an altogether more brutal representative of the occupying forces than Emil.

This letter, like the previous one, ends abruptly, with no sign-off other than Mimi's scrawled signature.

'Do you think we're going to find out what happened to Uncle Louis?' asks Florence as she reaches for the next envelope.

'Letter four,' says Matt. 'Have you got the stamina?'

She yawns, stretches, then leans into him. 'Go on then,' she says.

Matt opens the letter, and together they read on.

★   ★   ★

During the week, the Duchesnes all ate lunch at different times, but on Sundays they gathered in the dining room, with Germaine coming and going from the kitchen, fetching the vaguely tantalizing dishes she saved through the week for the occasion and spending rather more time gossiping than she would have dared before the war.

224

Heinrich Spätzer arrived during one such lunch in November 1943. He presented his papers with a click of his heels and a short bow, and apologized for interrupting their meal. By some administrative mishap, nobody had received prior warning of his arrival, but he was willing to be magnanimous. He would wait, he said. He would go out on to the porch and smoke, and they would show him his room when they were ready. There was really no need to hurry.

He displayed the same courtesy towards his hosts as Emil had two years previously, but his small stocky frame, his pale grey eyes and coarse, fleshy lips held none of the younger man's charm, and they all understood perfectly that his demurring was not to be taken literally. Eve, who had knocked over her water glass like a frightened child on his first appearing, rallied sufficiently to murmur that they would attend to the matter immediately. Germaine thought better than to offer a cup of contraband coffee. Mimi, whose conversations with Emil since his illness had consisted of no more than a handful of short horticultural exchanges, suddenly found herself thinking of him almost as an old friend. And Antoine, who over two years had grown quite used to Emil's presence in the house, to the point where he no longer actually turned away when their paths crossed, immediately stiffened his silent protest.

Alsacien by birth, if Spätzer was alive to the sensibilities of an invaded people, he never showed it, and he had little patience for the raw contempt with which Antoine treated him. He was coldly conciliatory at first, greeting Antoine politely whenever they passed each other (which was rare), and ignoring the fact that Antoine never responded. After a few days he tried to force the issue by addressing him with longer sentences, mundane platitudes in correct but heavily accented French about the weather or Eve's health. When Antoine still did not respond, Spätzer stopped in front of him at the foot of the stairs and asked a complicated question about local fishing practices. Still Antoine would not speak to him, but walked to the kitchen and ordered Germaine out to answer in his place. Spätzer considered this a victory of sorts, until Germaine launched into a lengthy explanation of how local fishing had all but ground to a halt, what with the appropriation of the fishing fleet, mining of waters, etc. If he wanted to know more about the subject, however, she had a cousin who had once been a fisherman, who might be willing to speak to him about it. He had been based in Rochefort, but that wasn't so far off, all things considered. And if the captain was interested in fishing himself, well, it might not be safe to take a boat out, but people still fished off the rocks, though she wasn't sure she had ever seen any German gentlemen do so. Spätzer had sufficient awareness to realize that to cross Germaine could make his life at La Pommeraie a great deal less comfortable and so, inwardly seething, he submitted to her fifteen-minute monologue with apparent good grace.

'How long will the old man keep this up?' he

asked Emil, a fortnight after his arrival.

'I've been here nearly two years and he's still never said a word to me.'

Spätzer wasn't sure what made him despise Emil more — the fact that he tolerated Antoine's behaviour, or that he had spent most of the war in La Rochelle. A veteran of several live action campaigns himself, in this war and the previous one, he made no attempt to hide the fact that the considered his posting to this quiet backwater of the war a humiliating comedown.

'Two years?' he asked. 'What the hell have you been doing with yourself?'

'I'm an engineer,' came the short reply. 'You've seen the base, I presume? It didn't build itself.'

'Have you not *tried* to speak to this man?'

'I couldn't care less whether he speaks to me or not.' Emil, who had no liking of Spätzer or his kind, strode off in a temper, and the older man was left with the distinct impression that he had been snubbed.

The fishing question marked the end of Spätzer's attempts at civility, and from then on he went out of his way to be unpleasant. I could tell that Emil was not happy about him. On the rare occasions that our paths crossed and they were together, he would hang back and make a show of letting me pass first while Spätzer just ignored me. But we didn't speak — I didn't *want* to speak to him — until one Saturday when Spätzer had particularly upset me, and Emil happened to come across me working by the wood-shed where he had left his car.

'Where is your woodcutter today?' asked Emil. 'Isn't chopping wood one of Jean's tasks?'

She paused in her work, and he considered with alarm the axe held high above her head. 'Jean can't work today,' she said shortly. 'Your *colleague* has upset him.'

'Strictly speaking, you know, Captain Spätzer is not my colleague. He is an army officer. I am — '

Down came the axe, making him wince.

' — an engineer. I know.'

'Would you like me to help you?'

'I don't need help.' The axe came down again, splitting a log into two perfect halves, and Mimi allowed herself a satisfied smirk.

'So I see,' said Emil. 'What did Captain Spätzer do?'

She threw an armful of firewood into the wheelbarrow as she considered the wisdom of telling the young man. She ought not speak to him. To repeat what Spätzer had said, to admit to being upset by it, would be to go far beyond her father's law of silence. And yet who else could she talk to? Certainly not Antoine, who would only shout, or Eve, who would cry, or Germaine, who would be upset. Not her friends in town, either, girls who lived in smart houses and laughed at Pov'Jean behind her back. Louis or France would have understood. So would Rémy, poor Rémy whose memory was now little more than a shadow.

228

'He said that people like Jean shouldn't be allowed,' she said in a rush. 'He called him disgusting, unnatural. He said he knew what he got up to in the woods and he made these really coarse, you know, hand gestures. He said that Jean should be neutered, and he shouted at him to go away before he castrated him himself. Then he laughed, and went back into the house. I think he's insane.'

She turned away from him to gather more wood and he rolled up his sleeves to help her. She made no comment, but moved aside to make way for him. 'Spätzer is a bully,' he said as they worked. 'He has frustrations of his own. He hates being here. Today he went to see the colonel to request a transfer. His transfer was refused. He was angry.'

'Don't,' she said angrily. 'Don't make excuses for him.'

'I am not. I am explaining his behaviour. A man like Spätzer, thus belittled, will seek to belittle, and he will pick on whoever is weakest.'

'Well he shouldn't.' Mimi threw the final log into the wheelbarrow and turned to face Emil. 'I know what to do with bullies. There were bullies at school. They picked on my little sister once, and I showed them. They never picked on her again. You have to stand up to bullies, you have to let them know you're not afraid. Only the rules are different now, aren't they? *How* can we stand up to you? How can *we* possibly stand up to *you?*'

'It will all finish,' said Emil awkwardly. 'It seems impossible to imagine, but one day life will be normal again. You know,' he smiled wryly, 'things are not going so well for us. That is why men such as Spätzer are here now. Older men, wounded men. Have you noticed how different they are to the fine young soldiers who first arrived? There are not so many of those fine young men now, and they are needed elsewhere, where the fighting is. Maybe the mighty Third Reich is not so mighty after all, eh? Maybe one day this will all finish.'

'Maybe.' She sniffed, and he offered her his handkerchief. 'A fine patriot you are.'

He shrugged. 'You know my feelings on this war already,' he said. 'I trust you not to broadcast them.'

'Of course.' She stared through the woods towards the river, trying to collect herself. 'You know, you once asked if it was possible to be friends across the divide?'

'I remember.'

'I stand by my answer,' she said. 'But I do think, if it weren't for the war, and we had met some other way, that we could have been friends. My brother would have liked you. You would probably have been one of his projects.'

Emil laughed, and Mimi thought, yes, *Louis would definitely have liked him. And France would probably have fallen in love with him.*

'Where is your brother now?' asked Emil.

Louis' instructions in the only letter they had from him had been clear. *Tell no one what I am doing. They will use you to get to me. For now, forget that I ever existed. You know nothing about me.*

'I don't know,' said Mimi. 'He disappeared in 1940. We're still waiting for news.'

'I'm sorry to hear that.' He obviously did not believe her. 'You should talk to your father again,' he said gravely. 'It is one thing to cut me, but Captain Spätzer does not admire him. He is angered by his attitude.'

'My father is his own man. I cannot control him.'

'Mademoiselle Duchesne . . . ' He held out his hand, his fingertips resting briefly on her sleeve, and she stared down, astonished. His arm dropped back to his side. 'Please. Talk to him. I am afraid . . . I am afraid that things will not go well if you do not.'

★   ★   ★

She spoke to Antoine again, and as she had predicted, he ignored her warnings. The battle of wills between the two men was escalating. Spätzer was too proud, and perhaps also too canny, to continue trying to force the issue directly. He stopped even trying to elicit spoken answers from Antoine, but made his authority felt in different ways.

Mimi returned from work one lunchtime shortly after her conversation with Emil to find that the lovely oak doors which separated the dining room from the *salon* were closed.

'What's going on?' she asked. She could not remember a single occasion when these doors had not been kept open.

'The captain,' said Germaine through uncharacteristically tight lips. 'He's taken over the *salle à manger*.'

'Why?'

'Said he needed more space. For entertaining.' The old cook was furious. 'And that's not all.'

'What else?'

'He says he's not comfortable under the roof. He says it's cold, and the noise of the rain disturbs him.'

'So . . .'

'He's taken *monsieur* and *madame*'s room . . .'

And so it went on. Not a day went by in which Spätzer, one way or another, did not find a way of humiliating his unwilling hosts. His presence infiltrated every area of their lives. He intercepted Mimi when she returned from one of her monthly visits to Germaine's cousins in the country, her saddlebags loaded with freshly butchered cuts of meat, a dozen goat's cheeses, three *saucissons* and half a pound of butter. He took her saddlebags under pretext of helping her, then opened them, quite calmly and leisurely, offering no reason for his gesture. He dropped the first bag clumsily to the ground, and a string of fat sausages spilt out. Perlette, Antoine's springer spaniel, bounded forward.

'Sausages,' said Spätzer.

'A gift,' she stammered. 'From cousins in the country. They have a farm. It's allowed,' she added childishly.

'Of course.' He picked up the sausages and held them out to her then, as she moved forward to take them, threw them to the dog, who caught them deftly between salivating jaws and bore them triumphantly to the laurel hedge.

Mimi would never have told her father about this episode, but Perlette was copiously sick that evening, and she was forced to explain why. The following morning, instead of going to work, Antoine marched to the butcher's shop and bought a string of sausages under the counter at six times their pre-war rate. He waited for Spätzer to return from work and then he made a great fuss of frying them himself, with the kitchen door wide open and the smell of fat wafting through the house.

On the day following this incident, Spätzer came home with a large party of colleagues and several bottles of champagne. They sang raucously until three o'clock in the morning, and spilt wine all over the table. Antoine retaliated by ordering Germaine to spring-clean the dining room in time for Spätzer's return. 'We will show him that his presence here is as nothing. Whatever he does cannot affect us.'

He cannot affect us. Father's response to all of Spätzer's transgressions. When Spätzer urinated on the porch, the steps were scrubbed down, and a pot of geraniums was planted jauntily over the offending space. When Spätzer ordered a tree cut in the park, Father planted three saplings in its place. Each petty action of Spätzer's met its quiet counterpart in Father's reaction, and still he would not speak. Spätzer grew angry and vented his temper on Germaine and me, barking orders at us, all pretence of polite conciliation quite vanished.

With Spätzer in the house, there was no question of Father pursuing his earlier activities. Different hiding-places were found for fugitives. The radio and guns were removed while Spätzer was away on exercises, and concealed above the choir stalls in the neighbouring church. At first Father had felt a certain triumph in his silent resistance to an enemy whom he finally considered worthy of the name, but his defiance grew dogged over time. Like the rest of us, he was worn down by Spätzer's persecution. He began to drink.

I avoided him. He was too angry, too bitter. Too often drunk. Sometimes, though, I had to speak to him and one night, while Spätzer was out, I went to his study. The harsh winter had vastly diminished our wood reserves, and the business' coal stocks were low. The BBC — we got our news now from the priest — suggested that the tide of the war was turning, but we couldn't be complacent. War or no war, we needed to stock up for the following winter.

You know the study at La Pommeraie. It hasn't changed much since Father's day, despite France's attempts to prettify it. It had the same solid dark desk with its square of green blotting paper, the same leather armchair, the same wood panelling on the wall. Rémy has changed the paintings — in those days there were just two, a portrait of a hunting dog my father had particularly loved, and a duck-shooting scene in the *marais poitevin*. And of course, on top of the bookcase, the tank of tropical fish, of which only two survived, swimming in gloomy circles above their secret drawer.

I hated that study. It was a sort of hallowed sanctum into which we children only ventured to be punished or rewarded. Even *maman* never went in unless she was specifically invited. Still, desperate times, desperate measures. I stuck my head around the door.

I could not enter the room at first. My father stood with his back to the door, a glass of eau-de-vie in one hand, his precious revolver from 1914–18 in the other. He was looking alternately from the gun to a framed photograph on his desk. It was a picture I knew well, a portrait of my mother as a young woman, her magnificent fair hair swept up in elaborate curls, her eyes full of laughter, her sweet mouth smiling gravely down at Louis, fat and splendid, standing on her lap. As I watched, I saw my father's shoulders sag. He staggered a little and let out a small moan, like a muffled sob. I went to him then and took the gun away from him. I tried to take the glass too, but he wouldn't let it go. He was muttering, and I had to lean closer to hear. The fumes of eau-de-vie on his breath were overpowering, but they could not stop me from hearing what my father said.

'I'll kill him,' he said. I left him then, to fetch water and to ask Germaine for a tisane. He was still muttering when I came back. *The bastards*, he was saying now. Just that. *The bastards, the bastards.* Over and over again.

Matt empties the last of the bottle into their glasses. 'We'll need another one,' he says, not because he means it, but just to say something, to remind himself of the here and now, the reality of life sixty years after the war. He finds them fascinating, these letters, but deeply disorienting. He would like to ask Florence how she feels about them, but she is already reaching out for the next one, her mouth set in the clamped, stubborn line he knows only too well. He knocks back the contents of his glass, pulls the throw on the sofa up around his shoulders, and settles down to read.

And so the war, which had been relatively gentle to La Pommeraie, finally found us. We still had not known real physical hardship, but at last we tasted what it is to mean nothing, to be completely insignificant. For Spätzer, we were dirt beneath his boot. He would not have noticed us had it not been for Father's silent resistance. From that point of view, I rather admired my father. He would not let that man, that embittered frustrated man, walk all over him. And yet he did let himself be affected by him. He drank and indulged in petty-minded tit for tat. They were both so caught up in it. Occupation, I learned, is a tedious business for occupied and occupier alike. Perhaps their personal war, their ridiculous vendetta, relieved the tedium for both of them. But for the rest of us, the atmosphere in the house grew unbearable. Germaine and I talked of little else. Fools that we were, we sat together in the kitchen, drinking chicory coffee — we no longer dared brew the coffee Emil gave us — and looked forward to a day when Spätzer would be gone, and life would be bearable. We knew from the priest that things were not going well for the Germans. But the Occupation had lasted so long we struggled to remember what life had been like before, and recalling it became one of our favourite pastimes, one we allowed ourselves now that the real possibility presented itself that the mighty Germans might one day be beaten. We did not realize then that these were still the good days.

Spring had returned, and the days were longer. France, still in Montpellier, wrote a plaintive letter to say that cramming for the *baccalauréat* had already started, and that she would come home the minute exams were over, whatever anybody did to try and stop her. *I really don't see, darling* papa *and* maman, *why I may not come home before. I can't see what possible use exams are to anybody with the world as it is.* Grand-maman, *incidentally, feels the same.* And then the cry which had been repeated throughout her exile, *it is* so *unfair that I should be here without you when you are all home together.* Others returned to La Rochelle, friends who had left town for the duration, sensing that the tide of war was changing, and venturing timidly back. Mimi joined them in the late afternoons at the café by the beach at the Concurrence, where they smoked makeshift cigarettes and made plans for the future. Everybody had a plan, it seemed. One girl was going to Poitiers to study medicine, another was going to travel, another to write. Sometimes they walked along the sea wall together, and on those occasions, the wind playing havoc with their hair, they talked of the island and how good it would be to go there again, of the sandy beaches and playful surf, quite forgetting that most of them had been there only a few times in their lives. *We'll get the little train to the end of the island and picnic in the dunes*, they said, and one of them, who had been particularly friendly with Louis, squeezed Mimi's arm and said *won't it be like old times, when Louis and France and Rémy get back?* Mimi, who had no plans for the future but who wanted to believe that it could be as golden as the girls described it, squeezed her back, and tried to ignore the voice in her head which whispered *if, if, if.* There had been no news of either Louis or Rémy for months now, but in this lovely springtime, with friends at her side once more and the air full of light, it was easier to be hopeful. The woods of La Pommeraie were a haze of tender green, their floor a carpet of violets and lily of the valley. Spätzer was away a lot that April, and in his absence Mimi thought that life was actually good.

On one such day, her work finished, she decided not to go into town to join her friends. It was the warmest day of the year so far, and the woods had never looked more appealing. To slip into their shade on a day such as this would be like swimming in the height of summer. Blissful, sensual joy. Rather than smoke and chatter and indulge in idle plans, she would go for a walk and gather bunches of violets for her mother's room. Then she might look out one of the old deckchairs, and curl up in a patch of sunlight to read.

★　★　★

On the same day, Emil's superior officer sent him home early.

Emil had never worked harder in his life. With talk of imminent Allied landings, the base, already busy, had gone into overdrive and all leave had been cancelled. Emil, who had secured and had been looking forward to a week with his parents, took the news badly. He had no objection to hard work. True, he still resented the forces which had brought him here. True also that, with news of the wavering fortunes of the Reich's army, it was harder than ever to find motivation for his work, less exciting anyway, now that the base was built and he was mainly engaged in its maintenance. But given that he was here, that as a newly qualified engineer he was still working on projects he could only have dreamed of in peacetime, that for all its folly he still loved his country and that under his watch the life of his workers was a little more bearable, he did not shy away from doing what was asked of him, and more. In the depths of his subconscious lay the confused thought that the harder they all worked, the more they gave, the quicker the end would be — whatever shape that end took. And, like Mimi, he longed for an end. Just as he wished that, for the space of a few days, his commanding officer could have found it in his heart to spare him.

News from home was not good. His father, who was never sick, who never had accidents, was suffering badly after falling from a bolting horse. His leg was broken, the doctor had ordered bed rest, and now he was complaining of headaches and loss of memory. Something in the tone of his mother's letter led Emil to suspect that the horse's bolting had not been an accident. Franz and Lisbeth had enemies, he was sure of it, devout party lunatics who resented their non-political stance. Emil, who had done his duty unstintingly if unwillingly for four years, actually toyed with the idea of going AWOL, then reluctantly dismissed it. The machine may have been under pressure, but it would still find him.

'I don't need you this afternoon,' said Emil's boss. A family man himself, it had grieved him to cancel the boy's leave. 'You've not had a break for months. Go on, take the afternoon, go down to the beach. Spend some money. Or go back to that grand house you're staying in and go to bed. You look done in.'

'If it's all the same to you, sir, I'd rather keep working,' said Emil.

'And if it's all the same to you, I don't want you here. Go.'

Leaving the base, Emil was overcome with exhausted indecision. Should he go down to the beach? The day lent itself to it. He could walk

240

along the sea wall, stop at the café. There would probably be somebody there he knew, with whom he could waste an hour or two, chatting or playing cards. Then again, his head was too heavy for conversation or cards. And, he suddenly thought as he swung his little car away from the base towards home, he didn't really want to be by the sea. The sullen Atlantic, with her mined waters, her wreck-strewn bed, her fortified beaches, had been diminished by men's war from elemental force to strategic position. He did not want to while away the hours watching the sea as if it were a source of pleasure, when he knew that all the while the U-boats whose existence he facilitated were slipping murderously into its depths. His eyes stung, and he was glad that he was alone, and that nobody could see him in his moment of weakness. He blinked fast several times to chase away the unexpected tears. What he wanted, he thought fiercely, was home. To be riding his own horse, Tolstoy, through the forest surrounding his father's estate, his dog Amber loping alongside, vanishing into thickets after game she never caught. To ride all day, tracking wolf and fox and hare, listening to pigeons and cuckoos, catching the occasional glimpse of playful red squirrels, before turning for home, where Lisbeth would be playing the piano and Franz would be working in his study and Lotte, their cook — their Germaine — would ply him with coffee and brandy and chocolate cake. He was aware that there was an element of fantasy to the scene — he could not honestly remember all of these elements ever having come together quite so perfectly in real life as they presented themselves to him now in his imagination — but that only made the dream more poignant.

He came to a crossroads and made his decision. Instead of heading west towards the beach, he swung eastwards for La Pommeraie. The woods there would have to serve as substitute for his father's forests. He would do something he had never done before, and walk in them. With any luck, if Antoine was out, the dog Perlette might even stand in for Amber.

* * *

Mimi had walked slowly around the property — it was too small, frankly, for a fast walk — and gathered sufficient violets and lily of the valley to make several posies for her mother's room. She planned to give one to Germaine too, and to put another on her father's desk. Her afternoon was proving to be every bit as delightful as she had imagined, and she was not at all pleased to stumble across Emil in a clearing close to the river.

He had taken off his jacket and lay upon it in the grass. He had removed his tie, too, and undone several buttons of his shirt. There was a book at his side, just out of reach of his hand where he must have dropped it when he fell asleep. For asleep he was, and deeply so. A branch cracked beneath her foot as she came to an abrupt halt a few feet from him, and he did not stir. Mimi watched him with annoyance. It

242

struck her as indelicate in the extreme for him to intrude on this perfect afternoon when she was happy and able to forget everything but the pleasure of the day. She would have expected more of him, she thought angrily, than to blunder in like this. At the same moment, the very fact that she *did* expect more of him surprised her, as did the realization that, along with the posies she intended to give the others, she had unconsciously planned one for him.

She stood staring at him, confused now. She had never thought much about how he looked — had never allowed herself to — but watching him now, asleep in the dappled shade of a horse-chestnut in full bloom, she realized that he was beautiful. He slept with his head thrown back and his fists closed in tight balls like a baby's. The skin on his face was tanned from being outside so much, but she could see through the gap in his unbuttoned shirt that his chest was white, and the sight made her feel unexpectedly tender.

The breeze picked up momentarily, shaking a chestnut blossom loose. Mimi watched as the pink flower spiralled down from the tree, down towards the sleeping man below, and settled on his mouth. Emil yelled out, and sat up, suddenly awake. Mimi burst out laughing.

He rubbed his face and yawned, then looked up at her. 'I fell asleep,' he said.

'I noticed. You looked like something out of *A Midsummer Night's Dream*.'

'Oberon, I hope, or Lysander.'

'More like Bottom, *I* was thinking,' she

retorted, and he laughed.

'I *was* dreaming,' he said. 'I was at home, in the forest. Something hit me.'

She crouched down, and picked up the chestnut blossom. 'A flower,' she said gravely. 'That is what hit you. You were attacked by a flower.'

'I can assure you, in my dream it felt like much more than a flower. It was extremely frightening.'

'Dreams can be deceptive.' It was too fine a day, Mimi decided, for the differences between them to matter. She sat down next to him on the grass.

'So they can,' he smiled. 'Though sometimes they can also offer insight.'

'My brother swears that once, when he had forgotten the combination to open the padlock on his locker in the changing rooms at school, the number came to him in his sleep. Just like that, and the next morning he went to school and was able to get his boots and shorts and go and play football.'

'I'd like to meet your brother,' said Emil. 'Everything I've heard of him makes me like him.'

'He'd have liked you,' she said. He smiled again, and she looked away, suddenly troubled by the look on his face, the utter sincerity which told her again that he liked her, that to him their differences meant nothing. 'Tell me about your forests at home,' she said, to change the subject.

'You want to know?'

'I do.'

'Very well then.'

They sat cross-legged like children, facing each other, a careful distance apart, and he told her everything. About Tolstoy, and Amber, the wolves and the squirrels. About felling trees in the autumn, and separating saplings in the spring. And then he told her about Franz and his bumbling good humour, and Lisbeth and her cosmopolitan friends. He told her about his travelling to Paris and London, and Lisbeth's long-held desire to live in New York. And in turn she told him about her childhood, about France and Louis whom she missed so much, and the excursions to Ré and into the *marais*, and her own dreams of Paris. And when they finally fell silent, they both realized at the same time that years had passed in their young lives since they had last had a conversation of this sort. The silence between them grew louder. They looked at each other, unsure where such confidences had led them. He glanced away first.

'You've been picking flowers,' he said.

She looked at her full basket, blushed to remember that she had considered giving some to him. 'For my mother,' she said. 'Poor flowers. They'd be so much happier outside. And yet along we come and cut them down.'

'It would be better, I agree, if we let things be. And yet if you had not picked the flowers, your mother would not have the benefit of them. If events had not pushed me here, you and I would not have met, would not be friends. Almost friends,' he corrected himself with a slight smile.

'I don't think one friendship can justify the

entire Occupation,' said Mimi primly.

'That's not what I meant.' She met his gaze, and found herself blushing again.

'I have to go and put these flowers in water,' she said. She leaped to her feet, smoothed down her skirt. Standing up, she could see through the trees towards the house. 'We have a visitor,' she said curiously. 'I wonder who it is.'

A man had just arrived on a bicycle. She watched him lean it against the side of the house, then pause with his back to her before climbing the front steps. Something about him worried her: the way he had carefully looked for a place to leave the bicycle, his pause, as if he were reluctant to go in. As if he brought bad news. 'I'd better go and see who it is.'

'I wish you'd stay.'

He was doing up the buttons on his shirt, and she was shocked at how the gesture affected her, at how much she wanted to be the one doing up those buttons. 'Lieutenant . . . '

'Shh,' he said. 'I know what you're going to say.'

'You understand?'

'That you don't want to be seen with me. That our conversation meant nothing. That we are not friends.'

'It's difficult . . . '

'I know.'

'Lieutenant . . . '

'Go.' He spoke harshly now, and she was grateful for it. She picked up her basket, and went.

Germaine opened the door to the man on the bicycle, and he told her his business straight away. It was not the first such message he had delivered, and he found that it worked best for everybody — well, for himself, at least — to be quick about it. They knew, as soon as he opened his mouth, what he had come to say. They knew that their worst fears had been realized, wanted only to know the when, the how, and to be rid of him.

'Disappeared,' he said. 'Over the North Sea. I'm afraid I didn't get more details. It's hard, you know, to get details. They wait a few days, after a plane goes down, you know, in case the crew get picked up, but . . . '

Germaine's head was ringing. 'I have to tell *madame*,' she said. And then she walked slowly up the beautiful winding wooden staircase, round and round to the top floor, and hot tears began to slide over her wrinkled old cheeks before she even reached the door to France's bedroom behind which Eve lay on her bed, oblivious to the hot day, detached from the world which no longer interested her.

She stood in the doorway to tell her, as if somehow not crossing the threshold could make it better. '*Madame Antoine*,' she whispered. '*Madame Antoine, c'est Monsieur Louis . . .* '

Eve's scream came from deep within her, a primitive, animal sound, terrifying and heart-rending. Mimi heard it, as she walked slowly away from Emil and their arrested friendship, and began to run, scattering flowers as she went. Antoine heard it, cycling through the front gates on his way home from the office, and threw his bicycle down to leap up the back stairs with the sudden athleticism of a much younger man. The messenger in the kitchen heard it, and wished, not for the first time, that they would not use him for such jobs. He had joined the network to blow up trains and kill Germans. It wasn't fair to subject him to other people's pain.

Antoine reached Eve before Mimi. She had fainted, and Germaine knelt beside her on the floor, cradling her head. He swept in like a tornado and gathered her in his arms. By the time Mimi arrived panting at her mother's door, Eve had regained consciousness. She lay on her bed with Antoine sitting beside her, and they were talking together in low voices, their intertwined hands tightly gripping each other, their heads close together, Eve weeping softly, Antoine murmuring words of comfort broken by the occasional sob. They did not hear Mimi come in. It was Germaine who broke the news, Germaine who took her in her strong old arms and told her she had to be brave.

'No,' said Mimi. She did not scream, as Eve had done. Her *no* came out like a whine, the plaintive, pitiful sound made by a child who hopes that a grown-up will put everything to rights. 'I don't believe you.'

She looked at her parents. '*Maman, papa . . .*' Eve carried on crying, and Antoine shook his head. She knew that expression. It was the automatic reaction to the children's whining. It meant, *not now*.

'*Maman* . . . ' she begged again, but Eve did not answer, and Antoine had turned his back on her.

⋆   ⋆   ⋆

She thought that grief would tear her apart.

She ran down the stairs from her parents' room and burst out of the front door, gasping for air. She continued to run blindly into the garden, across the lawn and towards the river. She did not think about where she was going. She knew only that she had to get away from the house, from the exclusion of her parents' sorrow. If she ran far enough, it might go away. If she hid, someone might come and find her, and tell her it was not true. She was dimly aware that the sun was still shining and she ran to escape the light, seeking shadows, seeking darkness to blot out the dreadful knowledge of her brother's death.

She did not think about Emil, but when she ran into him she knew also that she had been running towards him. His arms closed around her, and she pressed her face against his chest and told him, through muffled sobs, what had happened.

He kissed her tears first. Kissed them as they spilled out of her eyes, and caught one on the corner of her mouth. Delicately, like a cat washing her young, licked their salty tracks from her cheeks, and the wonder of what he was doing stopped her crying. She stared at him, a look both hard and tremulous, and his look back was hot with desire and defiance. She would not have kissed him back had he looked at her otherwise; had his face expressed pity, or sympathy, or sorrow. But the heat of that look kindled something in her, and she threw her arms around his neck and pressed her mouth to his.

His hands came up around her head, his mouth crushed hers almost violently, hurting her. She was glad of it, glad for the pain which confirmed that she, *she* was alive, which sent blood pulsing through her. She leaned heavily back against a tree, and he pressed against her, and she felt how hard he was, how much he wanted her. His mouth left hers, tracing a path down her neck to the opening of her blouse. His hands were at her waist, rucking up her skirt. She moaned, took his head in her hands, bit his lip gently. 'Not here,' she whispered.

'Where?'

'There's a place . . . ' Her words were coming out in short gasps. 'No one will see us . . . Go and wait for me by the door to the orchard.'

One last kiss, a long juddering sigh, and he went. Mimi ran on trembling legs through the woods around to the side of the house, in through the tradesmen's entrance where she silently picked up a small key from among the many which hung on hooks on the wall, before slipping away again like a shadow and running, as fast as she could before she changed her mind, back to the orchard where Emil was waiting for her by the entrance to the old forbidden tunnel.

* * *

'I can't read any more,' says Florence brusquely.

Matt has just reached out to pick up the next letter — the final letter, in fact. He puts the closed envelope back down on the coffee table, next to the pile of open letters, and turns towards her. 'Angel . . . '

She tries to control her shaking, finds that she can't. It starts from deep inside her, sending her stomach into spasms. She thinks she may be sick.

'Angel, I know it's difficult.' His voice, so sympathetic. So determined.

'No.' When did her own voice become so hard?

'Together,' he says. 'Remember? It'll be OK.' His arm around her, his hand gently stroking her hair, soothing her as he would an animal. Matt was good with animals. They trusted him. 'It'll be OK,' he repeats.

Emil von Fürst, the young lieutenant, was also good with animals. He loved his horse Tolstoy and his dog Amber. He wanted to befriend Perlette. And Rémy, with his dogs and hens and the ducklings which he protected so dramatically from their natural predators. Rémy, who had been Mimi's lover before the German officer, and who was now Tante France's husband.

'It's too much,' she whispers. 'Mimi and Rémy and the great-grandparents and the Germans. Why's she telling us all this stuff? It's doing my head in.'

'I think you know why.'

'Well I don't.' She stands up shakily. The

251

trembling has spread to her knees, and she has difficulty walking. The lump in her throat is sharp and hot. Her voice comes out in a painful whisper, but she is surprised to be able to speak at all. She has only one wish now, which is to make it to her bedroom before bursting into tears.

'I'm tired,' she says as steadily as she can. 'We can finish tomorrow. Can't we?' She looks up at him, unaware as she does so what a sad figure she cuts, her green eyes huge with supplication. Matt, whose first instinct had been that they press on now, feels too sorry for her.

'Of course we can. Flo, is it OK if I stay over? Only I've sort of not got anywhere else to go.'

She knows this is unlikely to be true. Matt not have anywhere else to go? There are probably a dozen places in London where he could turn up unannounced and be made welcome. He is here to watch over her. To protect her.

'You can have Cassandra's room,' she says. 'Since she's gone.'

Back in her room, she feels safe. She looks at the alarm clock on her bedside table. Half-past eleven. The time when she would normally wake Zélie for her final feed, the one Florence loves, when they lie together in the big bed in the soft light of her bedside lamp, when as often as not they both drift off to sleep until the small hours of the morning. At these times more than any other Zélie strikes her mother as a charm against the insidious dreams which, sooner or later, will pluck her from the delicious forgetfulness of sleep. Tonight, though, she is too tired, and decides to let the baby sleep. Shivering, she peels off her jeans and sweater, pulls on a thermal vest and an old pair of flannel pyjamas, wraps herself in her scarlet pashmina and crawls into bed. Not to think, that is the thing. Not to let the memories in, which currently clamour just on the limits of conscious awareness. Not to touch anyone, or to allow anyone to touch you.

She lies on her side, eyes wide open fixed on the cot where Zélie sleeps, arms flung above her perfectly formed head, a picture of concentration and peace. She would give anything to sleep like that, but the fear is too great. For the dreams will come. However hard she tries to stave them off, they *will* come.

Florence, curled on her bed facing her sleeping baby, loses her battle. The floodgates open, and the dreams come, and with them the memories.

La Rochelle, 1999

There was little chance, in a family such as the Grangers, for a secret such as Matt's to remain hidden for long.

Walking casually in from the street into the living room he found his parents, siblings and grandfather happily installed in front of a re-run of *La Grande Vadrouille*. He had seen the film countless times and it was no match for his mood. He was bubbling over with emotion, needing to talk yet with no idea of what to say. His elation was attended in no small measure by confusion, so that he did not know whether he should shout his new love or hide it. His parents greeted him amiably, but he could not sit with them. Hearing that Florence and Mimi were upstairs, he decided to join them.

His high spirits gave him wings, and he flew silently up the stairs towards Mimi's room, startling them as he bounded in. He took in their embrace, Florence's tear-stained cheeks, their position by the window, and he understood at once that they had seen everything. His expression, which had been jaunty, turned to embarrassment and alarm. Florence was looking at him as if she did not know him, as if she had never known him, her face a stormy conflict of disappointment and incomprehension. He turned to Mimi.

'I don't know what to say,' he stammered.

'Then say nothing,' she responded kindly.

'You saw . . .'

'I saw nothing that was my business, unless you choose to make it so.'

'I don't know what I choose.' His elation punctured, he looked very young as he revealed a bleakness beyond his nineteen years. 'I think it has chosen me.'

As Mimi's arms closed around Matt, Florence made her escape before he could see her cry again. She took refuge under her duvet, determined that no one should bear witness to the final breaking of her heart, her moment of utter humiliation. She had reckoned without Lily, who skipped into their bedroom during the adverts and promptly skipped out again to tell her mother that Florence was crying. Lily was followed by Claire, who put Florence's tears down to her disappointment over Matt's broken promise and stormed Mimi's bedroom to berate her son, only to find *him* in tears in his grandmother's arms. Whereupon Matt had no choice but to admit to his mother that he was gay, and Claire burst into tears too and told him that she had long suspected this and she was so proud of him for telling her and James, who had walked in to find out what all the fuss was about, said *proud of him for telling you what*, and Matt, looking rather dazed, had to repeat what he had just told his mother, whereupon James looked rather dazed as well but, under the ferocious glares of his wife and mother-in-law, managed to mutter something along the lines of *if you're happy son, that's all that matters*. So that by the time *La Grande Vadrouille* was

255

finished, the entire household was *au courant* with the state of Matt's love life, and went to bed that night with feelings ranging from surprise and excitement (his siblings and Ben), through concern and tenderness (his parents and grandparents), to despair (Florence).

★ ★ ★

Matt apologized to her the following day.

'I'm sorry we didn't get our drink yesterday. I really wanted to get back in time, but well . . . things rather took over.' He smiled up at her, his lazy grin sheepish.

Florence had spent much of the night brooding on the previous day's events. Gradually, the tears she was repressing because of Lily's presence in the bunk below had given way to anger, and then to the pressing problem of how to lessen what she perceived as her own humiliation. To have spent years carrying a torch for him, to have believed he returned her feelings, that he had been on the verge of declaring them . . . It seemed to her that everybody must have known how she felt, that everybody must have pitied her, not least Mimi yesterday as she waited for him to return.

The smile helped. Through it, she saw that Matt had already moved on. Yesterday's revelations made, he had sailed on with his customary ease, confident that he would always be accepted as he was, rather enjoying the temporary celebrity status they conferred on him, the glamour rather than the opprobrium of being

256

different. Tom had already drawn comparisons with Wilde, Gide and Vita Sackville-West; Lily, displaying understanding beyond her years, had asked if he could take her shopping. Claire and Mimi were being more than usually attentive to him. Matt, with his love of the limelight, was basking in his new-found notoriety, and the smile which accompanied his apology held more than a hint of smugness.

The smile annoyed her, but it helped. 'I had a perfectly lovely evening, as it happens,' she said haughtily. 'I certainly didn't spend it waiting around for you.' And then, because she couldn't resist, 'I knew you wouldn't keep your promise anyway.'

She managed to keep up her air of cool disdain until the afternoon, when they descended *en masse* on La Pommeraie for tea. France's vague formalities at the tea-table dispensed with, the cousins retreated to Louise and Camille's bedroom in the Warren, where the girls pounced on Matt and demanded that he *tell them everything*.

'When did you *know*? Was it love at first sight? I bet it was.'

'He's such a hunk. I am *so* mortally jealous.'

'Have you . . . you know . . . *done* it with him?'

'Was it the first time?'

He submitted to their barrage with good grace, answering some questions, batting away others. Florence felt her mask of indifference droop. There it was again, the enjoyment of the occasion, the rising to his new-found status. She

257

muttered something about needing the loo, and slipped quietly away.

The day was grey and blustery. Florence walked quickly through the woods, and thought longingly of Ré and the wide beach sweeping conch-shaped from La Rivière to Saint-Clément. She loved the island under the bright light of blue skies, but she liked it even better on days like this, when you could walk the length of the beach and barely see another soul. Once, on a day such as this, she had come across a man playing the saxophone, sitting alone on a rock facing the ocean. For a long time he had played a slow sequence of notes which were hardly a tune at all, each note coaxed out and held quivering in the diaphanous air until it died out and another took its place. The tempo had increased eventually, enough to form a simple melody. Florence had felt like a trespasser as she stood and listened. Then, seeing the rest of her family catching up — she had carried on walking alone while the others stopped to dig for clams — she had run back to them and made them walk through the dunes, away from the sea, so as not to intrude on the musician's solitude. She thought of him again as she marched through the woods of La Pommeraie. She wanted some of what he had. Something like his music, like the magic which elevated him to an undreamt-of sphere. Something extraordinary. Something life changing.

Ben found her disconsolately throwing pebbles

258

into the river. She was aware of him for a while before he spoke, but his words still took her by surprise.

'I can show you now, if you want.'

'What?'

'I tried to tell you before, but you wouldn't listen. The tunnel. I've found it.'

★ ★ ★

The entrance to the tunnel lay under a grubby piece of tarpaulin between the old compost heap and the walled orchard which had once been a part of the estate, but had long been sold to raise money for a punishing inheritance tax.

'I can't believe you found it,' she whispered, as she watched him carefully pull back the tarpaulin.

'I had a feeling it must be around here,' he replied in the same low voice. 'It makes sense for it to be close to a boundary, if it's an escape route. Close to a boundary, and out of view of the house. I searched everywhere else, but I couldn't look here until they moved the compost heap.'

'They moved it?' Florence had never noticed the existence of the compost heap, let alone that it had been displaced.

'Last summer. It's by the chicken range. I can't believe you didn't know.'

'I'm not exactly interested,' she retorted, and the ghost of a smile lit up his serious features. He had been carefully sweeping at a thin layer of dry earth and leaves, revealing the worn, grubby wood of an ancient trapdoor. Florence gasped and Ben's smile became a grin as he searched his jeans pocket for a key. The padlock was shiny and new. 'I had to saw through the old one,' he said. The padlock clicked open. He slipped it into his pocket. 'Ready?'

She expected the trapdoor to creak, but it opened silently on its recently oiled hinges, revealing a flight of roughly hewn steps leading downwards into impenetrable obscurity. Ben pulled a torch from his pocket, and by its thin light she saw that the steps were made of stone, their edges rounded and worn.

'Some are better than others,' whispered Ben. He held out his hand. 'Be careful not to slip.'

Later she would learn that there were only nineteen steps, but they were steep and that first descent felt very long to Florence. She was relieved to reach level ground, but gasped when Ben turned off the torch. 'Ben,' she hissed. 'Put it back on.'

He squeezed her hand. 'Just for the atmosphere,' he said. 'Trust me. You'll get used to it.'

She had caught no more than a glance of the tunnel before the light went out, had no more than a vague impression of a small chamber leading perhaps to another gallery beyond, with a low ceiling and walls of the same hard-packed earth as the ground on which she stood. The darkness pressed down on her, oppressive. She tried to control her rising claustrophobia by breathing deeply, and coughed as the cold clammy air entered deep within her lungs. Ben let go of her hand, and she cried out. 'For God's sake, Ben, turn the torch back on!' He laughed softly, and it occurred to her that he was enjoying himself, that this was something of a moment of triumph for him.

'I'm sorry,' she said. 'I'm sorry I never listened to you, I'm sorry I never took your searches seriously. I'm impressed. I'm really impressed. *Please* turn on the light?'

She heard the strike of a match, and turned towards the sound. Ben had moved away from her and was bent over the gentle glow, lighting a candle. As she moved closer she saw that the candle lit up an old-fashioned lantern, which stood on a shelf carved out of the wall. In its low-cast light she made out a mattress on the floor, cushions, an open sleeping bag. 'Yours?' she asked.

'There was another mattress here before, but it was kind of rank.'

'Where is it now?'

He gestured towards the second gallery. 'There was all sorts of stuff here. Burnt-out candles. Pillows. Empty bottles.'

She held her hand out towards the side of the chamber, and found to her relief that the walls were not made of packed earth, as she had imagined, but of stone, which a thick earth-like dust had covered over the years. 'What *is* this place?' she asked.

Ben sat down next to her. 'You know Dad's stories.' He rolled his eyes. 'Perhaps it was as protection from the Vikings,' he intoned, in a spoof documentary-style voice which failed to lighten the atmosphere. 'Just think about it.

Standing on a battlement, sighting those ships sailing in. Knowing your enemy, how merciless he is, how powerful. Knowing that if you don't run for cover, if you don't make it in time — and your own kind would sooner shut the door to you than risk their lives on account of a latecomer — you'll be killed on the spot if you are a man, raped then killed if you are a woman. At best, you'll be taken prisoner and become their slave until they grow bored with you and throw you overboard, or sell you on to an equally pitiless new owner. So you grab what you can, food, water, your children, and you run, you hide underground like an animal, a mole, a fox, a rabbit, and you wait, not knowing when it'll be safe for you to see the light of day, not knowing whether if they find you in there they will smoke you out or bury you alive . . . '

He had dropped the TV presenter act, and his voice was hypnotic, wrapping itself around her as surely as the darkness. She swallowed, laughed nervously. 'They'd have to do better than a little hole under the ground, wouldn't they? Wouldn't they have dug a proper tunnel, to escape?'

'Maybe they did. Maybe this one was longer, but part of it caved in. Or maybe it wasn't built for the Vikings at all, but during the last siege. All those people, trapped inside the city walls. The Catholics and the Protestants beating the hell out of each other, and meanwhile the towns-people starving to death, forced to eat their pets, to eat rats, maybe even each other . . . And then help coming to them through the tunnels, outsiders risking everything to bring them food and water, to help the rebellious town resist that much longer against the King . . . '

Her spellbound mind hung on his words. In the near-total obscurity, all her thoughts seemed to come from him, so that she lost all sense of where she ended and he began. He spoke, she listened. More than listened. He spoke, and she *was*.

He was standing closer to her, his faint shadow cast by the dim light of the lantern mingling with hers. He was still speaking, his voice more matter of fact now. 'Whoever built it, I'm fairly sure it was used during the war. You can just make out the label on one of those bottles, it was made in 1942. People must have hidden down here, *résistants*, Jews, waiting for their chance to get out, their chance to be free.'

Florence shivered. 'So much desperation. These walls. So much unhappiness and fear.'

He was right behind her now. She shivered again, and he brought his hands up to her shoulders. 'So much excitement,' he whispered close to her ear.

She didn't try to make sense of it. She didn't think *but this is Ben, and I love Matt, and this is wrong*. She knew only that he was warm and alive, that his body was hard with desire, that hers was soft and trembling, and as she turned to face him and his mouth found hers her only conscious thought, which was less a thought than a sensation, was that she was flying.

London, 2005

And now, once again, she dreams of nothing.

Walls she cannot see press in towards a body she cannot feel. There is quite literally nothing in the dream but fear, building wave upon choking wave. Nothing exists beyond it. That is what she has been reduced to, a receptacle for terror. She does not cry, or whine, or shout, or fight. She simply accepts. It rises in her like a mounting tide, ruthless and relentless, relentless and ruthless, until it becomes almost impossible to breathe. The light comes, as she knew it would, but she knows the dream now, and she hates the light almost as much as the darkness, hates it for raising her hopes before dancing away, forever out of reach.

Something has changed tonight. The light comes closer. It *is* a candle, and someone carries it. She can just make out the hands which hold it. They glow orange, and she cannot tell to whom they belong, whether old or young, male or female. They are deformed by the surrounding darkness, which is thick and still as the stagnant brackish waters in the *marais* surrounding La Rochelle. The hands repel and horrify her. She stops breathing completely as they raise the candle, upwards, upwards towards a face . . .

She screams.

★   ★   ★

Pierre is lying next to her. His arms are wrapped around her, so comforting. She turns to face him in her half-sleep, still whimpering but with a new smile on her lips now as relief floods her body, chasing away her fear. 'Darling,' she murmurs, and flings her arms around him, buries her face in his neck, that place she always returns to, which smells so much of him.

Something is wrong. In the split second before she opens her eyes, before Matt speaks and reality crashes in, she remembers. Relief, happiness, terror, anguish, all evaporate, leaving her with nothing but the small, bitter taste of disappointment.

'Shh,' says Matt, cradling her. 'Shh. It's all right. I'm here. It's all right.'

The baby is awake now too, and has passed in a matter of seconds from a state of catatonic slumber to one of clamorous protest. Matt hugs Florence closer as he whispers, awestruck, 'My but she is *loud*!'

Zélie's cries finally wrench Florence awake. 'I skipped her feed,' she says. 'I guess she's hungry. Pick her up for me?'

'Me?' Matt stares doubtfully at the red-faced spiky-haired little bundle, which does not deign to stare back but redoubles its howls.

'You're good with babies, remember?' says Florence.

He makes a big show of walking carefully up to the cot like a comedian in a silent movie, taking long exaggerated steps around the bed, raising his feet high before bringing them down on tiptoe, his finger on his mouth, blue eyes

265

opened large and round.

'Idiot,' laughs Florence shakily.

Zélie snuffles loudly as she latches on, and cups her mother's breast with both small hands. Matt laughs, and Florence smiles. She leans back against her pillow, glances over at the clock. Only half-past twelve. How strange, the way time is distorted by night.

Matt, who had left the room, returns bearing a tray laden with tea and half a Madeira cake. 'Let me guess,' he says. 'Cassandra. I can't imagine you baking, somehow.'

The tea is milky and sweetened with honey. She closes her eyes and feels its comfort running through her body, warming her limbs, her fingers and toes. Matt sinks down next to her on the bed and pulls the duvet around them both. She leans into him, and together they watch Zélie feed.

'You wouldn't feed her in front of me earlier,' he says, and she shrugs. 'Better now?' he asks.

'Better.'

'You know we can't just leave that last letter.'

'I know.'

'Shall we do it tonight? Now, while we're feeling brave?'

Is she feeling brave? Florence carefully searches her feelings, thinks about what she has read tonight, what she has dreamed and remembered. She feels too apprehensive to be truly brave, she decides, but she is surprised to find that despite this she is calm. Calm and, with Matt at her side, ready.

'Wait till she's finished feeding,' she says

266

quietly, and he nods. 'When she's back in bed. We'll read it then.'

★   ★   ★

Mimi never intended for Emil to become her lover.

The first time didn't count, she told herself. In a sense, it had not been her. No one saw her as she slipped away from the house and back into the woods, running the long way round in order to maintain the cover of trees. She met Emil by the door to the orchard, and they did not speak, did not even touch as she dropped to her knees and raised the grubby tarpaulin, half covered by the compost heap, which covered the old trapdoor. She heard his sharp intake of breath as the door opened to reveal the steps beneath, but she did not look back, and he followed her down in silence, down away from the indecent radiance of the day into the cold gloom of the ancient tunnel.

The first time they fucked fully dressed, standing up in the darkness, with her knickers around her ankles and his trousers around his knees. She stood with her back against the wall, and he lifted her up, his hands on her buttocks and the backs of her thighs as she wrapped her legs about him and clasped his neck. The rough stone of the wall dug into her back and made her gasp in pain, but she did not ask him to stop. She screamed when he came, the hot spurt of his semen hitting the wall of her womb, flooding her. He carried on thrusting until she came

267

herself, shuddering and gasping, crying and laughing, and they sank to the floor next to each other, leaning against the wall, not talking, panting, each wondering in the absolute darkness what forces had brought them here.

'Will it be all right?' he asked eventually.

'You mean . . . yes, it should be. I'm . . . it's due any day now.'

'That's good.' They sat without talking for a while longer.

'I want you to know . . . ' he began eventually, but she held up her hand, felt for his mouth in the dark and laid her finger gently on it.

'Shh,' she said. 'Not a word.'

He took the hand, turned it over, pressed his lips to the palm. They left the tunnel as silently as they had entered it. She slipped out first, checked the ground was clear, and he crept out after her. A glance, a grave acknowledgement, the trace of a smile. And Emil and Mimi parted, going their separate ways in the dying warmth of the afternoon.

★   ★   ★

No, the first time did not count. She had needed comfort and he had offered it, the real, physical comfort of his body. The emotions involved had been different from subsequent occasions. Then, there had been desire and excitement, tenderness, even love. But that first time, their coupling had felt more transcendent. It had been about life and death, about loss and finding, about grief and elation, and as they fucked it had seemed to

Mimi that she understood all the contradictions of creation, that they were in fact all a part of one complete whole. Whenever her mind wandered back to her first brief encounter with Emil in the tunnel, this was the feeling she remembered, much more than the sex. She clung to it in the days that followed, bleak days that crawled past to the sound of Eve's weeping and Germaine's sighing, with Antoine barricaded in his study. It felt to Mimi, pouring her heart out in a letter to France, that the inhabitants of La Pommeraie had never been more fragmented. Spätzer and his cold, contemptuous anger, Antoine barely containing his rage, Eve in the isolation of her grief, Jean still smiling and uncomprehending as he roamed the garden, Germaine tight lipped and dry eyed, throwing herself into ever more desperately creative ways of cooking the endless same dreary food. *We all live in our own little separate worlds, all orbiting the house and yet never coming into contact. Every now and then we catch a glimpse of another planet, but before we can truly size it up for what it is, it has passed and we are alone again. You must come home soon, darling. I miss you so much.* She did not mention Emil because really, what could she say?

The second time, she told herself, happened by accident. A chance encounter in the woods, though later, when they were honest enough to admit it, they both confessed that there had been very little chance involved and that each had known exactly where the other was. They met again in the clearing where they had sat and talked on *that* afternoon several days before. They had not spoken since.

'I've been wanting to tell you,' he said awkwardly. 'About the other day. I am ashamed of myself for taking advantage of you, of your emotional state, of your grief.'

Mimi, who was rarely embarrassed, blushed scarlet.

'I wanted to assure you that the entire incident has been erased from my mind,' he continued, his face an almost comical blend of formality and anxiousness. 'For me, it is as if it never happened. I will not mention it again.'

'That's good,' she said firmly. 'Thank you.'

'Except that it's not true.' His words tumbled out in a rush, and his voice grew hoarse as he stepped towards her. 'I can't stop thinking about it, about you. You are the first real thing that has happened to me since I left home. I remember everything about it. It's driving me mad.' He was standing very close to her, and the only feeling she had now was of unadulterated lust. She took his hands in hers, and raised them to her lips. They stood perfectly still for a moment, not speaking, not looking at each other, not touching except for his hand pressed to her mouth. It all hung in the balance at that moment. To continue, or to stop? A beginning, or a goodbye?

Their eyes met. There was no going back.

The second time, she brought candles and matches and a rug, and they lay kissing for a long time first on the mattress Antoine had brought for his fugitives. Their love-making was quicker but less urgent, more like the fumbling she remembered with Rémy, but it left her wanting more. The third time, they finally undressed completely. She intercepted him on his way home with the key to the vault already in her pocket. They had both drunk a little, he with dinner at the hôtel des Étrangers, she with Germaine in the kitchen, sharing a small glass of eau-de-vie, *to boost morale* as the old cook said. The alcohol made them adventurous, and their love-making grew bolder and more playful. After that, they stopped counting, and met as often as they could without arousing suspicion, each driven by an insatiable appetite for the solace of the other's body.

★　★　★

Six weeks passed. Six weeks of a strange fragmented life, which continued as before, days made up of work in the office and the house, punctuated by the occasional meeting with her girlfriends, her mind almost constantly domi-nated by thoughts of her lover. Sometimes she wondered how she could be so obsessed with him, when surely her grief for Louis should be her only care. Later, she came to understand that the affair with Emil had been a part of her grieving.

At the beginning of June, news reached them of the Allied landings.

'You see,' said Emil, nuzzling Mimi's neck. 'I told you it wouldn't last for ever. This is the beginning of the end, you know.'

271

'You *are* a strange sort of patriot,' she said affectionately.

'I've told you before, I am a true patriot. Germany will suffer now, but ultimately it must be better for her. Imagine if we won, what that would mean for Europe. For the world. No, it is all over for us, and all I can hope is that the end comes soon.'

She turned on her side to look at him. 'What will happen to us, when the end comes?'

'We'll go to Paris first, then I'll take you home to meet my parents. We'll ride in the forest. We'll swim naked and make love in the sunshine . . . ' His mouth left her neck, moved to her throat, her collarbone, down towards her breasts. She closed her eyes and let him, trying not to think of what else would happen when the end came. Of Rémy, who would return from Germany, of how Antoine would react to the news of a German lover.

Emil was rolling on a condom. 'I wish we didn't have to use these,' he said.

'You'd like it, would you, to have your own little Franco-German baby?'

'I wouldn't mind.' He lay down beside her and put his hand on her stomach. 'I think I *would* like it.'

She wanted to say, *do you know what they do to women like me, to their children? How they mock them and beat them, shave their heads, spit at them?* She had heard stories from towns already clawing back their freedom in the north. Some women had been killed for what she was doing now.

Emil mistook her shiver of fear for the tremors of desire, and pulled her close. She let him take her, but for the first time her body did not respond immediately to his, and as he fucked her, her mind wandered, to the world outside, to the coming changes, to the possibilities of victory.

★ ★ ★

Spätzer was angry.

He called Emil into the dining room late one evening as the younger man bounced up the steps on his return from dining at the hôtel des Étrangers. He'd noticed the new energy radiating from the engineer, his lighter step, his brighter eyes. Being a man of little imagination, he attributed it to the object of his own obsession. Germany was losing the war. Spätzer despaired. Fürst rejoiced. The man was an unpatriotic coward.

'You know what pisses me off the most?' he said.

He sat at a precarious angle, balanced on the back legs of one of the cherry-wood dining chairs which had been a wedding present to Antoine's grandmother. His feet, still in their boots, rested on the table. 'You know what pisses me off the most?' he repeated.

'I'm sure you're going to tell me.' Emil had been hoping for a meeting with Mimi and was feeling impatient.

Spätzer leaned forward and spilled red wine on the carpet. 'Too fucking right I am. D'you

273

know what's going on right now all over Europe? Fucking Armageddon, that's what. Germany fighting for her life. Germany magnificent, defending herself. And here? Here we fight a barefoot army of terrorists, what do they call them? *Maquisards*.'

Emil deduced from this that Spätzer's latest transfer application had not been successful. 'You know,' he offered, 'for what it's worth, I should think most fighting now is composed of minor skirmishes. Surely the time for great battles is past?'

'That man,' Spätzer bulldozed on: 'He thinks it's all over. He looks at me differently now. Smugly. He has this . . . *triumphant* look.'

Relations between Antoine and Spätzer had not improved since the news of Louis' death. Antoine had grown more sullen. He no longer taunted Spätzer by redressing the effects of his acts of defiance. There were no more pots of geraniums, no more illegally bought sausages fried under the officer's nose, but the scorn he felt for the German captain had never been more obvious. Spätzer continued to behave as he always had. Antoine barely seemed to notice he was there.

'I'm sure Monsieur Duchesne is as realistic as the rest of us about the future,' said Emil wearily.

Spätzer had moved on to schnapps, spilling it on the exposed wood of the table. 'Leave it,' he snapped, as Emil moved to wipe it up. 'The old bitch can do it in the morning. Or the tight-ass daughter. She won't look at me, either. Whore.' Emil bristled, and Spätzer laughed. 'What's the matter, got the hots for her? Fuck her while you can, mate. All French girls are whores. Well-known fact.' He knocked back his schnapps and belched loudly. 'I'll tell you what though, Fürst,' he said. 'I'll make him talk to me. If it's the last thing I do before I leave this . . . this fucking backwater shit-hole of a place, I will make him talk to me.'

★   ★   ★

August came, bringing a new wave of bombardments on La Pallice. On the 20th, the German First Army received orders to withdraw from Charente-Maritime. On the 22nd, they left nearby Rochefort. On the 27th they came back, only to leave again on 12 September.

At La Pommeraie, Antoine followed the news closely. The priest, well informed as ever, had already warned him not to get his hopes up. The garrisons at La Rochelle and Royan further up the coast weren't going anywhere, he said. Both ports — like Bordeaux to the south, and Lorient and Saint-Nazaire to the north — were still a part of the German strategic defence. All were to be defended to the last man. For the inhabitants of these towns, the war was far from over. On 13 September a group of *maquisards* ambushed a German patrol in the village of Ferrières. On the 16th the Germans retaliated, and several men were executed. And meanwhile, La Rochelle battened down for the fifth siege of its ancient history. Those who could leave did so. Others, who could not or would not abandon their homes, prepared themselves for the long, dark months ahead.

Until now, Mimi had managed to separate her affair with Emil from the war and the world at large. But too much was going on, in this early autumn of 1944. Too many hopes had been raised only to be dashed, too many men — and not just young ones — had vanished into the countryside to take up arms. Friends who had trickled back to La Rochelle over the course of the war had gone again, back to their country houses or their relatives in liberated villages not thirty miles away. Even Germaine was beginning to threaten that she might go and stay with her cousins, and that the only thing stopping her was *pauvre madame et l'état dans lequel elle est.* And Eve's state was pitiful, it was true. Mimi spent more and more time with her now. Not talking, for Eve talked barely more than her husband these days. Mimi just sat with her, working at her side, on her accounts, on mending, very occasionally on her knitting. She avoided Emil. He had been — she had to admit it — a lifeline for her when she needed him most, after the news about Louis. But now, she recognized sadly, it was over. The differences between them were not, as he had maintained, reconcilable, but grew more evident with each passing day.

She would have to tell him. She would rather he worked it out for himself, preferably by telepathic communication, but this seemed unlikely. He was already taking too many risks: on two separate occasions, he had asked Germaine where she was, a message the old cook had relayed to her with eyes full of questions and a mouth set into something between fear and disapproval. 'Can't think what he wants,' Mimi had shrugged, but she knew Germaine suspected something, and braced herself for her final conversation with Emil.

In the end, he intercepted her by the side door, the one which led into the scullery. She nodded at him coolly, the way she always did when they met in public, but instead of responding likewise, he seized her hand.

'I have to see you,' he said.

'Let go of me,' she hissed. 'Someone'll see.'

'I don't care. Please, meet me tonight. It's important.' His eyes were pleading, the hazel eyes with his mother's thick lashes. 'Please,' he repeated.

'All right,' she relented. 'I'll try to get away after dinner.'

'Thank you,' he said. On impulse, he raised her hand to his mouth. Her heartbeat quickened. They stood together for a moment, close but not touching except for her hand in his against his lips, and right then she felt a tremor of excitement, and wished that things could be different again. 'Go,' she murmured. 'I'll see you later.' He went, melting into the shadow of the old yew. She knew that he would slip round the house and re-enter from the back, making as much noise as possible, and smiled despite herself at the childishness of the subterfuge.

When she looked up, Germaine was standing on the step, looking at her, and this time her face was full of sorrow. 'Be careful,' she said. Nothing else. *Be careful.*

★ ★ ★

Something was different. He did not kiss her as soon as they reached the bottom step, did not sweep her into his arms, did not hold her tight as he buried his face in her neck, her hair, did not seek to make love to her immediately like a starving man finally offered food. He walked to the bottom of the vault to light the candle, and stood for a moment with his back to her, watching the dancing movement of the flame.

'We're leaving tonight.' He turned to her at last, and she was shocked to see that he looked frightened. 'I only found out today, I'd have told you sooner otherwise. The whole Todt crew, we're leaving. Just like that. Four years of work, four years of *life* here, and we're leaving like thieves in the night.'

'Where are you going?'

'I don't know.' He sank heavily down on to the mattress. 'I'd worked it all out, you know? I was going to finish the war here, then I was going to take you home and introduce you to my parents, and ask you to marry me.'

She walked over and sat down quietly beside him. 'It's over, isn't it?' he said.

'Yes.'

'You won't come to Germany, after the war.'

'No.' And then, because despite their differences she did love him in a way, she leaned over and kissed him.

* * *

Antoine had made up his mind.

It had not taken him long to reach his decision, which was not to say that it had been easy. There was talk of an evacuation. It had been months since trains ran from the station in La Rochelle, but as soon as they did, he was going to make sure Eve was on one headed south. There was no way he was leaving La Pommeraie now, but nor was there any doubt that harsh times lay ahead, no matter how efficiently Mimi managed the fuel stock or Germaine doctored their food. Power cuts were already a plague on their lives, and would only get worse as winter advanced and supplies were stretched. Winter at La Pommeraie would be damp and bitter. With all the patrols going out in the *marais* — *maquisards* attacking the Boche, the Boche executing the *maquisards* — it was becoming impossible to get out into the country, and their small steady supply of meat and butter had dried up. Meals seemed to boil down to two options: soup, made from whatever vegetables were to hand; and seafood according to what was available at market. The price of fish was prohibitive now, but there was no shortage of shellfish. They didn't taste the same though without their accompanying sauces. Mussels needed white wine and *crème fraîche*, as much as *palourdes* needed butter and garlic and oysters needed lemon. Antoine ate his share readily enough. He no longer really cared what he ate, just swallowed whatever was presented to him without even noticing it, but it was different for Eve. The first time he had brought her a bowl of Germaine's steamed mussels — *moules au naturel,* the old cook called them, with that peculiar twist of her mouth which was almost a smile — she had gagged pitifully. Eve, who in her youth could demolish a *plateau de fruits de mer* faster than any man. She had asked plaintively if she might not have soup instead, and he had had to tell her that no, she couldn't, that Germaine had not been able to make it because the gas had only just come back on. She had eaten the mussels then, like an obedient child, and he had turned away from her, stared out of the narrow attic window down at the trees beneath, blinking back his tears of pity.

No, he could not subject Eve to another winter of freezing cold and bad meals cooked at the whim of power cuts and fuel shortages. And so as soon as he could, he would take his wife to the station, his wife from whom since the end of the last war he had never been parted, and he would send her to Montpellier with Mimi. She could go to her sister's until it was all over. She would be looked after there, with her two daughters. And it would be a joy for her to see France again. A mother ought not to be separated from her children. His decision made, he burst out of his study, calling for his daughter.

'Mimi!' he roared. She did not answer. He stood in the hall and called up to the floor above, then, cursing, climbed the stairs two at a time and knocked on her bedroom door. Still no answer. He opened the door, but she was not in her room. She was not with her mother, either, nor in the bathroom, nor the living room. He thundered downstairs to the wood-cellar. Logs lay stacked from floor to ceiling, each pile neatly covered with a sheet of tarpaulin, but still no sign of Mimi. 'Damn it, Germaine, where the hell is she?' he demanded, storming into the kitchen.

'Mimi?'

'Well obviously Mimi! Who the devil else would I be talking about?'

'I think she went for a walk.'

'In this weather? At this time? For Chrissakes, woman, it's dark outside, and it's pouring with rain. Who goes for a walk in the rain?'

'Perhaps she went to see about the wood.'

'The cellar's full of wood.'

Germaine would not meet his eye, but carried on painstakingly podding the last of the summer's white beans, ready for drying. Antoine looked out of the kitchen window.

Who goes for a walk in the rain?

A memory, of Eve and himself walking on a beach, wrapped in coats and hats and scarves, hands entwined, wet faces turned towards the open heavens. The two cars of the German officers sat side by side under the old yew tree. Two cars. Unbidden, his mind retraced the evening. He knew that Spätzer was in his room. He always knew exactly where the pig was in the house, what he was doing. He had a vague memory of hearing Emil, hours before, coming in through the back door by his study, but nothing since. 'Did the lieutenant go out again?' he asked. 'Because his car's here.'

'I haven't seen him.'

Lovers walk in the rain.

He went back to his study, his mind reeling from the answer, the obvious answer which suddenly explained so much. Mimi's absences, unnoticed until now but suddenly remembered. A glow about her, a secrecy. Not the look of a recently bereaved sister. The look of a woman . . . a woman . . . He could not bear to think about it. He stood in his study, clenching and unclenching his fists, breathing in sharp, painful gasps, and his hand moved like an automaton's towards the secret drawer beneath the fish tank.

★   ★   ★

They made love with the slow, concentrated tenderness of old lovers. No time for playfulness now, no teasing games, no suggestive gestures full of promise, no whispered secret fantasies. No rush, either, no clothes pushed aside in eagerness, no sweaters peeled off in haste getting knotted and stuck, no biting or feverish thrusting. Just Mimi and Emil lying naked in the light of a lantern, kissing softly as he rolled on top of her and they gently rocked together, their bodies perfectly attuned. She closed her eyes, and in the darkness she relived their whole history, saw him pale and exhausted in bed refusing to be dismissed as just another Nazi, saw him waking up under the tree on the day they learned of Louis' death, remembered the desperation of their first love-making and the awkwardness of their second, the ease with

282

which they talked together, the joy of finding a new friend. It didn't seem right, at this moment, with his strong young body stretched along hers, with his warm mouth in her hair, it didn't seem right to say goodbye. His breathing quickened and she knew that he was close. He was starting to moan, and she adjusted her hips beneath him, changed her rhythm so that her climax should coincide with his.

He stopped suddenly, with a strangled noise she had never heard before. She opened her eyes and tried to scream.

Her father stood behind Emil, his old revolver pressed to her lover's head.

La Rochelle, 1999

Almost overnight, Florence's love for Matt became a distant blur, the memory of something painfully childish. Lust, which had somehow never entered her feelings for him, now consumed her. She and Ben couldn't get enough of each other in the days running up to Tante France's lunch party on the *quinze août*. They met in secret, inventing reasons to stay behind when the others went out, or disappearing for solitary walks and bicycle rides to meet up in quiet places, pressed up against walls, trees, the fortifications of the old town. She went to him with sweating palms and beating heart, short of breath and melting, propelled by a desire that excited her and alarmed her too, because after all Ben was her cousin and surely, she now realized, this sort of thing was wrong?

Ben struggled to understand her. 'Cousins do fall in love, you know. Even marry. I don't see why we have to be so cloak and dagger about it.'

'Not *first* cousins. Jesus, Ben, do you want to give them all heart attacks? If they knew what we'd been up to, what we're doing . . . '

'Like this?' He pressed his mouth against hers, rolled his tongue slowly around hers as his left hand came up to her breast.

Her knees went weak. 'Just like that,' she gasped.

'I can't help it,' he mumbled. 'You're

everything to me, Flo. I've been in love with you for as long as I can remember. Nothing can hurt me when I'm with you.'

She was barely able to think when she was with him, but when they were apart she tried by whatever means she could to counter the heat of their love-making.

'You can't be *that* dirty!' said an exasperated Tom one day, as she slunk out of the bathroom, skin wrinkled and shrivelled like a prune after yet another hour's soak in a cooling bath.

'Wanna bet?' she muttered.

At the beach, she floated on her back, entirely focused on the physical sensations of the salt drying on her face, and the cold tugging each strand of her hair fanning out around her. She did not want to feel anything else. More importantly, she didn't want to *think*. Ben, her cousin, the lonely geek she had befriended, who loved her and trusted her. Ben, whose wounded puppy eyes followed her as she studiously ignored him in front of the others, who told her again and again how he felt as he panted above her in the secrecy of the empty house, whose breath came out in long ragged sobs when he came, who told her he couldn't live without her. Ben whose soft skinny body so improbably set her on fire, whose love she did not return but who had woken something in her which could not be sated. She went to him, and moaned at the touch of his fingers, mouth to mouth, hip to hip, her body bucking under his, and with each rolling climax, as Ben incandescent with happiness told her again how he loved her, she

285

hated herself a little more. Each time he touched her, she yielded to him. Each time, when it was over, she told herself that she would not go to him again. Slowly, her resolve to end it hardened within her. On the night of 14 August, as she lay in bed waiting for sleep, she decided that tomorrow would be the day.

*   *   *

On the morning of the lunch party, Florence came down to breakfast to find the adults arguing over logistics.

'Remind me again why *you* can't pick Gilles up from the station?' Mimi asked Claire crossly.

'Because I said I would fetch the ice-cream,' explained Claire with the exaggerated patience of the person who has had to repeat the same information several times already. 'I promised France I would pick up the ice-cream from Luca's by eleven-thirty, and take it straight there. Why can't you or Dad go?'

'I'm having my hair done,' said Mimi grumpily.

'Well, can't he get a taxi? Or — heavens above — a bus?'

But Mimi didn't like that idea. 'How would you like it if nobody came to meet *you?*'

'Frankly, if I knew it made life easier for everybody else, I couldn't care less.'

'Well *that's* nice,' huffed Mimi. Florence picked up a croissant. Mimi moved the jam pot. 'Plate,' she said automatically. Florence dunked her croissant in her hot chocolate instead. 'I'll get the ice-cream,' she said. 'I'll go on my bike.'

'Brilliant!' cried James from behind his newspaper. 'Give that child a medal. I know you're sticking your tongue out at me, Flo, put it away.'

'I'll come with you,' said Ben.

'Nah, don't worry,' she said. 'Don't you want to go to the station and pick up your dad?'

'I'll see him later,' said Ben steadily. 'It's not fair you going to town all alone.'

★   ★   ★

As they cycled into town through the parks, he told her that he had spoken to his father late the previous evening.

'Mum's set a date for the wedding. He called to tell me.'

'What!' Florence skidded to a halt, and a man cycling behind them swerved to avoid her, swearing loudly. 'Why didn't you say anything?'

Ben shrugged. He looked miserable. 'You'd already gone to bed. I thought of coming in to see you, but I didn't want Lily to hear. It's supposed to be a secret.'

'But why didn't your mum tell you herself?'

Another miserable shrug. 'Dunno. Time difference, maybe. Apparently they're in San Francisco.'

'Right.' Florence, seething, bit back her opinion of Karen. For all her faults, Ben was protective of his mother and wouldn't let anybody criticize her but himself. 'Does anyone else know?'

'Mimi. I think that's why she was so out of sorts this morning. You know how personally she takes things like this. And Dad was in a really bad way last night. Like, crying and everything. He told me the biggest mistake of his life had been letting Mum go. That she was the love of his life.'

'Oh for God's sake! Your parents . . . '

Ben looked close to tears, and Florence sighed. She reached out, put her hand over his. 'Come on,' she said. 'Let's go and get this stupid ice-cream and deliver it to Tante France. Then you can tell me all about it.'

★   ★   ★

It wasn't difficult to slip away at La Pommeraie. The ice-cream safely stowed in the freezer, Florence looked out of the kitchen window at the lawn where a harassed France was issuing orders to her granddaughters. Two long trestle tables had been brought out from the garage, dusted and hosed down, before being covered with long white linen cloths. The girls were laying them now with their grandmother's best china and silverware, the same that had survived being buried during the war and would hopefully, said France raising her eyes heavenwards, survive handling by Louise and Camille. Marie-Jo had been dispatched to pick dahlias, and Paf was in the garden keeping the dogs out of the way. Inside, Rémy sat at the dining room table in fine form drinking champagne, opened ahead of the festivities to celebrate his morning's achievement, his first killing of a coypu. He was cleaning his gun, and gleefully recounting his exploit to Christophe, who listened in long-suffering silence, unable to get a word in edgeways, bored and irritated but bound by his own strict laws of proper etiquette to suffer his father-in-law's eccentricities to the end. In the kitchen, Agnès was busy opening oysters and laying them out on beds of ice on a table already groaning under the weight of food, bowls of *crevettes grises*, loaves of bread, platters of langoustines and rich yellow home-made mayonnaise, tomato salads, green salads, rice salads, fruit tarts and *charentais* melons cut in half, their hollowed-out centres filled with *pineau*, all covered with clean crisp cloths to keep out the flies that hovered hopefully *en masse*, ignoring the yellow fly-catcher hanging from the ceiling and dodging Agnès' occasional half-hearted attempts with the swatter.

'Yum,' said Florence, reaching out for a shrimp. 'I can't think why you wanted the ice-cream.'

'Tradition,' said Agnès. 'I said the same to *maman*, and she said the *quinze août* wouldn't be the *quinze août* without Luca's pear sorbet and chocolate ice-cream.'

'A fair point,' conceded Florence. 'What can I do?'

'Nothing right now, *chérie*. Nothing at all. Later, you can help with the chairs.'

Ben was standing on the front porch, leaning against one of the pillars with his arms crossed, scowling. Paf crouched on the gravel driveway with his arms around Kitty, the chocolate Labrador, who was enthusiastically licking his face. 'It's all right, girl,' he said, scratching her ears and shooting murderous looks at Ben. 'I've got you now, it's all right.'

'What's going on?' asked Florence.

'Ben kicked Kitty,' said Paf accusingly.

'She fucking jumped on me,' snarled Ben.

'It means she likes you!' cried the little boy.

'Well I don't like her.' Ben jumped down from the porch and strode off towards the woods. Florence followed him.

'Flo!' She turned back towards Paf, who was still petting the dog. 'D'you think she'll be OK? I mean he kicked her really hard.'

'She looks fine to me, Paf,' said Florence shortly. 'I gotta go see Ben.' She caught a fleeting glance of Paf's face as she ran off. He looked angry and tearful and disappointed. She felt sorry for him. In normal circumstances she would have stayed, made a big show of checking over the dog, given her a treat. But right now, Ben needed her more. She found him where she knew she would, by the wall of the old orchard. He was kneeling at the tarpaulin, unlocking the padlock. He held out his hand silently. She overcame her reluctance and took it.

Underground, his defences melted away, and he wept. They sat together on the mattress, and she put her arms around him with his head on her shoulder as he cried for the mother who was slipping away from him and the father who didn't understand. When his tears subsided he began to kiss her, and between kisses he repeated the words she had come to dread, *only you . . . only you.* She did not want to make love, but she submitted to his embraces, knowing that not to do so now would be cruel, even though she was aware in a confused recess of her mind that she was only shoring up more complications for later.

Above ground Paf, accompanied by Kitty, silently crept away.

★ ★ ★

Up at the house, people were starting to arrive. Mimi, her newly washed hair twisted into a heavy chignon, with Hector leaning heavily on a cane but beaming, pleased to be out. Matt, dropped off at the main gates by Jean-Marc. Claire and James, with Tom and Lily and Gilles, just picked up from the station, large and jolly as ever, showing not a hint of heartbreak, calling for his son.

'He was around earlier,' said France vaguely. 'I'm sure he must be somewhere.'

The girls pressed round to hug their favourite uncle, and he kissed each of them enthusiastically in turn. 'Where's my Florence?' he asked.

'Here she is!' said France as Florence emerged from the woods. 'And here's Ben. They must have gone for a walk.'

Rémy emerged from the house waving one half-empty bottle of champagne and brandishing another. Everybody laughed, and moved towards him. Nobody saw Paf sidle up to Lily and

Marie-Jo, and nobody saw the three of them slipping off together into the woods.

★ ★ ★

The party was just getting going when Agnès, suddenly aware that two of her brood were missing, sent Camille and Louise out to find them. Shortly afterwards, the two older girls came running back, bursting with excitement and the news that Paf had found a trapdoor in the woods.

'It's got a padlock, but Paf's sawed through it! There are steps going down and everything, we've come to get more torches!'

Florence felt as though all the blood had suddenly been drained from her body. Her mouth went dry, her palms were clammy, her head rang. She gripped the back of Mimi's deckchair, forcing herself to breathe normally. As her eyes came back into focus she noticed that Matt was watching her, and she smiled at him weakly.

A party was already on its way towards the mysterious trapdoor, consisting of Camille, Louise and Tom among the younger generation, Christophe, James, Gilles, Claire and Rémy among the grown-ups. Only Mimi sat perfectly still in her deckchair. Hector had raised himself painfully out of his, and held her hand. France occupied his vacated seat, and was anxiously looking at her sister.

'Flo!' called Matt. 'You coming?' She shot Ben a stricken look, and he nodded dumbly.

Lily and Marie-Jo were standing rather crossly with the grown-ups at the top of the steps. 'It's not *fair*,' Lily complained loudly. 'We got here first with Paf, and then Camille and Louise spoiled *everything* by sticking their noses in, and now *they* get to go down before us because they're big fat bullies and I *hate* them.'

A shout came up from below. Lily hurried to the entrance of the trapdoor but made no move to go down. 'Are there skeletons?' she called out cautiously.

Gilles' head popped up above ground. 'No skeletons,' he said cheerfully. 'But it looks like you've got trespassers, Rémy. Someone else has been down there, and recently too by the looks of things.'

Paf had come back up now too, and was looking straight at Ben. Ben narrowed his eyes at him.

'There's a mattress!' said Camille, jumping out of the trapdoor. 'And candles!'

'A vagabond?' wondered Rémy. 'We've never seen anybody.'

Florence, trembling, was watching Paf, but he did not take his eyes off Ben. She remembered his look as she left him with the dog, disappointed and hurt. Had he followed her? How else could he have found the tunnel, so quickly, so soon after they had left it?

Rémy was indignant now. 'Well how can we find out? How will we know?'

'Lie in wait,' advised Gilles. 'It's our only hope. Vigils. Night watches.'

Ben and Paf were still staring at each other.

293

Paf smirked. *Oh God, he knows!* panicked Florence. *He followed us, he saw us. He knows.*

Florence did the only thing she could think of. She turned on her heel, and ran.

★ ★ ★

Ben went after her.

'Where are you going?' he asked.

'I don't know. To get my bike. Home. Anywhere. I've got to get out of here.'

'Hey!' He tried to pull her towards him, but she resisted, shaking. 'It's not so bad. I mean, I'm pissed off about the tunnel and stuff, but it's OK.'

'But don't you see? They're going to *know*. Paf saw us, I'm sure he did, he's going to tell them, they're going to *know* . . . '

'So they'll know.' He stepped towards her, and she took a little step back. 'So what?'

'So *everything*.' He was standing right in front of her now, his hands reaching out to her waist. She brushed him off impatiently.

'Someone'll see,' she said.

'I don't care.'

'Well I do!' she shouted suddenly. 'I do care. And I can't go on. With this . . . weird, weird thing between us. It's not right.'

'But we love each other,' he frowned.

'No. I don't. I don't love you.'

'But just now . . . why would you do that if you didn't love me? When you know how I feel about you? Why would you do that?'

Florence started to cry. 'I don't know.'

'I get it.' His face, which had been pale and uncomprehending, settled into the familiar defensive scowl. 'You felt sorry for me.'

'It's not like that,' Florence wept. 'I do love you, Ben, but you're like my brother. I can't sleep with my brother . . . Ben! Where are you going?'

He was striding away from her. 'The fuck you care!' he yelled angrily. 'You're just like all the others, Flo. Taking what you want and pissing on the rest.'

'I'm not! Ben, please . . . '

He wheeled round to face her. 'Two words,' he spat. 'Fuck. Off. Got it?'

⋆   ⋆   ⋆

She had to find Mimi.

Mimi would know what to do. Florence would tell her everything, about the crush on Matt, the comfort of Ben, the shameful lust. She would explain how she wanted to stop it, but couldn't, and she would tell her how fragile Ben was, how upset by his parents, how deeply hurt. Second to her, Mimi understood him better than anybody. She would find Ben, and bring Mimi to him, and Mimi would look after him and make everything all right. And then maybe Florence could explain herself to him too, and they could be friends again — maybe.

Florence found her grandmother in the living room, wrapped in a shawl and holding a glass of brandy. She entered the room hesitantly. 'Mimi, are you OK?'

'I'm fine, *chérie*.'

'Good.' With the innate selfishness of adolescence, Florence took her grandmother's words at face value, dismissing as mere oddities the shawl, the brandy and the fact that Mimi was sitting indoors in an armchair on a radiant August afternoon when everyone else was outside. 'Mimi, can I talk to you? It's kind of important.'

Mimi closed her eyes and leaned back in her chair. Hector intervened. 'Your grandmother's tired, darling,' he said. 'Maybe later, eh?'

'Please, Mimi?' wheedled Florence. 'It's about Ben. And sort of about the tunnel they found.'

Mimi opened her eyes. Her look was cold and hard, shocking Florence into silence. 'You heard your grandfather,' she said. 'Not now.'

'But . . . '

France swept into the room. 'We're ready to eat, Mimi,' she said anxiously. 'Will you be all right?'

Mimi stood up slowly, holding Hector's arm. 'I'll be fine,' she said. She turned to Florence. 'Come and eat, *chou*,' she said, not unkindly. 'Come and eat, and we'll talk later.'

★   ★   ★

She worried that someone would ask why she had run away, but no one did, and in the familiar chaos that followed, Florence could almost believe that everything was all right. Paf had clearly not said anything, had chosen to keep the glory of the tunnel's discovery to himself. The others suspected nothing, and chattered about the tunnel excitedly until France, in icy tones nobody had dreamed she was capable of, ordered them to change the subject. There were more chairs to be got from the house, drinks to be taken from the fridge, food to be brought to the table. There were *oohs* and *aahs* as the extent of the feast was revealed, and satisfied murmurs as corks were pulled and wine glugged into glasses. Everybody sat down, then immediately stood up again as Christophe began to intone a lengthy grace. Matt winked at Florence across the table, and she giggled despite herself. When Christophe had finished and the eating began, he reached across the table to pour wine into her glass.

'Drink,' he smiled. 'It'll help, whatever it is.'

She looked up quickly, anxious as to his meaning, but he had already turned to Agnès, who was sitting next to him and was offering him a plate of tiny *crevettes grises*.

'Where's Ben?' asked Gilles. 'Honestly, that son of mine. Here, there, never where he's meant to be. Off sulking, I expect. Kids!' he exclaimed cheerfully, draining the *pineau* from his melon in one gulp.

'Rémy!' France called out to her husband, who had stood up and was heading back towards the house. 'What now? We've only just sat down at last, what are you looking for?'

Rémy frowned and rubbed his temple. 'I've forgotten something,' he said. 'Only I don't know what.'

'Well sit down, you silly old man, and eat your melon before the wasps get to it. It can't be that important if you've forgotten it.'

'You're right, dear.' Rémy sat down obediently, seizing a langoustine from a passing plate.

'*Grand-père!*' Camille called out from her place at the far end of the table. 'Marie-Jo wants to know if we're going to *eat* the coypu!'

'Yum, yum,' said Louise. 'Fried water-rat, my favourite.'

Marie-Jo, overcome with anguish at the fate of the coypu, whose status death had already elevated from pest to martyr, burst into tears. Rémy leaped to his feet again with a cry.

'*Mais voyons, Rémy!*' complained France. 'He is like a yo-yo,' she announced. 'Up and down, just like a yo-yo.'

'I've remembered!' he shouted, already half-way back to the house. 'I'll be right back!'

Lily distracted them by announcing that she was going to eat an oyster, a feat she had never yet accomplished. Her cousins and siblings gathered around her. Matt speared the delicate, quivering flesh on a little silver fork and held it before her. 'Eat! Eat! Eat!' chanted the others and Lily, holding her nose and giggling helplessly, opened her mouth to the sound of cheers and stamping feet.

Nobody, not even Florence, thought any more about the whereabouts of Ben until Rémy rushed panic-stricken out of the house.

'My gun!' he cried as he reached the table. 'Which of you children has hidden my gun?'

★　★　★

Antoine watched her as he pulled the trigger. She would never forget that. He would not even give Emil the dignity of knowing who killed him, but kept his eyes trained on his daughter's face, his lip curled with scorn, his mouth twisted into something resembling satisfaction. Emil lay perfectly still above her, slightly raised on his arms, his body trembling. He stared at her too, his eyes wide with shock, and in them she read the question, *who?*

When Antoine pulled the trigger, he grabbed Emil by the hair first, so that he looked up, straight ahead, still unable to see his aggressor. He yanked the young man's head back so that when he shot him there would be no risk to Mimi, but that was as far as his protective instinct went. The noise ripped round the stone vault, sharp and terrifying. Mimi screamed. Emil slumped lifeless on top of her. He twitched once, twice, then lay motionless, his still beating heart pumping out the strong young blood which gushed through his shattered skull, soaking her.

★　★　★

No one paid Rémy any attention at first. They were all watching Lily as she tried to swallow her oyster, and they only listened properly when he repeated his question. Then, even as France told him not be so melodramatic, and Gilles asked him what he meant, and Lily gave a loud squeal of triumph, Florence knew what had happened to the gun. She rose from the table and began to run as fast as she could towards the tunnel

299

where, in the momentary silence between the deafening explosion of the gun and the tumult of discovery, Ben lay far beneath the ground in a place born of desperation.

★   ★   ★

Violent death, like secrets, runs in families. Louis, Emil, Ben. I would like to think the cycle was complete. I would like to see you again. Before it is too late, and darkness does for us all.

PART III

Florence found out she was pregnant one evening in the middle of July.

Outside, New York was melting in the summer heat. Gasping tourists littered the shaded grass of Central Park, and workers in short sleeves and light dresses were leaving the air-conditioned havens of their offices and heading for bars to get drunk on the promise of vacations to come. She and Pierre were leaving two days later, for a beach house in Maine where his parents were to join them for a week.

'Time to legitimize our relationship,' Pierre had said when he'd suggested the plan. She'd resisted at first, of course, just as she'd resisted meeting his friends and colleagues, but he had convinced her, as he always did.

The friends, after all, had been friendly. The colleagues, though patronizing, less intimidating than predicted.

'*Really?*' one of them had asked, peering at her curiously through impossibly thick glasses. 'No university education *at all?*'

'And why should she?' a large hairy woman had boomed. 'With a figure like that, I bet you earn more than any of us, eh, dear?' she had added with an unmistakable leer.

More than all of you put together, I should think, Florence had wanted to retort. Pierre had roared with laughter when she told him about the exchange. 'Eric is an intellectual snob, and Joanna obviously fancied you.'

'They're nothing like you,' said Florence crossly.

'I'm glad you've met them,' he said. He picked up a strand of her hair and wound it round his own throat. 'They're nuts, but they're part of my world. I want you to know everything about me.'

Everything about me. It was Pierre's mantra, the driving force in their relationship. He wanted to give himself to her completely, and in doing so he was forcing her to open herself up too, to look beyond the immediate safety of what she knew, the circuit of fashion shows and go-sees and photo shoots, the intimate anonymity of the photographer's lens. The acquaintances who knew her only as the modestly successful English girl who didn't go to parties.

She could not remember ever feeling so happy or so confident. With each new hurdle overcome, Florence felt herself returning to something closer to normality, to how she had once been, to how she might have become had things turned out differently. And she was glad when he convinced her to meet his parents. Meeting his family was one step closer to him meeting hers. She fantasized about this sometimes. Fantasized about it, yet vowed that it would never happen. Her future would never collide with her past, and Pierre would never learn the truth.

'You don't need to worry about that lot anyway,' Pierre had added with a touch of arrogance which amused her. 'They're pretty much irrelevant. Or will be, when the film project comes off.'

The film project. In the few months she had known him it had developed from a distant threat, growing gradually more alarming as it gathered momentum, until the night when Pierre had made the twin announcements that it was really happening, and that he wanted her to go with him.

'You will, won't you?' he asked anxiously as he refilled the champagne glass she had drained in a few gulps to recover from her shock.

'To the Orinoco delta?' she said, not because she didn't know, but because it seemed so unutterably strange that life should take her to such an unlikely place. 'But what would I do there?'

'Whatever you want. Read poetry. Learn poker. Help me.'

'Help you?'

'You speak Spanish.'

'Pierre, I did Spanish *A Level*. I don't use it except to order *breakfast*.'

'You can do a crash course. With your French, it'll be easy.'

'But I don't know anything about anthropology!' she wailed.

'Nothing to it,' he said airily. 'I'll tell you what to do. What questions to ask. I'm serious!' he protested as she began to laugh. 'You'd really help me, with the women. They'll open up to you, much more than to me. Please?' he wheedled, closing in on her, sensing weakness. 'Say you'll come, say it . . . '

'All *right!*' she shouted, still laughing. 'All right, all right, I'll come!'

That night as she lay in his arms he told her stories of the delta. Of the Warao Indians and their dugout canoes, of freshwater dolphins and brightly coloured macaws, of the darkness of night filled with the cries of the forest, and as she fell asleep her mind was full of pictures, like a child's after a bedtime story.

That had been six weeks ago. And now here she stood, in the tiny bathroom in Pierre's flat in Manhattan's concrete jungle, Eminem competing with Ella Fitzgerald from the open windows of neighbouring apartments, holding the wand from a home pregnancy test and staring at the two thin blue lines which confirmed the hunch she had secretly been harbouring since that night. She looked up from the wand at the bathroom mirror, surprised to find that she looked no different to before. She moved closer to the mirror, systematically checking her skin, her eyes, her hair for signs of change, but there really were none. She reached out and traced the outline of her face in the mirror.

'Pregnant,' she said out loud. The word seemed improbable. '*You are pregnant,*' she repeated, and this time a smile broke out, radiant and unexpected. Her legs gave way and she sat down on the closed toilet seat, knees drawn up to her chest, arms clasped around her legs. She did not think of the Orinoco delta then, nor of her compromised modelling career, nor even of Pierre and how he would react. She thought only of the incomprehensible new life growing inside

306

her, and of the incontrovertible, terrifying, dizzying knowledge that everything was about to change.

'A new beginning,' she whispered, as her hands instinctively came to rest, protective and caressing, on her belly. 'A new beginning, for all of us.'

★   ★   ★

She had thought she would tell Pierre immediately, but when he came home the news felt too momentous to divulge without preparation. He burst into the apartment with the smell of the street still on him, a smell of sweat and heat and traffic and excitement quite at odds with her own almost meditative calm. She would wait, she decided. Wait for him to tell her about his day and calm down, then curl up next to him on the sofa, the way he liked it, with her back against the cushions and her legs hooked over his body, his arms around her and her head on his shoulder, too deliciously languorous to move, their very breathing synchronized. Pierre would open a bottle of wine, would question why she wasn't drinking, and it would just slip out, softly, easily, and he would know how right it was because he always felt the same as her.

In fact, Pierre showed little sign of slowing down that evening. Preparations for the trip were in full swing, and he had spent the day interviewing cameramen. He wanted as small a crew as possible, and intended to do without completely for the first couple of months, filming as much as he could himself. He came home bursting with information on which material he should take, excited to have found a team he could work with. As he spoke, reality slowly crept back into Florence's focus. The crew. The delta. The jungle. Alarming tales came back to her, of children eaten by caymans, of malaria and yellow fever, of primitive sanitation and oppressive heat. She couldn't stop him going, not when he wanted it so much. But she couldn't go with him. Could she?

Pierre padded back from the kitchen, a couple of bottles of beer in hand. 'Want one?' he asked. *Tell him, tell him now.*

'How would you feel,' she asked with forced lightness, 'about having a baby?'

Pierre choked on his beer. '*What* did you say?'

She repeated the question, willing her voice steady. 'I'm just asking,' she added. 'You know, in theory. How you feel, about the . . . general concept of babies.'

'Oh, right.' He sank down on to the sofa, pulling her on top of him, his relief palpable. 'Well, I want — let me see.' He kissed her forehead. 'One.' Her nose. 'Two.' Her eyes, each in turn. 'Three, four.' He buried his mouth in her neck, started raining a collar of kisses along her throat. 'Five, six, seven, eight . . . '

He looked up at her, enjoying the game, and her mask must have dropped, because he looked suddenly anxious. 'Flo, tell me you're not . . . '

'No way!' she assured him quickly, because what else *could* she say when he looked at her like that, and he laughed.

308

'You had me worried there for a minute. God, a kid now, can you imagine? Disaster.'

I don't think it would be a disaster, she wanted to say, but Pierre was talking about their holiday, looking forward to it now that everything was falling into place. *I don't think it would be a disaster at all.*

She didn't sleep that night. She lay beside Pierre in the stifling darkness, listening to the soft whirring of the overhead fan, and she thought about her options. *Tell him. Tell him why you want it. Tell him everything.* She reached out more than once, determined to wake him, but each time her courage failed her. *Leave him.* He looked like a child himself when he slept, she thought tenderly. So full of confidence, so sure of his path. What right did she have to alter it, she who had known him so little time?

Even as she thought this, she knew that it was an excuse, that if she left it would be because leaving was the easiest option, because to cut and run now would mean avoiding questions and escaping the truth. She got out of bed and curled up in an armchair in the living room. Dawn came, pink and gold streaking across indigo before settling into a luminescent opal. For the short time that Florence sat watching the changing sky, she pretended that everything was all right. She tried to visualize her happiness, a ball of fire, glowing and bright inside her, lighting her up. Pierre, and her, and a baby. A family, strong, united, loving. But dread gnawed, and fear rose, and as the implacable sun rose higher reality reasserted itself, and her decision was made.

★   ★   ★

'Flo, you have to wake up!'

Florence groans. Matt's voice is urgent and pressing. There is no place for it in Florence's mind, already full of agonizing decisions long taken but revisited under the muddling cloak of darkness. As her thoughts gradually straighten themselves, the problems of the past recede only to be replaced by questions of the present. She is tired, and wants to sleep. The baby — she has had the baby, she remembers, and her name is Zélie — is not crying, so why should Florence awake?

'Flo!' hisses Matt. 'I know you can hear me.'

Suddenly she remembers everything. The letters, refusing to read them, the tears. Oh God, the tears, Matt rocking her in his arms, falling asleep surprisingly quickly, at least she assumes so, she remembers nothing but a duvet being pulled up over her, a warm body holding her.

'Flo!'

'Leave me alone!' she groans. She tries to blot out his voice, rolls over to pull a pillow over her head. 'I'm sleeping,' she says. 'Go away.'

'Flo, we have to go to France.'

'What?' She flings the pillow down and sits up. The sudden movement, ripping her out of a short disturbed night's sleep, makes her feel physically ill, and she leans back weakly against her pillow, wincing at the memory of the two

310

bottles of Nuits-St-Georges consumed the previous evening. Matt, she notices with surprise, is naked but for a damp towel wrapped around his waist. A small, uncharitable part of her brain registers detachedly that although his arms and legs look toned and strong, his father's genes are winning their battle for his midriff. 'Jesus,' she says. 'You've showered. What time is it?'

'Six o'clock. I waited to wake you. Flo, listen!' Florence has sunk back down into her mattress, whimpering softly. 'Do you know what day it is?'

'Tuesday,' comes the reply, once again muffled by the pillow. 'Only just.'

'But the date. It's 21 March. Tuesday, 21 March.'

'First day of spring,' grumbles Florence. 'Lovely. So?'

'So it's Mimi's birthday.'

★ ★ ★

He makes coffee while she showers. She comes out to join him in the kitchen, still yawning but dressed, towelling her damp hair. 'I still don't see what all the fuss is about,' she says as he places a large bowl of café au lait in front of her. 'What are you going to do, travel across France to sing her Happy Birthday?'

'She asked me to,' he admits. 'She asked me to come and see you, and bring you back for her birthday.'

'I thought Cassandra asked you.'

311

'Her too.'

'All these people,' says Florence, a note of sarcasm creeping into her voice. 'Worried about me. Why didn't you tell me before?'

'I didn't think you'd listen. I'm sorry to spring it on you now. But we have to go. I'm worried about Mimi.'

'You're worried about her too?'

'Don't you see? As we were reading the letters, a part of me kept asking myself, *why is she writing these?* At first I thought it was to help *you*, but now I see that she's the one who's crying out for help. And it's her birthday, the first without Grampy.'

'Well won't the others be there, Claire and Gilles and Mum?'

'I don't think so. Mum said something about going to see her later, but she's in Cambridge, and Gilles never goes go to La Rochelle any more. I don't know about Catherine . . . Anyway, she shouldn't be alone.'

'Well *you* go then,' says Florence irritably.

'The letters were addressed to you. She wants you.'

Last night Florence shook like a leaf as they read the final letter. It started with her hands, then spread over her whole body, until her very stomach was racked with spasms and she thought she was going to throw up. She shivered with cold and Matt wrapped a rug around her shoulders, but the palms of her hands were damp with sweat, and even breathing hurt. Afterwards, when the first shock had passed, she cried, silently at first, then huge racking sobs as

312

Matt held her close, pulling her on to his lap and wrapping her in his arms. She cried as she never had, not once since 15 August 1999, the day of Tante France's lunch party, the beautiful, radiant, perfect summer's day when Ben died and her childhood ended. And as she cried, she was aware of a curious feeling, that she was somehow being more genuinely herself through these tears than she had been for years. Pierre, Zélie, New York, Venezuela, the lonely years away from home, her absolute rejection of her family — last night's torrid wave of emotion roared through them all, obliterating them, crashing through her fragile defences to unlock her heart's grief, and in the violence of her response she had heard her sixteen-year-old self screaming to be let out. She remembers now the moment before falling asleep, cradled in Matt's arms. Feeling drained, utterly exhausted and unexpectedly at peace.

That was last night. Today, Florence's defences are up again, more prickly and impregnable than before. Today, she will not let her family reclaim her, not when she has fought so hard to keep them away.

'I can't go,' she says. 'I've got a *baby*.'

'She can come too. I'll help you.'

'Frankly,' she declares, 'I think those letters are unbelievably manipulative.'

'What?'

'You want to know why she's writing to me? It's to make me feel bad. To punish me. *I want to see you. Before darkness does for us all.* What do you think she's going to do, top herself?' Even

313

she cringes at the words but there, she has said them. Coarse, brutal, vulgar, but she has said them.

Matt's temper is up now. 'Jesus, Flo, I can't believe you of all people . . . I mean, Christ!'

'Me of all people *what*?'

'Could *say* that like that. So . . . coldly.'

'Yes, well.' She gets up, walks over to the counter where the bread bin sits, removes a bag of bread with a shaking hand and puts two slices in the toaster. The gesture soothes her by its familiarity, though she knows she will not eat.

'You have to stop this,' he says as she glares at the toaster, willing back tears. His voice is even, but she can sense the anger behind it. 'This whole guilt trip thing, you have to stop it. I mean fuck, you read the letters, how can you think Mimi's trying to punish you?'

Florence opens her mouth to speak, realizes that she can't, and shuts it again as Matt ploughs on.

'You've got to come, Flo. You've got to respond. You owe it to her.'

Florence fishes the toast out of the toaster, throws it on to a plate. 'I'm not going,' she says, finding her voice at last. 'And that's final.'

⋆ ⋆ ⋆

Matt is leaving. He has gathered the last of the belongings strewn around the flat over the course of his short visit, and he has left, slamming the door behind him with no consideration for the neighbours, presumably all awake anyway following the screaming row which has just taken place. He finally flipped as she began to butter the toast, actually snatched the plate from her hands and slammed it so hard on the counter that it broke, split straight down the middle.

'You are fucking unbelievable,' he shouted, and went into a long rant which she only partly heard because she was covering her ears with her hands, but the general meaning of which she grasped. *When are you going to realize it's not all about you . . . when did you turn into such a selfish little cow . . . I used to feel sorry for you . . .* and the final straw, *God help that poor baby if this is what she has to look forward to,* at which point Florence roared back that how dare he talk to her like this, that she never asked him to come, that she was quite happy on her own and that the one thing Zélie wouldn't have was a mad family subjecting her to emotional blackmail and suffocating her, that was the word, that was how she felt when she was with them and that was why she had cut herself off, and it had bugger all to do with Ben's suicide and everything to do with them and their overwhelming need to dominate everything.

'And it's so bloody typical of you to come barging in here thinking everybody's going to go down on their knees to *worship* you like you're God's fucking gift or something . . . ' she had finished, rather frightened of her own rage and at the same time relishing its magnitude. 'Because you're not!' she yelled, exulting in the raw power

315

of her fury. 'You're not, you're nothing to me, nothing at all! None of you are, none of you!'

And then Matt had slung his rucksack over his shoulder and said *nobody does denial like you do, Flo,* followed by *fuck you, then, I'm going,* and then he had slammed the door. Florence stands in the middle of the flat, quivering, exhausted and breathless. *Free!* That is her first thought. Throwing Catherine out had been relatively easy, another variation on the timeless pattern of rows between parents and children. Getting rid of Matt, though . . . Golden boy Matt, teenage heart-throb, director of operations, natural leader. She smiles to herself grimly. Getting rid of Matt had felt good. Nobody would bother her now. Nobody would pester her to call Mimi, to come to family occasions, to take her place among them and their miserable memories. She has seen off the top dog, their strongest weapon. She is free.

She hears another door slam downstairs. He has gone. In the bedroom, Zélie sleeps on undisturbed. Somewhere outside, a car's engine starts up, sufficiently isolated in the early morning for the noise to echo through the empty street. The flat is very quiet. Florence — her tears spent, her rage subsided — tells herself that this is what she wanted.

And then a memory, raked from its depths by the storm, rises to the murky surface of her consciousness. Another row, a stamped foot, the declaration, stoutly made, that *she would not go.* Twelve years old, refusing to go to

France, feeling lost and rejected.

She remembers Mimi's uncompromising acceptance, and she thinks *this has to end*.

★ ★ ★

Matt walks fast, one hand deep in his coat pocket, the other hooked through the straps of the rucksack which he carries over one shoulder. He walks fast because he is worried, and because he is in a hurry, but mostly he walks fast because he is furious. With himself, largely, because he feels that he has handled the situation with Florence very badly. But also with her, for being so intractable.

Matt knows his limitations. He is not clever like Tom, nor sharp like his little sister, but he is straightforward and good with people, as his boss has been quick to notice. He can't understand why things went so wrong with Florence. Surely it should be a relief, after all these years of hiding, to know that she is understood and loved and wanted, that she need not be alone. He is confronted once again with a reality with which he is not comfortable, that women are complicated, and not to be reasoned with.

'Bring her back for my birthday,' Mimi had asked, and like a fool he had tried to scare Florence into agreeing, his instinct telling him — wrongly, as it turns out — that she would never come if he let her think about it for too long.

As he nears the end of the street, he is dimly

aware of somebody shouting, and that what is being shouted is his name.

'Matt! Matt, wait!'

His mouth set to a grim line, he carries on walking. She has thrown him out of her flat. She has told him that he is nothing, that he means nothing to her, she has insulted him. He shan't stop, he shan't even look back. Not even for Mimi.

The voice persists, louder still, matched by others, all exhorting her in rich, colourful language to keep the noise down. Florence ignores them.

'Matt, wait!' she bellows. 'Wait! You have to help me pack!'

★ ★ ★

Florence and Matt sweep into the ticket office at Waterloo International half an hour before the next train's departure. Florence pushes Zélie in her pram, a bulging tote slung across the handles. Matt carries his rucksack, and pulls a wheelie suitcase the size of a small trunk.

'I still don't understand why you needed so much stuff,' he grumbles. 'You didn't have to take your entire wardrobe.'

'Sweetheart, you would need a lot more than one case to hold my wardrobe, even one that size,' retorts Florence. 'Besides, there are two of us.'

'Two second-class tickets to Paris, please,' says Matt to the ticket clerk. 'For the next train.'

'Make that three tickets,' says Florence.

'First-class. Open return.' She slaps down her credit card.

'Oh, the extravagance!' sighs Matt.

'It's Zélie's first trip,' she answers primly. 'I want it to be special.'

'Perhaps it's not necessary to book a seat for the baby, madam,' suggests the clerk.

'I like to spread out,' she snaps.

'Methinks you were a tad brusque with the poor man,' says Matt mildly as they walk briskly through the ticket barrier. 'And I still don't see why we had to splash out on first class.'

Florence is gurgling at Zélie in her pram. Now that they are on their way, she feels exhilarated. 'I always travel first class,' she says, surprised. 'It's so much nicer. Besides,' she adds, conciliatory, 'they'll give us breakfast. Cooked, I shouldn't wonder. And champagne!'

'Champagne,' says Matt. 'Aren't you the princess.'

★   ★   ★

'You see,' she says twenty minutes later, installed in their comfortable seats in an empty carriage, Zélie in her carrycot next to her mother fast asleep and totally oblivious to the expense of her surroundings. '*So nice.*'

A steward has already poured out two glasses of champagne and orange juice and she raises hers to Matt.

'To you,' she says. 'For dragging me out, for making me cry, for shouting at me. This is fun.'

'You are completely impossible,' he replies. He drinks, then raises his glass at her. 'To you, I suppose. For screaming at me, for insulting me, for agreeing to come. What made you change your mind?'

'Just saw sense, I guess.' She fusses over the baby for a moment, tucking in an unnecessary blanket. 'Isn't she good?'

'Flo.'

She fiddles with the blanket a moment longer and sighs. 'You came,' she says at last. 'After everything I did, after all the harm I caused you. Don't say anything,' she adds as he opens his mouth to protest. 'I know you say nobody blames me, but they do, and if they don't, they should. I ruined everything, and you came. And I've been so lonely. After you'd gone, I realized I never wanted to be lonely like that again. And I'm sorry I said all those things and shouted at you.'

Matt's mouth twitches. 'I'm sorry I was an arrogant brute.'

'Have you spoken to Mimi?'

'She's not answering the phone.'

'Maybe she's gone away.'

'I don't think so. She didn't mention any plans.'

'And we'll turn up and have nowhere to stay.'

'There's always La Pommeraie.'

'Have you spoken to Rémy and France?'

'No answer there either.'

'Great.'

'Don't worry. I've got a key.'

'I wasn't worrying.'

The champagne has induced somnolence in Matt, and reverie in Florence. He sleeps, his head at an alarming angle, occasionally lurching with the movement of the train. She picks up a stirring Zélie, puts her to the breast and feeds her, leaning back into her seat, one leg cocked up against the table. Her mind wanders as she watches the gentle Kent countryside roll by. Yesterday's tears and this morning's anger have had a cathartic effect. The curious feeling of peace she experienced last night has returned, and she vaguely attributes it to the fact that she has finally relinquished control and is allowing herself to be carried, by this train, by time, by Matt's determination.

He wakes with a start as they enter the Channel Tunnel.

'How long have I been asleep?'

'About forty-five minutes. I'll ask for some coffee.'

The steward brings orange juice as well, and croissants. Florence waits for Matt to eat his fill before putting the question she has been wanting to ask all morning.

'Will you tell me about Grampy's funeral?'

'Hasn't Catherine told you about it?'

'I wouldn't let her.'

So he tells her. About the congregation that packed the old Romanesque church at Esnandes, and the two flags, British and French, that draped his coffin. About the poem Lily had written, which Tom had to read instead because she was crying too much. About James' address, emphasizing the gentleness, the generosity, the dignity of his father-in-law, and about the music, chosen by Mimi.

'It ended with the wedding march from *Figaro*.'

'So Mimi,' says Florence.

He tells her about the burial, the gravel cemetery surrounded by acres of windy marshland, the wide sullen grey skies, summer temporarily suspended to mourn Hector's passing. About the Pommeraie cousins, all present, tear-stained and subdued, entirely out of character, and about Amandine's dress, a black couture number so stylish and simple that a number of mourners just had to enquire about it discreetly later on at the wake. He describes the garden roses picked by Claire to strew the grave, and the dreadful hollow sound of the first clod of earth hitting the coffin. Finally, he describes Mimi, pale and frighteningly elegant in her old Chanel suit and triple string of pearls, a black lace mantilla draped over her head and throat.

'Every inch the Catholic widow,' he says. 'Except perhaps a tad *too* theatrical.'

'Did *she* cry?'

'Not then. She was incredible. All those people filing past, and she kissed them all, and kept smiling and thanking them for coming. Then they all came home for champagne and lunch, and the party went on until the evening. And then we cleared up, and ate some more, and everybody stayed up really late, like they were afraid of leaving her to go up to bed alone. And then Catherine put the twins to bed, and Lily went up to read them a story, and Tom went to have a shower, and we all had to get on with things. And she only cried much, much later, when she thought everyone was asleep and couldn't hear her.'

'You did, though.'

'Yes.'

'Did you go in to her?'

'Yes.' He hesitates. 'You know, it was the first the time we were all together since . . . well, since Ben's funeral.'

'Except for me,' she says wistfully.

'You could have been,' he says, his voice involuntarily harsh. 'I'm sorry,' he adds more gently. 'But you could have. People wanted you there, you know.'

'It was difficult.'

'New York's not *that* far away. Not when you have the money,' he adds pointedly.

'I wasn't in New York.'

'Where were you?'

'I was in London.'

⋆ ⋆ ⋆

'I don't understand.' He looks upset. 'If you were only in London, why didn't you come?'

'I couldn't.' She bites the inside of her cheek, and stares out of the window at the black walls of the tunnel, the amazing tunnel under the sea which Hector always marvelled at but through which he never travelled.

'Couldn't or wouldn't?'

'A bit of both, I suppose.'

And then she tells him about Pierre. About how they met, and how she loved him immediately, and his job at NYU and the plans for the delta. She tells him about falling pregnant and agonizing over how to tell Pierre, and the perfect July morning watching dawn break over the Manhattan skyline, and how she reached her decision but could not move from her chair, not to pee, or make tea, or embrace Pierre when he finally stumbled into the living area, sleepy and dishevelled.

'How long have you been up?' asked Pierre.

'A while. I couldn't sleep.'

'Are you OK?'

'Fine. Really.'

She had hoped that he would see through her. That he would ask questions, push her to tell the truth, to tell him everything. But it was the early morning of a busy day and Pierre was barely awake. Rather than ask questions, he yawned something about coffee and shuffled sleepily towards the kitchen, while Florence continued to sit in her armchair by the window, not moving because to move would mean that everything was over.

Showered and breakfasted, Pierre was back to his cheerful, energetic self. 'One more day of Manhattan madness,' he said, dropping a kiss on her head as he headed out of the flat. 'Then vacation, sun, sea, sex' — another kiss, in her neck, just beneath her ear, the last word whispered, the sibilants drawn out, the tone

324

joking but suggestive. 'And off to a madness of our own making!' He picked up the rucksack which served him as briefcase. 'Sure you don't want to come with me today? We'd have fun.'

'I've got things to do. Gotta drop by the agency, finalize things with them. Shop.'

'See you later then.' Another kiss. 'I'll be home around five. You?'

'Same.'

But by the time Pierre returned that afternoon, Florence was already gone.

★ ★ ★

'What d'you mean, *gone*?'

'I left him.'

'Just like that?'

'Yes.'

'But does he know about the baby?'

'No.'

'Didn't he try to find you? Didn't you tell him *anything*?'

'I left a note. I said he wasn't to look for me, that I was sorry, that I had to go away.'

'But that's terrible!'

'I couldn't stay,' she said stubbornly. 'He didn't want a baby, and I did. I didn't want to get in his way.'

'Bollocks. I think that's the most selfish thing I've ever heard!'

'Well I'm sorry but . . . '

'Taking a man's baby away from him. You can try to dress it up as altruism as much as you like, but I'm not buying it. You were running away. Again.'

Florence starts to cry. Matt sighs, hands her a tissue, and takes her hand.

'This guy, this anthropologist,' he asks eventually. 'Do you still love him? Was it the real thing?'

'Yes.'

'Sweet Jesus,' says Matt. 'You are one fucked-up little chicken.'

⋆ ⋆ ⋆

Florence stands up as the train emerges from the tunnel. 'France!' she exclaims.

'At this point, not so very different from England.'

'Bigger,' she says. 'Different cows. *Totally* different.'

'Whatever you say, princess. Welcome back.'

He waits for her to wander off to the bathroom, then pulls out his mobile phone.

Tom, for all his bookishness, is very popular with the ladies. Matt doesn't see it himself, but apparently the lean, bespectacled look can work. 'They get turned on by my intellect,' Tom has explained candidly. 'And they think they can protect me.' In addition to his unexpected sex appeal, Tom possesses the knack, which Matt has never mastered, of remaining on excellent terms with his small army of doting ex-lovers. One in particular interests Matt at this moment, a loud large-breasted Texan named Holly, a lecturer several years his senior whom Tom fucked cheerfully for most of her short secondment to his Oxford college. Holly, Matt is fairly sure, is now back in New York, having secured her tenure at NYU.

Tom answers after the second ring. 'Hey Tom,' says Matt. 'It's me. I need your help.'

★　★　★

Mimi is tired.

She sits on a broken bench in an overgrown clearing. The entrance to the tunnel is hidden from view by a profusion of young hazels, but light streams down through the sparsely leaved branches above her. Hector worried terribly about changing weather patterns but right now, after her morning underground, she is grateful for the unseasonal warmth of the late March sun.

She glances down at Hector's watch, heavy and reassuring, too large for her thin wrist. She is thinking, not for the first time today, about Matt and Florence and whether they will come. If Matt has convinced his cousin, if she has read the letters, if they caught a mid-morning train . . . She shakes herself briskly. They will come in their own time, if they come at all, and no amount of speculation will make them arrive sooner.

The vault is ready. Yesterday she asked the gardener to carry out the old mattress, and she watched with Rémy and France as he doused it with petrol and set it alight, the fuel roaring through the damp fabric, purging it. Now that it is done, she can't believe that they did not think of doing it before. The tunnel's reopening will be brief. Until now they have tried to ignore it, locked and abandoned, but men are coming tomorrow to block it off properly. The entrance will be filled in, the ground turfed, trees will be planted. Today, its final act will be played out, and tomorrow it will be given back to the earth. And then — a difficult decision this, painfully reached — La Pommeraie will be sold. *Too big,* Rémy has said with unconvincing firmness to a tearful France, and Mimi has agreed. *Too many bills. And it's not as if anyone comes here any more.*

Mimi's stomach gives a loud rumble. It does not do, at her age, to skip meals. She should go back to the house, prepare something to eat, lie down. It occurs to her at last that Matt may have tried to call her, that in fact in this age of advanced technology and mobile phones she could call him to tell him where to find her.

Oh yes, there are many reasons for going back to the house, but it is pleasant here in the sun, in this hidden glade, away from the world. Let *them* seek her out, she thinks rebelliously. Today is her day, and she has chosen to spend it honouring her dead. Ben, Louis, Emil. Her parents. Hector. It is a day of remembrance. She forces her mind away from sorrow and violence, down happier paths, mentally wandering the grounds of La Pommeraie, memories of different eras jumbled together by their common topography. *Here I hid from Louis, and he didn't find me until tea-time, and here Papa taught me to ride a bicycle . . . Here France got stuck up a tree, and here Claire took her first steps towards her brother, and here I kissed Rémy, and here Emil . . .*

Here Spätzer cut down the trees, and here Father found us . . .

It is no good. The happy memories dance out of reach in the shadows cast by the darker ones. It is their day, after all. Resigned, Mimi closes her eyes and lets them come.

★   ★   ★

She had grown careless.

Germaine was not the only person to have noticed what was going on. It never occurred to Mimi to glance towards Jean's little cottage when she slipped silently through the side door to run the long way round the woods, and she never noticed when he followed her, because Jean could move as silently as a fox when he wanted to and he weaved through shadows in her wake. Jean meant Mimi no harm. Jean loved Mimi, for her grace, and her kindness, and the wild suppressed longing he sensed in her. He knew what she was doing with the young German officer, the one who was also kind and always smiled when he saw Jean, and asked him how his work was going. It did not occur to Jean to be jealous, or to condemn what they were doing. Usually, they arrived at the tunnel separately, but once Jean had seen the young German officer surprise her, and he had watched as they kissed,

329

mouths open, tongues entwined, and he had seen the bulge in the young German officer's trousers and the way he pressed it against her. He liked to think of the two of them doing it together under the ground, like rabbits. It made him feel warm. Often, when they were down there, he unbuttoned his own flies and played with himself, and it made him feel happy to think that they were all doing it together. Afterwards, he would slink back to his cottage and curl up under his blankets, and sleep the sleep of the dead.

On the night when Emil died, the night before the siege began, the night when nobody should have been out on account of the diluvian rain, Jean saw Mimi slip out of the side door to meet her lover for the last time, and he followed her.

★　★　★

Spätzer was in a foul mood again. He was no closer to knowing whether he would be transferred, which meant that he probably wouldn't be. He had supper early at the hôtel des Étrangers, where he drank too much, finding the company lacking and the atmosphere morose. People, he suspected, were beginning to avoid him, and this evening an elderly colonel had snapped at him to stop complaining. *Stop whingeing*, in fact, was what he said. As if he, Captain Heinrich Spätzer, ever whinged . . .

And so he had driven home, if you could call the dark, freezing house with its equally chilly inhabitants home, planning to collar Fürst and carry on drinking with him. Fürst loathed him as much as he loathed Fürst, of course, but for some reason seemed to want to humour him. Spätzer wasn't particularly interested in knowing why this might be. He simply accepted it as a convenient fact.

The young lieutenant's car was in the drive, but he wasn't in his room. *Blast the boy*, thought Spätzer. *Where the devil is he?* Downstairs, he could hear the boorish Frenchman calling for his stuck-up daughter. Mimi. *Stupid name*, he thought, back in his own room, uncorking a bottle of schnapps. The glass on his table was half full of water. He crossed over to the window to empty it, and froze.

Antoine, bare-headed and coatless, was marching across the lawn.

★   ★   ★

Jean was gibbering.

He had seen Antoine arrive at the trapdoor in his soaking wet clothes with his hair plastered to his head and his beard full of drops, and he had wanted to stop him, to run and catch him and tell him not to disturb Mimi and the young German officer who always smiled when he said hello, but to leave them alone like rabbits in their burrow. But his trousers were round his ankles and his cock was in his hand, and he remembered in the confusion of his mind that Germaine and Mimi had told him this was wrong, and anyway, with his trousers like that, he couldn't run, and something about the situation,

331

the night, the dark, the rain, the look on Antoine's face and the gun in his hand, something about all this paralysed him so that he stood rooted to the spot, opening and closing his mouth like a goldfish. Jean knew that what he had seen was not good. He knew that Mimi did not want to be found, and that Antoine looked angry, and he knew that something bad was going to happen. The knowledge pressed against his skull, expanding like damp oats in a sack growing rapidly too small. He began to moan softly to beat them back, but still they grew, filling his head. He moaned louder, then louder still. He sank to the ground with his trousers still undone and he rocked to and fro with his hands over his ears, pressing the side of his head to stop it exploding, and the sound of his keening drew Spätzer to the trapdoor.

★   ★   ★

Spätzer enjoyed what came next.

He kicked Jean, forcing him to his feet, and grabbed a handful of his hair, pulling his head back, his pistol against the terrified boy's head. Then, holding his human shield close, he kicked open the trapdoor and began his descent.

He had not brought a torch, but a lantern glowed dimly at the foot of the stairs. In the flickering darkness he saw the figure of a woman, half dressed, kneeling in a corner retching. *The daughter*, he registered. *Of course.* Her father stood with his back to the wall, his white face livid in the shadows. He appeared to be crying, thought Spätzer. *Interesting.* His eyes came to rest, with little surprise and some satisfaction, on the naked body of Emil, slumped forward in a pool of blood. At the sight of the body, Jean began to wail, and Spätzer twisted his arm to shut him up. No weapons, he noted, except for a revolver on the ground by the body. A Mas 1892, French issue, last war. No question who the owner was. He pushed Jean roughly and the boy fell to the ground, sobbing softly and rubbing his arm. Spätzer kicked him again, picked up Antoine's revolver and slipped it into his jacket.

'So,' he said softly. He kept his pistol cocked, but did not point it at them. If they tried anything, he would surprise them with the rapidity of his reaction.

Mimi looked at her father. Her father, whom she had watched as a child, imbued with grace as he danced with her mother, her father the unlikely pacifist and silent *résistant*, her father the murderer who was staring blankly ahead, his tears dried, the violent trembling which had seized him after pulling the trigger apparently under control.

'So,' repeated Spätzer, and Mimi knew that Antoine would not answer.

'It's not what you think.' The words, clichéd, preposterous, came out in a faint pleading gasp.

'You don't know what I think,' said Spätzer shortly. Keeping one mistrustful eye on Jean, he walked slowly over to Antoine. 'Tell me what happened.'

Antoine continued to stare stonily ahead. Spätzer sighed, raised his pistol thoughtfully, stroked the barrel. Mimi watched in horrified fascination as he stepped closer to Antoine, stepped right up to him so that his mouth was practically touching her father's ear. Antoine barely flinched. Despite herself, Mimi found herself straining forward to hear what Spätzer was saying.

'You will talk,' he was murmuring softly. 'As God is my witness, I will make you talk. If it's the last thing either of us do in this pathetic excuse for a war, *I will make you talk.* So tell me what happened.' The pistol came up, the barrel pressed into Antoine's neck, and the soft voice grew harder. 'Tell me what happened.'

Still Antoine did not speak. They stayed like that for what seemed an eternity, Mimi standing alone in the middle of the vault, Antoine and Spätzer looking almost intimate, the German officer pressed right up against the stony Frenchman, Jean cowering on the floor, Emil's broken body in the corner. Spätzer was smiling, a tight complacent little smile, but she could tell that Antoine's continued resistance was straining his patience. *If none of us move,* she thought, *nothing will happen. We will just stay here, and everything will be all right.*

And then Jean screamed again.

★ ★ ★

She never knew why he screamed. It was one of those Jean things, one of those actions with no apparent cause which fitted into his curious logic. He screamed, and the tension was broken.

Spätzer stepped away from Antoine, his gun still trained on him, and grabbed the boy by the neck with a cruel smile.

'I'll tell you, shall I?' He looked almost relaxed now, certain of victory. 'This is what happened. Your whore daughter was here, screwing . . . ' he lingered over the word, watching Antoine's face for a flicker of emotion, but none was forthcoming ' . . . screwing Fürst. Probably not for the first time. No, now I come to think of it, definitely not for the first time. And they had an audience. Didn't they?' He shook Jean, who moaned, rolling terrified pleading eyes at Mimi. 'Maybe they even knew they had an audience. Maybe they even enjoyed being watched. But maybe they didn't realize, as they *screwed* each other, that this disgusting creature was eaten up with jealousy. So eaten up that tonight, unable to bear it any more, he crept down the stairs and shot a man in cold blood, a young man doing what young men do, enjoying the spoils of war, taking his due. An officer of the Reich. Do you know what they do to people who shoot officers of the Reich?' He twisted Jean's arm sharply, and the boy yelped. 'He won't get away with it. If he's lucky, they'll shoot him. I'd prefer to see him hang. What do you say, Duchesne? What do you think of my version of events?'

Antoine was shaking.

This is a nightmare, thought Mimi. I am living a nightmare. Any moment now, I will wake up, and I will realize that it has all been a bad dream — the war, Louis dying, Emil, Spätzer. I will wake up in my pretty bedroom, and Rémy will

335

come round, and we will all go to the beach.

The sound of Jean crying brought her back to reality. She noticed with dismay that there was a large dark patch on one of his trouser legs where he had wet himself. 'Please let him go,' she begged. 'He doesn't understand what's happening.'

Spätzer did not look at her, but he did let Jean go. The boy cowered whimpering next to Mimi, and she took one of his hands.

'Shh,' she whispered. 'It'll be all right. Don't worry. *Papa* will sort it out.'

Except that *papa* wouldn't sort it out. *Papa*, shaking and pale, was still staring grimly ahead, refusing to acknowledge Spätzer's presence. *Papa*, who had pulled the trigger on Emil, who had killed a man for loving his daughter, *papa*, who had always told his children to take responsibility for their own actions, was going to let Jean take the blame, and what could she do to stop it without condemning her own father? And now Spätzer had collared Jean again and was bundling him towards the stairs, and Jean was screeching and fighting back, and another shot rang out, and the boy's body crumpled on to the hard stone floor.

Mimi screamed. Antoine flinched. Even Spätzer looked momentarily shocked, before turning to Antoine, lip curled in a cold, contemptuous sneer that she would never forget.

'An eye for an eye,' he said flatly. 'Isn't that what they say? Two deaths on your conscience. Think of that as you brood silently on your hatred for me. I win here tonight. I always win.'

336

* * *

'Don't speak to me,' Antoine said when Spätzer had gone. 'Don't speak to me, don't look at me, don't ever call me father again. You are not my daughter. I am not your father. I will not know you.'

The following day, Spätzer finally got the news he had been waiting for, and was transferred with immediate effect to a fighting unit in the east. Emil's body was taken away. His colleagues, as planned, had all left town overnight, and the harried authorities, busy organizing the beginning of a siege and the evacuation of civilians, were too busy to question Spätzer's version of events, that Jean had shot Emil before turning his gun on himself. Antoine, forced out of silence at last, bore grudging witness to his statement.

* * *

If Mimi has learned one lesson over the years it is that guilt, if ignored, will fester, and cannibalize grief.

Mimi and Eve travelled to Montpellier as Antoine had planned. Mimi said nothing to her mother, but told France everything.

'Promise you won't tell anyone else,' said France. 'Swear it. For your own sake as well as *papa's*.'

She had promised. And then at the end of the war, when Antoine refused to hear of her coming home, she had hitched a ride to Paris with some Americans, and got a job in a bar, and met

337

Hector. And on the night he asked her to marry him, as they lay together on the narrow single bed in her tiny *chambre de bonne*, she told him everything.

He was silent for a long time. Mimi steeled herself for his reaction and held her breath.

'I survived two hits at sea,' he said at last. 'I was the doctor, I was supposed to save people, and both times I clawed my way into a lifeboat and listened to people screaming for help until they drowned. I have nightmares about those people.'

Mimi breathed out.

'It wasn't my fault, though. I didn't launch the torpedo or drop the bomb. I didn't kill them.'

'Jean and Emil died because of me.'

'Maybe. But you didn't kill them. You can't let guilt rule your life, Mimi. You have to let it go.'

Her lifeline, the steelier side of Hector, his absolute refusal to linger on the past, his determination only to look forward. She followed him to England and built a life with him, and each new milestone, each house lived in, and child born, and anniversary celebrated, convinced her that together they had triumphed over history. France — still at La Pommeraie, nursing ailing parents, married to Rémy who had returned from prison camp to find one sister gone only to fall in love with the other — ended all her letters the same way, sorry that Father still would not hear Mimi's name mentioned. *Don't be sorry, Mimi* wrote back. *We have moved*

wanted me to come back. Hopefully with you.'

'Plans change,' says Florence. 'Even when you don't have any.'

'Maybe.'

★ ★ ★

There are no taxis at the station.

'Jesus,' says Matt. 'This town out of season.'

'There'll be one in a minute.' Florence tries to speak calmly, but his anxiety is infectious, and she is worried too. 'Look, there's a phone over there, I'll ring for one.'

'I'm going to hire a car.'

'That's ridiculous . . . ' she begins, but he is already striding off towards the rental agency.

Ten minutes later they are bowling down the avenue Général de Gaulle towards the old harbour. Florence catches her breath as the old towers come into sight. 'I'd forgotten,' she says. 'It's so pretty. How could I forget how pretty it is?'

'Too much baggage,' replies Matt. He drives hunched over the wheel. 'Home first, I think. If she's not there, we'll go to La Pommeraie.' He pulls his mobile out of his jacket pocket. 'Here, try her again.'

'But we're nearly there!'

'Flo, just do it.' But there is still no answer.

Zélie's whimpering is a welcome distraction for Florence as they drive through the tall iron gates which shield Mimi's house from the avenue Carnot. To look at the house now, to linger on the moment of arrival, would be too painful.

341

Better by far to fuss over the baby, to spill out of the car as she always has done, arms full, thoughts elsewhere, taking for granted the pink and grey gravel and the gnarled branches of the lime tree and the solid red-brown reassurance of the front door. It is harder though to ignore the smell of the house as they walk in, the smell of coffee and beeswax and lavender unchanged over all these years. Zélie starts to cry, and Florence tells herself firmly that she must sit down and feed her, and resist the temptation to close her eyes and inhale her childhood and bawl her eyes out herself.

'She had breakfast,' announces Matt. 'There's a plate in the sink, and a cup. She didn't wash up.'

'There you go then,' says Florence. She sits in Hector's armchair with Zélie at her breast, and she feels warmed by the nearness of his presence. 'She can't be far.'

'The Golf's not in the garage,' says Matt grimly. 'She could be anywhere. Let's go.'

'The baby!'

'Feed her in the car.'

★   ★   ★

'I still don't see what the fuss is,' she says plaintively, as they speed around the outskirts of town towards Lagord. 'I mean, Mimi can look after herself, can't she?'

'Jesus, Flo,' mutters Matt through clenched teeth as he jumps a red light. 'Try to see things from someone else's point of view for once.'

342

'Meaning what exactly?'

'Meaning you're not the only one who's suffered from Ben's death,' he says sharply. 'Everything changed that summer, Flo. It's not just you. Gilles hasn't come to La Rochelle once since Ben's funeral, the Pommeraie cousins can't bear to come back either, France and Rémy are selling up. The rest of us come when we can, but I don't have that much holiday, and Tom has his own life, and Lily — well, you can imagine what it's like for her with none of us around. It's all gone, Flo. The holidays, the picnics, the *clan*. And now with Grampy dead ... Mimi's changed, Flo. She's eighty-four today, for fuck's sake, she's fragile. She always thought she'd grow old with us around her, and instead she's all alone. Those letters, they're almost like a ... '

'Like a goodbye,' Florence finishes sombrely.

'Exactly.'

★ ★ ★

The gates to La Pommeraie are open. Matt swings through them much too fast and skids to a halt under the old yew tree by the trademen's entrance.

'There's the Golf,' says Florence.

'But no other car. Which means she's here on her own.'

'Or that she's gone out with Rémy and France.'

'That's possible too,' he concedes.

'But they wouldn't have left the gates open,' points out Florence. 'Would they?'

343

'Certainly wouldn't have left the front door unlocked,' says Matt. He calls out as he steps into the house, but his voice echoes in the silence.

'No sign of a meal here,' says Florence from the kitchen. She stands by the window with the baby on her hip, and it is a measure of her anxiety that she does not think of the countless times she has stood here before, does not linger on the memories of afternoon *goûters* dispensed by Tante France and oysters opened by Agnès, does not bring to mind the recently evoked image of a young man in German soldier's uniform drinking clandestine coffee prepared in secret by a wrinkled cook, but focuses entirely on the matter at hand, the finding of her grandmother.

'She's not in the house,' says Matt, running back down the stairs.

'D'you think . . . '

They look at each other. Nothing more need be said. They look at each other, and then they run.

They run down the steps of the crumbling front porch, over the lawn still dotted with ducks where so many plans were made for endless summer holidays, so many lunches eaten at long trestle tables, so many games played. Through woods lighter and less dense than Florence remembered, the consequence of the big storms at the turn of the new century, a mere few months after Ben's death, woods in which tree-houses were built, and friendships forged, and in which romance blossomed. They run without stopping. Matt has taken Zélie and she hinders his progress, so that the two cousins arrive at the old orchard wall at the same time, hearts beating fast and breath coming short, while the baby howls with indignation.

They run until they reach the open trapdoor, and Florence stops short, whipped to a standstill by memories roaring darkly from its yawning mouth.

★ ★ ★

It was Matt who found Ben. He sprinted after Florence, passing her easily, and by the time she reached the tunnel he was already down there, his panic-stricken crying the first of the many sounds she remembers from that day.

Gilles, corpse-white, stammering questions, *but what, but how, but why.* Christophe, unsurprisingly efficient, *back to the house children, I'll call the police.* Lily complaining, wanting to stay, Claire pleading with her, Agnès murmuring words of comfort to Paf, Paf who was sobbing *I didn't mean to, I didn't mean to, I didn't know* ... Someone retching, Matt, over and over, on his knees on the grass, James holding him, *my boy, my boy.* Above it all her own voice, screaming at a completely silent Mimi, *I told you to talk to him, I told you, I told you* ...

It all came out at the inquest, of course. The affair, its strange beginning, its clumsy end. Florence gave evidence, her eyes as dry as her mouth, her breathing difficult, her words no more than whispers, flanked by her parents, her baffled father and her mother who could not quite look at her.

'You mustn't blame yourself,' Mimi said gently, coming into her room the night before she left for home. 'It was not your fault.' She hesitated. 'What you did . . . you were confused.'

Florence lay facing the wall, and squeezed her eyes tightly shut, shunning the solace of tears. If she started to cry, she knew she would not be able to stop, and so she huddled around her grief, holding on to it, refusing comfort, hoping only for numbness.

'Flo, speak to me.'

Please, thought Florence miserably. *Please, please go away.* And then, to say something, anything, to get Mimi to leave, she said words she did not mean but which she would hold on to for years to come. 'I asked you to speak to him,' she said in a small voice. 'I did ask. If you'd spoken to him, he might not have done it.'

'He might not,' agreed Mimi quietly. She reached out, and Florence flinched. Mimi sighed, and quietly left the room.

There was a funeral, of course. After the cremation in Paris, Gilles returned to La Rochelle with Karen, and together they went to Aix and threw his ashes over the ocean, watched the wind lift and scatter them carelessly far and wide. Mimi and Hector went too, with the cousins and aunts and uncles, but by then Florence had fled with her guilt-swollen grief, back to London where she cut herself off from her friends and plunged herself into her studies and refused to talk about what had happened, did not speak a word of it to anyone. The family, some respecting her desire for privacy, some too shocked to approach her, did not try to speak to her. After trying unsuccessfully to get her to talk, dragging her to doctor's appointments and to counsellors, her parents learned that it was easier never to mention the events of the summer. Her friends drifted away, and at last she was alone.

She has always thought of the tunnel as his grave. They hadn't wanted her to see him, but she had fought them, and in her mind's eye, he is still here, with the makeshift bed and the candles stuck into old wine bottles, perfectly still, asleep one could think except of course for the hole blown through his head, his blood a slick pool seeping slowly into the dusty hard-packed earth.

She stands here now, at the edge of Ben's grave, the scene of her childhood's demise, her baby in her arms, and she is overwhelmed by her own helplessness. She fights the visceral response of her body, the urge to retch and run, and thinks bleakly that she has no idea what she is doing here.

Matt, bravely, has gone down while she has been thinking. He climbs back out, frowning.

'Someone's been doing housework,' he says.

'How, housework?'

'It looks — tidy. Swept. No rubbish, no rubble, no cobwebs.'

'Who?' Florence frowns.

'Me,' says Mimi.

So this is it, the first meeting in six years. A slow, painful heartbeat, palms clammy with sudden sweat, breath trapped, the urge to hide stronger than ever. These form the prelude to the first words she will speak to her grandmother since that short cruel sentence, *you are as much to blame as anybody.* She turns towards the voice, the voice which is thinner than she remembers but which is still unmistakably Mimi's, even now stamped with authority despite the gentleness with which she has spoken. Florence turns, head swimming, senses lurching, but as her eyes settle finally on the figure before her the urge to run gives way to a sudden, violent desire to cry.

How has Mimi changed so much? How can a mere six years, only just over half a decade, have wrought such a transformation? The woman before her has grey-white hair cut short to the top of the neck, the waves across her forehead fastened above the ear with a pin. She is smaller than Florence remembered, the slim athletic body still straight but reduced, not just because the excess flesh has melted from her bones but because the bone structure itself has grown more fragile.

'It was me,' repeats Mimi, with an apologetic wave of the hand to indicate the dusty navy trousers, the soiled white blouse, the large smudge of dirt across her face, and in that modestly coquettish gesture Florence glimpses the Mimi of always.

'Mimi.' Matt buries his face in his hands, rubs

his eyes, exhales deeply before kissing her, his young hands too strong on her bony shoulders. 'Thank God. We tried to call you,' he adds reproachfully.

'Ah yes.' Another vague wave. 'I was going to ring you on your portable phone . . . ' She tails off as Florence approaches.

They stand before each other, Florence and Mimi, and there is nothing they can say. How do you greet each other after six heavy years of silence? What do you say to a woman who has told you her darkest secrets, or to one who blames you for a crime you didn't commit? How do you introduce the baby squirming uncomfortably in your arms, kiss the cheek you have taught yourself to hate, offer belated condolences for a loss you should have shared? How do you ask the stranger who was once a child you loved if they have understood you, why you acted as you acted, why you wrote what you wrote? How do you ask for absolution and how, more importantly, do you receive it?

'Come,' says Mimi, and she holds out her hand. 'Let's go together.'

'Not the baby, I think,' she adds quietly to Matt, and Florence, with faltering understanding, makes a tiny gesture of agreement. Matt takes Zélie, raises her high above his head towards the canopy of trees, makes rumbling engine noises at which she gurgles appreciatively. He laughs, an easy, happy laugh which fills Florence with envy.

From the basket she has been carrying, Mimi

pulls three candles. 'The symbolism is a little crude,' she says ruefully. 'But I couldn't think what else to do.'

'What *are* we going to do?' whispers Florence faintly.

They are going to pray, says Mimi. Pray, and remember. They are going to honour the dead, and consign their memories to rest. They are going to light the candles, one for each of the tunnel's dead, for Emil and Ben and another man called Jean whom she will tell her about, and they are going to illuminate this place of nightmares, and bring it peace. And when they have finished, they are going to come out of the darkness together, and they are going to talk. And finally they will know that the earth beneath La Pommeraie is no longer the custodian of guilty secrets and bloody memories, but just, simply, only earth, as it always has been and always will be. And thus it will all end.

'I can't,' says Florence. 'I can't go down there.'

Mimi does not answer. She puts two of the candles under her arm, holds the third awkwardly in her left hand and leans over it, sheltering the tiny blue flame of the lighter she has pulled from her trouser pocket. She gives a pleased little grunt as the wick catches, cups her hand around it protectively, looks up. 'Come,' she says gravely. 'Please.'

It is an end, but also a beginning. Mimi begins her descent, the glow from the candle throwing shadows on the rough walls. In the few seconds it takes for her silver head to disappear beneath the ground, Florence thinks of Ben, her first lover, and the intensity with which he lived. Of Matt, her teenage crush, still here for her, and of Pierre, her true love whom she has lost. She thinks of the past which was shattered and the future it destroyed, of her years of hiding and exile, of the girl she was and the woman she is becoming. She thinks at last that she has run enough, and that it is time to embrace her history.

At the bottom of the steps lie demons, waiting to be slain. Florence takes a deep breath of sweet woodland air, of new leaves and heady sap, then turns her back on the day and heads into the darkness, following the candle's flickering light.

EPILOGUE

La Rochelle, May 2005

'I've changed my mind,' announces Mimi. 'I don't want to go into town at all, I want to go to Ré for a picnic.'

Florence, having arrived with no plans, decided to stay with Mimi. She has written to Greta to ask her to keep an eye on the flat, and to Cassandra to thank her for the strange part she played in bringing her family back to her, and she has taken over the big green bedroom upstairs. Zélie's pram sits in the garage now among the beach paraphernalia and the old bicycles, her sheets and babygros and muslin cloths hang out to dry on the line, the bathroom is full of baby products. 'An invasion,' says Mimi regularly with satisfaction. 'Whoever would have thought a baby would have so much *stuff*?'

Others have come back since her return, and now to Mimi's exasperation France and Rémy are dithering about whether to change their plans, and not sell La Pommeraie after all. Agnès has come, bringing Paf and Marie-Jo, all clamouring to see the baby. Camille and Louise have paid a flying visit too, with talk of returning for a week's holiday. Catherine is due with the twins for half-term, and even Gilles is expected. 'A little miracle-worker,' Mimi keeps saying, prodding Zélie who smiles adoringly. The reunions, though ultimately joyous, have also been tearful and often painful. There is no absolution, Florence has discovered. There is only acceptance, but it is a first step.

'A picnic?' she says. 'I thought you wanted to go into town to see the parade.' This weekend marks the sixtieth anniversary of the liberation of La Rochelle. Great celebrations are planned, ancient tanks oiled back to life, music, fireworks, a parade of veterans, the inevitable cycle race and feast.

'Fireworks,' says Mimi. 'Bicycle races. It's got bugger all to do with the war. I've changed my mind,' she repeats. 'I want a picnic. A good, big picnic like we always used to have on the first day of the holidays.'

'Matt!' Florence shouts upstairs. 'Change of plan. *Madame* desires a picnic.'

Matt has joined them for the weekend. He walks into the living room, frowning as he types a text. 'For heaven's sake, Matt, you've been on the phone all morning.'

'It's work.'

'It's Saturday!'

'Not in my world.'

'Mimi wants to go to Ré for a picnic.'

'Good idea.'

'But I thought you wanted to see the parade. I don't think Zélie's ready for a picnic on the beach.'

'She'll be fine.'

'But . . .'

'Flo. It's Mimi's day. Just humour her?'

★   ★   ★

They pack a 'First Day' picnic: cold *rôti de porc*, *tartes au gruyère*, tabouleh, *salade de chou*. In the picnic basket it all goes, with a huge bar of chocolate, a melon, a *quatre-quarts au citron* and a bottle of champagne.

'When did you *get* all this food?' asks Florence.

'Yesterday at the market. I thought it would come in handy.'

'Handy for what?'

The look Mimi exchanges with Matt is not so quick that Florence does not notice it. He shakes his head briefly, frowning.

'I just fancied it,' says Mimi defensively. 'I'm allowed.'

The car is loaded up for a day at the beach, with parasol and windbreak, blankets, Mimi's camping chair and Zélie's carrycot.

'Who's going to swim in *May*?' protests Matt as Mimi dumps a pile of towels into his arms.

'You never know,' she answers breezily. The prospect of the picnic has brought a new glint to Mimi's eye, and she seems to have grown taller. The food packed, she takes to her room, to emerge half an hour later looking radiant, perfectly made up and draped in swathes of cream-coloured cashmere.

'It's only a picnic,' says Florence.

'Nonsense,' says Mimi. 'It's a special occasion. You should make a little effort yourself.'

Florence looks down at her jeans and the oversize chocolate-coloured cable-knit sweater which reaches down almost to her knees. She gropes into her bag for her scarlet pashmina and sunglasses. 'There,' she says. 'Perfect.' Mimi sighs.

Matt's mobile beeps. 'Fuck,' he says.

'Ignore it,' begs Florence.

'No, it's all right.' He is reading a text message. 'It's from Tom.'

'Well?' asks Mimi.

'Nah, nothing.' He flashes her a quick smile, and she beams back.

'What's going on?' asks Florence. 'Why are you both grinning like Cheshire cats?'

'Honestly, *puce*,' says Mimi indignantly as she sweeps off towards the garage. 'You sound like the Gestapo.'

★ ★ ★

They drive to the usual place, right at the end of the island at La Rivière. 'I'll have to put her in the sling,' says Florence. 'And carry the cot. There's no way the buggy's going up those dunes.'

'Can't you just lie her on a blanket?' Matt, loaded down with the rest of their paraphernalia, squirms impatiently.

'She'll be more comfortable in her carrycot. The sand . . . '

'Whatever, whatever. Just hurry up.'

'Relax, can't you. I don't know what's got into the pair of you today.'

Mimi, claiming infirmity and great age, has stridden ahead of them empty-handed, and already stands at the top of the dunes in her flowing coat and large sunglasses, gesticulating wildly with her walking stick for them to follow.

'Move it!' says Matt.

It is the first time in six years that Florence has returned here, and she also stops in the dunes to take in the view. Beneath her, the beach stretches out, unchanged. To the left, the perfect conch-shaped sweep of golden sand with the lighthouse on the distant point. To the right, the rock pools, glinting darkly and full of promise. The May breeze is fresh, but the sun is warm, and she tilts her face up to greet it, breathing in the salty tang of the air mingled with the fresh clean smell of the pines behind her. *Home*, she thinks. She could stand here for ever, but already the others are calling and the baby is stirring, and it is time to move on.

★ ★ ★

'This,' announces Mimi, 'is what the war was fought for.'

They have spread themselves out on the sand, sheltered from the wind by their usual *blockhaus*. Mimi sits back in her little deckchair, a rug tucked around her legs, another draped around her shoulders, drinking champagne and watching the sea. 'All we need now,' she says, 'are a few of those jolly Americans we got at the end of the war.'

'Mimi!' warns Matt.

Florence is busy settling Zélie into her carrycot and fussing with parasols. 'What do you mean?' she asks.

'Nothing!' they chorus. 'Why?' asks Mimi.

'You're both being very odd today.'

'Well that's nice,' says Mimi. She sounds offended, but tries hard not to grin.

'You are!' protests Florence.

Matt is grinning too now, looking down the beach towards the shoreline. 'What's so funny?' demands Florence. Mimi has started to giggle, and Matt snorts nervously with suppressed laughter.

Florence turns then to follow their line of vision. She takes in the sand, the breaking waves, the sailing boats zipping along in the distance, a couple of dogs, a few families playing on the beach. She shrugs grumpily. 'I don't see what's so funny,' she says. And then she sees them.

Two figures, walking towards them along the shore. One is tall but slight, a little stooped, the sunlight reflecting off his glasses. The other stands straight, but walks with his broad shoulders hunched against the wind, hands deep inside the pockets of his leather jacket.

'Pierre,' she whispers. 'And Tom.' She bites her lip and stares. Turns to Matt and Mimi, then back to Pierre and Tom approaching along the sand, then back once more to Matt and Mimi.

'How?' she stammers. Matt holds up his mobile. 'Only a phone call away, princess.'

'Are you pleased?' asks Mimi eagerly.

'I think . . . ' Florence is having difficulty breathing. 'I think you're both playing a very dangerous game.'

'Risk worth taking,' says Matt smugly.

on . . . Moved on so much in fact that when they did go back after Antoine's funeral, she was surprised by how little she thought of the past, even during the first visit to La Pommeraie, an emotional moment but not an unhappy one, Eve falling into her arms in tears, laughing as her grandchildren, quite unaware of the importance of the occasion, clambered over her. It had been Hector's idea to stay on, but she had agreed readily, happy to be home. It was an exciting time, La Rochelle still full of Americans, Hector setting up a practice, the house being built, the children all-consuming. It only dawned on her gradually how much she had missed the town, her mother and sister, but if ever her thoughts strayed towards the shadowy landscape of the past, they did not allow them to linger there.

But guilt, she has learned, has no permanent cure. It lies dormant, a cancer in abeyance, smothered by happiness and normality, by babies and picnics and holidays, by walking to school and helping with homework. It waits as children grow up, bides its time through marriages and funerals, through changing seasons and speeding years until something gives which cuts through the safety of these layers, right through to the sickness at the core, and then it spews up like a rush of blood to a wound and taints even the truest sorrow.

With Hector gone, there is no one to keep it at bay. No one, that is, except Florence. Florence who also knows about guilt, what it means to have blood on her conscience. Mimi could not

339

bear to write the final instalment of her story. But if she and Florence are to be each other's salvation, she will have to tell her when she comes.

If she comes. The afternoon is growing old, and Mimi's clearing is no longer in the sun. She thinks of the tunnel waiting in the gathering shadows, and hopes her granddaughter will come before it is too late.

★ ★ ★

They change trains in Paris, crossing the capital by taxi.

'So beautiful,' sighs Florence, as they pass in front of the Louvre, its modern glass pyramid glittering in the midday sun. She holds the baby up to look. 'One day, my child,' she says solemnly, 'all this will be yours.'

They are in buoyant mood as the taxi shoots across the Seine, feeling like tourists on a day trip, but once installed in the TGV — second class, this time, with Zélie on her mother's lap and only the prospect of the buffet car for sustenance — they grow more sombre, as Matt tries calling avenue Carnot and La Pommeraie again.

'Fuck, fuck, fuck,' he grumbles. 'Where the bloody hell *is* she?'

'She's probably just gone out for the day. With some friends.'

'She specifically told me she had no plans. That she couldn't face it. Grampy always made a really big deal of her birthday. That's why she

340

'Go,' nudges Mimi. 'Go, go, go. We'll look after the baby.'

The baby. 'No,' says Florence. Her voice sounds distant, not a part of her at all. She kneels, and picks Zélie out of her cot. Holds her tightly, her mouth pressed against her soft, sweet-smelling head. Any minute now, she thinks, she will wake up. Tom is walking towards them. He stops in front of her, says something she does not hear, kisses her on the cheek. She feels the scratch of stubble, the cold steel of his glasses. Not a dream, then.

Florence stands very still for a moment which is probably quite short, but which feels like an eternity. And then she starts to walk.

Away from the protection of the *blockhaus*, the wind picks up. It whips her hair out of its fastenings and across her face. She pushes it back, and finds that her hand is wet with tears. She wants to run, but she forces herself to go slowly, because she also wants this moment to last for ever.

★   ★   ★

He waits for her by the shore, staring out to sea. She walks carefully, holding Zélie, her eyes fixed firmly on the sand until she stands just a few feet away from him. And then at last they look at each other, serious and questioning, knowing that everything hangs in the balance of this moment. They look at each other but do not move until Pierre, with a groan which sounds like a sob, reaches out and pulls her towards him, and she stands with his arms wrapped around her and her arms wrapped around their baby, and they clutch each other, still silent but both crying now, beside the grey-blue waters of the Atlantic Ocean.

Other titles published by
The House of Ulverscroft:

GLITZ

Louise Bagshawe

The four Chambers girls are rolling in money, care of the fund set up by their super-rich Uncle Clem. Social climber Juno, scruffy academic Athena, wannabe actress Venus and trendy It Girl Diana take their extravagant and glamorous lifestyles for granted. But then Uncle Clem announces his engagement to Bai-Ling, a woman young enough to be their baby sister — and the Chambers girls know the party could be over. They must stop the wedding — by destroying Bai-Ling. But could Uncle Clem have a bigger plan up his sleeve? Will the four of them unite against the threat of Bai-Ling, or is it every woman for herself? Without the money, who will learn how to stand on her own two feet — and who will fall?

ALL WE EVER WANTED WAS EVERYTHING

Janelle Brown

In the heat of a West Coast summer, three very different women, each poised for success, find themselves failing spectacularly. Janice, a devoted mother and housewife who's approaching fifty, finds she has been abandoned by her husband; her elder daughter Margaret, a magazine editor, is driven back home by towering debts; and her teenage daughter Lizzie is humiliated by the boys whose affections she has embraced. At first they hide their crises — bankruptcy, addiction, promiscuity — from one another, but as the curtain-twitching world they inhabit begins to intrude, they find their secrets exposed. In the midst of the manicured lawns and country club whispers, the Miller women cloister themselves in their suburban home for the summer and confront first their personal downfalls, then each other . . .

AN ARSONIST'S GUIDE TO WRITERS' HOMES IN NEW ENGLAND

Brock Clarke

Sam Pulsifer spent ten years in prison for accidentally burning down poet Emily Dickinson's house — and unwittingly killing two people in the process. He emerged aged twenty-eight, went to college, found love, got married, fathered two children, and made a new start — and then watched as the vengeful past caught up with him, right at his own front door. As the homes of other famous New England writers are torched, Sam knows that this time he is not guilty. To prove his innocence, he sets out to uncover the identity of this literary-minded arsonist. Sam learns that the truth has a way of eluding capture, and then, when you finally get close enough to embrace it, it turns and kicks you in the ass.